KU-298-285

Conclave

Robert Harris

W F HOWES LTD

This large print edition published in 2017 by
W F Howes Ltd
Unit 5, St George's House, Rearsby Business Park,
Gaddesby Lane, Rearsby, Leicester LE7 4YH

1 3 5 7 9 10 8 6 4 2

First published in the United Kingdom in 2016
by Hutchinson

Copyright © Robert Harris, 2016

The right of Robert Harris to be identified as
the author of this work has been asserted by him
in accordance with the Copyright, Designs and
Patents Act, 1988.

All rights reserved

A CIP catalogue record for this book is available
from the British Library

ISBN 978 1 51006 005 0

Typeset by Palimpsest Book Production Limited,
Falkirk, Stirlingshire

P

HAMPSHIRE COUNTY LIBRARY

C015949557

WITHDRAWN

9781510060051

C015949557

To Charlie

AUTHOR'S NOTE

Although for the sake of authenticity I have used real titles throughout this novel (Archbishop of Milan, Dean of the College of Cardinals, and so on), I have used them in the sense that one might when writing about a fictitious U.S. President or British Prime Minister. The characters I have created to fill these offices are not intended to bear any resemblance to their present-day incumbents: if I have erred, and if there are some coincidental similarities, I apologise. Nor, despite certain superficial resemblances, is the late Holy Father depicted in *Conclave* meant to be a portrait of the current Pope.

'I thought it wiser not to eat with the cardinals. I ate in my room. At the eleventh ballot I was elected Pope. O Jesus, I too can say what Pius XII said when he was elected: "Have mercy on me, Lord, according to thy great mercy." One would say that it is like a dream and yet, until I die, it is the most solemn reality of all my life. So I'm ready, Lord, "to live and die with you". About three hundred thousand people applauded me on St Peter's balcony. The arc-lights stopped me from seeing anything other than a shapeless, heaving mass.'

POPE JOHN XXIII, DIARY ENTRY,
28 OCTOBER 1958

'I was solitary before, but now my solitariness becomes complete and awesome. Hence the dizziness, like vertigo. Like a statue on a plinth – that is how I live now.'

POPE PAUL VI

CHAPTER 1

SEDE VACANTE

C ardinal Lomeli left his apartment in the
Palace of the Holy Office shortly before
two in the morning and hurried through
the darkened cloisters of the Vatican towards the
bedroom of the Pope.

He was praying: *O Lord, he still has so much to
do, whereas all my useful work in Your service is
completed. He is beloved, while I am forgotten. Spare
him, Lord. Spare him. Take me instead.*

He toiled up the cobbled slope towards the
Piazza Santa Marta. The Roman air was soft and
misty, yet already he could detect the first faint
chill of autumn. It was raining slightly. The Prefect
of the Papal Household had sounded so panicked
on the telephone, Lomeli was expecting to be met
by a scene of pandemonium. In fact, the piazza
was unusually quiet, apart from a solitary ambulance parked a discreet distance away, silhouetted
against the floodlit southern flank of St Peter's.
Its interior light was on, the windscreen wipers
scudding back and forth, close enough for him to
be able to make out the faces of both the driver
and his assistant. The driver was using a mobile

1

phone, and Lomeli thought with a shock: they haven't come to take a sick man to the hospital, they've come to take away a body.

At the plate-glass entrance to the Casa Santa Marta, the Swiss Guard saluted, a white-gloved hand to a red-plumed helmet. 'Your Eminence.'

Lomeli, nodding towards the car, said, 'Will you please make sure that man isn't calling the media?'

The hostel had an austere, antiseptic atmosphere, like a private clinic. In the white-marbled lobby, a dozen priests, three in dressing gowns, stood around in bewilderment, as if a fire alarm had sounded and they were unsure of the correct procedure. Lomeli hesitated on the threshold, felt something in his left hand and saw that he was clutching his red zucchetto. He couldn't remember picking it up. He unfolded it and placed it on his head. His hair was damp to the touch. A bishop, an African, tried to intercept him as he walked towards the elevator, but Lomeli merely nodded in his direction and moved on.

The car took an age to come. He ought to have used the stairs, but he was too short of breath. He sensed the others looking at his back. He should say something. The elevator arrived. The doors slid open. He turned and raised his hand in benediction.

'Pray,' he said.

He pressed the button for the second floor; the doors closed and he began to ascend.

If it is Your will to call him to Your presence and

2

leave me behind, then grant me the strength to be a rock for others.

In the mirror, beneath the yellow light, his cadaverous face was grey and mottled. He yearned for a sign, for some infusion of strength. The elevator lurched to an abrupt halt but his stomach seemed to go on rising, and he had to grip the metal handrail to steady himself. He remembered riding with the Holy Father in this very car early in his papacy when two elderly monsignors had got in. Immediately they had fallen to their knees, stunned to find themselves face-to-face with Christ's representative on earth, at which the Pope had laughed and said, 'Don't worry, get up, I'm just an old sinner, no better than you . . .'

The cardinal raised his chin. His public mask. The doors opened. A thick curtain of dark suits parted to let him through. He heard one agent whisper into his sleeve, 'The dean is here.'

Diagonally across the landing, outside the papal suite, three nuns, members of the Company of the Daughters of Charity of St Vincent de Paul, were holding hands and crying. Archbishop Woźniak, Prefect of the Papal Household, came forward to meet him. Behind his steel-rimmed glasses his watery grey eyes were puffy. He lifted his hands and said helplessly, 'Eminence . . .'

Lomeli took the archbishop's cheeks in his hands and pressed gently. He could feel the younger man's stubble. 'Janusz, your presence made him so happy.'

Then another bodyguard – or perhaps it was an undertaker: both professions dressed so alike – at any rate, another figure in black opened the door to the suite.

The little sitting room and the even smaller bedroom beyond it were crowded. Afterwards Lomeli made a list and came up with more than a dozen names of people present, not counting security – two doctors, two private secretaries, the Master of Papal Liturgical Celebrations, whose name was Archbishop Mandorff, at least four priests from the Apostolic Camera, Woźniak, and of course the four senior cardinals of the Catholic Church: the Secretary of State, Aldo Bellini; the Camerlengo – or Chamberlain – of the Holy See, Joseph Tremblay; the Cardinal Major Penitentiary, or confessor-in-chief, Joshua Adeyemi; and himself, as Dean of the College of Cardinals. In his vanity he had imagined that he had been the first to be summoned; in fact, he now saw, he was the last.

He followed Woźniak into the bedroom. It was the first time he had seen inside it. Always before, the big double doors had been shut. The Renaissance papal bed, a crucifix above it, faced into the sitting room. It took up almost all the space – square, heavy polished oak, far too big for the room. It provided the only touch of grandeur. Bellini and Tremblay were on their knees beside it with their heads bowed. Lomeli had to step over the backs of their legs to get round to the pillows where the

Pope lay slightly propped up, his body concealed by the white counterpane, his hands folded on his chest above his plain iron pectoral cross.

He was not used to seeing the Holy Father without his spectacles. These lay folded on the nightstand beside a scuffed travel alarm clock. The frames had left red pinch-marks on either side of the bridge of his nose. Often the faces of the dead, in Lomeli's experience, were slack and stupid. But this one seemed alert, almost amused, as if interrupted in mid-sentence. As he bent to kiss the forehead, he noticed a faint smudge of white toothpaste at the left corner of the mouth, and caught the smell of peppermint and the hint of some floral shampoo.

'Why did He summon you when there was still so much you wanted to do?' he whispered.

'*Subvenite, Sancti Dei . . .*'

Adeyemi began intoning the liturgy. Lomeli realised they had been waiting for him. He lowered himself carefully to his knees on the brightly polished parquet floor, cupped his hands together in prayer and rested them on the side of the counterpane. He burrowed his face into his palms.

'. . . *occurrite, Angeli Domini . . .*'

Come to his aid, Saints of God; race to meet him, Angels of the Lord . . .

The Nigerian cardinal's basso profundo reverberated around the tiny room.

'. . . *Suscipientes animam eius. Offerentes eam in conspectu Altissimi . . .*'

Receive his soul and present it in the presence of the Most High . . .

The words buzzed in Lomeli's head without meaning. It was happening more and more often. *I cry out to You, God, but You do not answer.* Some kind of spiritual insomnia, a kind of noisy interference, had crept over him during the past year, denying him that communion with the Holy Spirit he had once been able to achieve quite naturally. And, as with sleep, the more one desired meaningful prayer, the more elusive it became. He had confessed his crisis to the Pope at their final meeting – had asked permission to leave Rome, to give up his duties as Dean and retreat to a religious order. He was seventy-five, retirement age. But the Holy Father had been unexpectedly hard on him. 'Some are chosen to be shepherds, and others are needed to manage the farm. Yours is not a pastoral role. You are not a shepherd. You are a manager. Do you think it's easy for me? I need you here. Don't worry. God will return to you. He always does.' Lomeli was hurt – a manager, is that how he sees me? – and there had been a coldness between them when they parted. That was the last time he saw him.

'. . . *Requiem aeternam dona ei, Domine: et lux perpetua luceat ei . . .'*

Eternal rest grant unto him, Lord: And let perpetual light shine upon him . . .

When the liturgy had been recited, the four

cardinals remained around the deathbed in silent prayer. After a couple of minutes Lomeli turned his head a fraction and half opened his eyes. Behind them in the sitting room, everyone was on their knees with their heads bowed. He pressed his face back into his hands.

It saddened him to think that their long association should have ended on such a note. He tried to remember when it had happened. Two weeks ago? No, a month – 17 September, to be exact, after the Mass to commemorate the Impression of the Stigmata upon St Francis – the longest period he had gone without a private audience since the Pope had been elected. Perhaps the Holy Father had already started to sense that death was close and that his mission would not be completed; perhaps that accounted for his uncharacteristic irritation?

The room was utterly still. He wondered who would be the first to break the meditation. He guessed it would be Tremblay. The French Canadian was always in a hurry, a typical North American. And indeed, after a few more moments, Tremblay sighed – a long, theatrical, almost ecstatic exhalation. 'He is with God,' he said, and stretched out his arms. Lomeli thought he was about to deliver a blessing, but instead the gesture was a signal to two of his assistants from the Apostolic Camera, who entered the bedroom and helped him stand. One carried a silver box.

'Archbishop Woźniak,' said Tremblay, as everyone

started getting to their feet, 'would you be so kind as to bring me the Holy Father's ring?'

Lomeli rose on knees that creaked after seven decades of constant genuflection. He pressed himself against the wall to allow the Prefect of the Papal Household to edge past. The ring did not come off easily. Poor Woźniak, sweating with embarrassment, had to work it back and forth over the knuckle. But eventually it came free and he carried it on his outstretched palm to Tremblay, who took a pair of shears from the silver box – the sort of tool one might use to dead-head roses, thought Lomeli – and inserted the seal of the ring between the blades. He squeezed hard, grimacing with the effort. There was a sudden snap, and the metal disc depicting St Peter hauling in a fisherman's net was severed.

'*Sede vacante*,' Tremblay announced. 'The throne of the Holy See is vacant.'

Lomeli spent a few minutes gazing down at the bed in contemplative farewell, then helped Tremblay lay a thin white veil over the Pope's face. The vigil broke up into whispering groups.

He moved back into the sitting room. He wondered how the Pope could have borne it, year after year – not just living surrounded by armed guards, but this place. Fifty anonymous square metres, furnished to suit the income and taste of some mid-level commercial salesman. There was nothing personal in it. Pale lemon walls and curtains. A parquet floor for easy cleaning. Standard-issue table, desk, plus sofa and two armchairs, scallop-backed and upholstered in some blue washable fabric. Even the dark wooden prie-dieu was identical to a hundred others in the hostel. The Holy Father had stayed here as a cardinal before the Conclave that elected him Pope, and had never moved out: one look at the luxurious apartment to which he was entitled in the Apostolic Palace, with its library and its private chapel, had been enough to send him running. His war with the Vatican's old guard had started right here, on that issue, on his first day. When some of the heads of the Curia had demurred at his decision as not being appropriate for the dignity of a Pope, he had quoted at them, as if they were schoolboys, Christ's instruction to his disciples: *Take nothing for your journey, no staff, nor bag, nor bread, nor money; and do not have two tunics.* From then on, being human, they had felt his reproachful eye upon them every time they went home to their grand official apartments; and, being human, they had resented it.

The Secretary of State, Bellini, was standing by the desk with his back to the room. His term of office had ended with the breaking of the Fisherman's Ring, and his tall, thin, ascetic frame, which he usually carried as erect as a Lombardy poplar, looked as if it had been snapped along with it.

Lomeli said, 'My dear Aldo, I am so very sorry.'

He saw that Bellini was examining the travelling chess set that the Holy Father used to carry around in his briefcase. He was running a long, pale forefinger back and forth over the tiny red and white plastic pieces. They were crowded intricately together in the centre of the board, locked in some abstruse battle now destined never to be resolved. Bellini said distractedly, 'Do you think anyone would mind if I took this, as a keepsake?'

'I'm sure not.'

'We used to play quite often at the end of the day. He said it helped him relax.'

'Who won?'

'He did. Always.'

'Take it,' urged Lomeli. 'He loved you more than anyone. He would have wanted you to have it. Take it.'

Bellini glanced around. 'I suppose one should wait and ask for permission. But it appears that our zealous Camerlengo is about to seal the apartment.'

He nodded to where Tremblay and his priest-assistants were gathered around the coffee table laying out the materials he needed to affix to the doors – red ribbons, wax, tape.

Suddenly Bellini's eyes filled with tears. He had a reputation for coldness – the aloof and bloodless intellectual. Lomeli had never seen him show emotion. It shocked him. He put a hand on Bellini's arm and said sympathetically, 'What happened, do you know?'

10

'They say a heart attack.'

'But I thought he had the heart of a bull.'

'Not entirely, to be honest. There had been warnings.'

Lomeli blinked in surprise. 'I hadn't heard that.'

'Well, he didn't want anyone to know. He said the moment word got out, they would start spreading rumours that he was going to resign.'

They. Bellini didn't have to spell out who *they* were. He meant the Curia. For the second time that night, Lomeli felt obscurely slighted. Was that why he knew nothing of this long-standing medical problem? Because the Holy Father had thought of him not only as a manager, but as one of *them*?

He said, 'I think we'll have to be very careful what we say about his condition to the media. You know better than I do what they're like. They'll want to know about any history of heart trouble, and what exactly we did about it. And if it turns out it was all hushed up and we did nothing, they'll demand to know why.' Now that the initial shock was wearing off, he was beginning to perceive a whole series of urgent questions that the world would want answering – indeed that he wanted answering himself. 'Tell me, was anyone with the Holy Father when he died? Did he receive absolution?'

Bellini shook his head. 'No, I'm afraid he was already dead when he was discovered.'

'Who found him? When?' Lomeli beckoned to

Archbishop Woźniak to join them. 'Janusz, I know this is hard for you, but we'll need to prepare a detailed statement. Who discovered the Holy Father's body?'

'I did, Your Eminence.'

'Well, thank God, that's something.' Of all the members of the Papal Household, Woźniak was the one who had been closest to the Pope. It was comforting to think that he had been the first on the scene. And also, purely from a public relations point of view, better him than a security guard; better him by far than a nun. 'What did you do?'

'I called the Holy Father's doctor.'

'And how quickly did he arrive?'

'Immediately, Eminence. He always spent the night in the room next door.'

'But there was nothing to be done?'

'No. We had all the equipment necessary for resuscitation. But it was too late.'

Lomeli thought it over. 'You discovered him in bed?'

'Yes. He was quite peaceful, almost as he looks now. I thought he was asleep.'

'This was at what time?'

'Around eleven thirty, Eminence.'

'*Eleven thirty?*' That was more than two and a half hours ago.

Lomeli's surprise must have shown in his face, because Woźniak said quickly, 'I would have called you sooner, but Cardinal Tremblay took charge of the situation.'

Tremblay's head turned at the mention of his name. It was such a small room. He was only a couple of paces away; he was beside them in an instant. Despite the hour, his appearance was fresh and handsome, his thick silver hair immaculately coiffed, his body trim and carried lightly. He looked like a retired athlete who had made a successful transition to television sports presenter; Lomeli vaguely remembered that he had played ice hockey in his youth. The French Canadian said, in his careful Italian, 'I'm so sorry, Jacopo, if you feel offended by the delay in informing you – I know His Holiness had no closer colleagues than you and Aldo – but I felt as Camerlengo that my first responsibility was to secure the integrity of the Church. I told Janusz to hold off from calling you so that we could have a brief period of calm to ascertain all the facts.' He pressed his hands together piously, as if in prayer.

The man was insufferable. Lomeli said, 'My dear Joe, my only concerns are for the soul of the Holy Father and the well-being of the Church. Whether I am told a thing at midnight or at two is neither here nor there as far as I'm concerned. I am sure you acted for the best.'

'It's simply that when a Pope dies unexpectedly, any mistakes made in the initial shock and confusion can lead to all manner of malicious rumours afterwards. You only have to remember the tragedy of Pope John Paul I – we've spent the past forty years trying to convince the world he wasn't murdered, and all because nobody wanted to admit his body was discovered by a nun. This time, there must be no discrepancies in the official account.'

From within his cassock he drew a folded sheet of paper and handed it to Lomeli. It was warm to the touch. (Hot off the press, thought Lomeli.) Neatly printed on a word processor, it was headed, in English, 'Timeline'. Lomeli ran his finger down the columns of type. At 7.30 p.m., the Holy Father had eaten with Woźniak in the cordoned-off space reserved for him in the dining room of the Casa Santa Marta. At 8.30, he had retired to his apartment and had read and meditated on a passage from *The Imitation of Christ* (Chapter 8, 'Of the dangers of intimacy'). At 9.30, he had gone to bed. At 11.30, Archbishop Woźniak had checked to see that he was well and had failed to observe any vital functions. At 11.34, Dr Giulio Baldinotti, seconded from the Vatican's San Raffaele Hospital in Milan, commenced emergency treatment. A combination of cardiac massage and defibrillation was attempted, without result. The Holy Father had been pronounced dead at 12.12 a.m.

Cardinal Adeyemi came up behind Lomeli and began reading over his shoulder. The Nigerian always smelled strongly of cologne. Lomeli could feel his warm breath on the side of his neck. The power of Adeyemi's physical presence was too much for him. He gave him the document and turned away, only to have more papers thrust into his hand by Tremblay.

'What's all this?'

'The Holy Father's most recent medical records. I had them brought over. This is an angiogram conducted last month. You can see here,' said Tremblay, holding up an X-ray to the central light, 'there is evidence of blockage . . .'

The monochrome image was tendrilled, fibrous – sinister. Lomeli recoiled. What in God's name was the point of it? The Pope had been in his eighties. There was nothing suspicious about his passing. How long was he supposed to live? It was his soul upon which they should be focused at this moment, not his arteries. He said firmly, 'Release the data if you must, but not the photograph. It's too intrusive. It demeans him.'

Bellini said, 'I agree.'

'I suppose,' added Lomeli, 'you'll tell us next there will have to be an autopsy?'

'Well, there are bound to be rumours if there isn't.'

'This is true,' said Bellini. 'Once, God explained all mysteries. Now He has been usurped by conspiracy theorists. They are the heretics of the age.'

Adeyemi had finished reading the timeline. He took off his gold-framed glasses and sucked on the stem. 'What was the Holy Father doing *before* seven thirty?'

Woźniak answered. 'He was celebrating vespers, Eminence, here in the Casa Santa Marta.'

'Then we should say so. It was his last sacramental act, and implies a state of grace, especially as there was no opportunity for the viaticum.'

'A good point,' said Tremblay. 'I'll add it.'

'And going back further – the time before vespers,' Adeyemi persisted. 'What was he doing then?'

'Routine meetings, as far as I understand it.' Tremblay sounded defensive. 'I don't have all the facts. I was concentrating on the hours immediately before his death.'

'Who was the last to have a scheduled meeting with him?'

'I believe, in fact, that may have been me,' said Tremblay. 'I saw him at four. Is that right, Janusz? Was I the last?'

'You were, Eminence.'

'And how was he when you spoke to him? Did he give any indication he was ill?'

'No, none that I recall.'

'What about later, when he had dinner with you, Archbishop?'

Woźniak looked at Tremblay, as if seeking his permission before replying. 'He was tired. Very, very tired. He had no appetite. His voice sounded hoarse. I should have realised—' He stopped.

'You have nothing to reproach yourself with.' Adeyemi returned the document to Tremblay and put his glasses back on. There was a careful theatricality to his movements. He was always conscious of his dignity. A true prince of the Church. 'Put

16

in all of the meetings he had that day. It will show how hard he was working, right up to the end. It will prove there was no reason for anyone to suspect he was ill.'

'On the contrary,' said Tremblay, 'isn't there a danger that if we release his full schedule, it will look as if we were placing a huge burden on a sick man?'

'The papacy *is* a huge burden. People need to be reminded of that.'

Tremblay frowned and said nothing. Bellini glanced at the floor. A slight but definite tension had arisen, and it took Lomeli a few moments to realise why. Reminding people of the immense burden of the papacy carried the obvious implication that it was an office best filled by a younger man – and Adeyemi, at just over sixty, was nearly a decade younger than the other two.

Eventually Lomeli said, 'May I suggest that we amend the document to include the Holy Father's attendance at vespers, but otherwise issue it as it stands? And that as a precaution we also prepare a second document listing the Holy Father's appointments for the entire day, and keep it in reserve in case it becomes necessary?'

Adeyemi and Tremblay exchanged brief looks, then nodded, and Bellini said drily, 'Thank God for our Dean. I can see we may have need of his diplomatic skills in the days to come.'

Later, Lomeli would look back on this as the moment when the contest for the succession began.

All three cardinals were known to have factions of supporters inside the electoral college: Bellini, the great intellectual hope of the liberals for as long as Lomeli could remember, a former rector of the Gregorian University and former Archbishop of Milan; Tremblay, who as well as serving as Camerlengo was Prefect of the Congregation for the Evangelisation of Peoples, a candidate therefore with links to the Third World, who had the advantage of seeming to be an American without the disadvantage of actually being one; and Adeyemi, who carried within him like a divine spark the revolutionary possibility, endlessly fascinating to the media, that he might one day become 'the first black Pope'.

And slowly, as he observed the manoeuvring begin in the Casa Santa Marta, the realisation came upon Lomeli that it would fall to him, as Dean of the College of Cardinals, to manage the election. It was a duty he had never expected to perform. He had been diagnosed with prostate cancer a few years earlier, and although he had supposedly been cured, he had always assumed he would die before the Pope. He had only ever thought of himself as a stopgap. He had tried to resign. But now it seemed he would be responsible for the organisation of a Conclave in the most difficult of circumstances.

He closed his eyes. *If it is Your will, O Lord, that I should have to discharge this duty, I pray that You will give me the wisdom to perform it in a manner that will strengthen our Mother the Church . . .*

18

He would have to be impartial – that first and foremost. He opened his eyes and said, 'Has anyone telephoned Cardinal Tedesco?'

'No,' said Tremblay. 'Tedesco, of all people? Why? Do you think we need to?'

'Well, given his position in the Church, it would be a courtesy—'

'A courtesy?' cried Bellini. 'What has he done to deserve courtesy? If any one man can be said to have killed the Holy Father, he did!'

Lomeli had sympathy for his anguish. Of all the late Pope's critics, Tedesco had been the most savage, pushing his attacks on the Holy Father and on Bellini to the point, some thought, of schism. There had even been talk of excommunication. Nevertheless, he enjoyed a devoted following among the traditionalists, which was bound to make him a prominent candidate for the succession.

'Still, I should call him,' said Lomeli. 'It will be better if he hears the news from us rather than from some reporter. God knows what he might say off the cuff.'

He lifted the desk telephone from its cradle and pressed zero. An operator, her voice shaky with emotion, asked how she could help him.

'Please put me through to the Patriarch's Palace in Venice – to Cardinal Tedesco's private line.'

He assumed there would be no answer – after all, it was not yet three in the morning – but the phone didn't even finish its first ring before it was picked up. A gruff voice said, 'Tedesco.'

The other cardinals were talking quietly with one another about the timetable for the funeral. Lomeli held up his hand for silence and turned his back so he could concentrate on the call.

'Goffredo? It's Lomeli. I'm afraid I have terrible news. The Holy Father has just passed away.' There was a long pause. Lomeli could hear some sort of noise in the background. A footstep? A door? 'Patriarch? Did you hear what I said?'

Tedesco's voice sounded hollow in the cavernousness of his official residence. 'Thank you, Lomeli. I shall pray for his soul.'

There was a click. The line went dead. 'Goffredo?' Lomeli held the phone at arm's length and frowned at it.

Tremblay said, 'Well?'

'He already knew.'

'Are you sure?' From inside his cassock Tremblay took out what appeared to be a prayer book bound in black leather, but which turned out to be a mobile phone.

'Of course he knew,' said Bellini. 'This place is full of his supporters. He probably knew before we did. If we're not careful, he will make the official announcement himself, in St Mark's Square.'

'It sounded as though there was someone with him . . .'

Tremblay was stroking his screen rapidly with his thumb, scrolling through data. 'That's entirely possible. Rumours that the Pope is dead are already trending on social media. We shall have to move quickly. May I make a suggestion?'

And now came the second disagreement of the night, as Tremblay urged that the transfer of the Pope's body to the mortuary should take place straight away rather than be delayed until the morning ('We cannot allow ourselves to fall behind the news cycle; it would be a disaster'). He proposed that the official announcement should be released at once and that two film crews from the Vatican Television Centre plus three pool photographers and a newspaper reporter should be allowed into the Piazza Santa Marta to record the transfer of the body from the building to the ambulance. His reasoning was that if they moved quickly, the footage would be broadcast live and the Church would be sure to have maximum exposure. In the great Asian centres of the Catholic faith it was morning; in Latin and North America, evening; only the Europeans and the Africans would be obliged to wake to the news.

Again, Adeyemi objected. For the sake of the dignity of the office, he argued, they should wait for daylight, and for a hearse and a proper casket that could be taken out draped with the papal flag. Bellini countered sharply: 'The Holy Father would not have cared a fig about dignity. It was as one of the humble of the earth that he chose to live, and it is as one of the humble poor that he would wish to be seen in death.'

21

Lomeli concurred. 'Remember, this was a man who refused to ride in a limousine. An ambulance is the nearest we can give him now to public transport.'

Nevertheless, Adeyemi would not change his mind. In the end he had to be outvoted three to one. It was also agreed that the Pope's body should be embalmed. Lomeli said, 'But we must ensure it's done properly.' He had never forgotten filing past Pope Paul VI's body in St Peter's in 1978: in the August heat, the face had turned greyish-green, the jaw had sagged, and there was a definite whiff of corruption. Yet even that ghoulish embarrassment wasn't as bad as the occasion twenty years previously, when Pope Pius XII's body had fermented in its coffin and exploded like a firecracker outside the church of St John Lateran. 'And another thing,' he added. 'We must make sure no one takes any photographs of the body.' That indignity, too, had been inflicted upon Pius XII, whose corpse had been shown in news magazines all over the world.

Tremblay went off to make the arrangements with the media office of the Holy See, and less than thirty minutes later, the ambulance men – their phones confiscated – came and took the Holy Father out of the papal apartment in a white plastic body bag strapped to a wheeled stretcher. They paused with it on the second floor while the four cardinals went down ahead in the elevator so that they could meet it in the hotel lobby and escort it off the premises. The humility of the body in death, the smallness of it, the little rounded foetus shape of the feet and the head, seemed to Lomeli to make a profound statement. *And he bought fine linen, and took him down, and wrapped him in the linen, and laid him in a sepulchre* . . . The children of the Son of Man were all equal at the last, he reflected; all were dependent on God's mercy for the hope of resurrection.

The lobby and the lower flight of the staircase were lined by religious of all ranks. It was their silence that imprinted itself most indelibly on Lomeli's mind. When the elevator doors opened and the body was wheeled out, the only sound – to his dismay – was the click and whir of phone cameras, interspersed with an occasional sob. Tremblay and Adeyemi walked at the head of the stretcher, Lomeli and Bellini at the rear, with the prelates of the Apostolic Camera in a file behind them. They processed through the doors and into the October chill. The drizzle had ceased. There were even a few stars. They passed between the two Swiss Guards and made towards a crucible of multicoloured light – the flashes of the waiting ambulance and its police escort streaking like blue sunbeams around the rain-slicked piazza, the white strobe effect of the photographers, the engulfing yellow glare thrown up by the lamps of the TV crews, and behind all these, rising out of the shadows, the gigantic illuminated glow of St Peter's.

As they reached the ambulance, Lomeli tried to picture the Universal Church at that moment – some one and a quarter billion souls: the ragged crowds gathered around the television sets in the slums of Manila and São Paulo, the swarms of commuters in Tokyo and Shanghai hypnotised by their mobile phones, the sports fans in the bars of Boston and New York whose games were being interrupted . . .

Go forth and make disciples of all the nations, baptising them in the name of the Father, the Son and the Holy Spirit . . .

The body slid head-first into the back of the ambulance. The rear door slammed. The four cardinals stood at solemn attention as the cortège pulled away – two motorcycles, then a police car, then the ambulance, then another police car, and finally more motorcycles. It swept around the piazza for a moment and disappeared. The instant it was out of sight, the sirens were switched on.

So much for humility, thought Lomeli. So much for the poor of the earth. It could have been the motorcade of a dictator.

The wails of the cortège dwindled into the night.

Behind their rope line, the reporters and photographers started calling out to the cardinals, like tourists at a zoo trying to persuade the animals to come closer: 'Your Eminence! Your Eminence! Over here!'

'One of us should say something,' announced Tremblay, and without waiting for a response, he

24

set off across the piazza. The lights seemed to impart to his silhouette a fiery halo. Adeyemi managed to restrain himself for a few more seconds, and then went in pursuit.

Bellini said, under his breath and with great contempt, 'What a circus!'

'Shouldn't you join them?' suggested Lomeli.

'God, no! I shan't pander to the mob. I think I would prefer to go to the chapel and pray.' He smiled sadly and rattled something in his hand, and Lomeli saw that he was holding the travelling chess set. 'Come,' he said. 'Join me. Let us say a Mass for our friend together.' As they walked back into the Casa Santa Marta, he took Lomeli's arm. 'The Holy Father told me of your difficulties with prayer,' he whispered. 'Perhaps I can help. You know that he had doubts himself, by the end?'

'The Pope had doubts about God?'

'Not about God! Never about God!' And then Bellini said something Lomeli would never forget. 'What he had lost faith in was the Church.'

CHAPTER 2

CASA SANTA MARTA

The story of the Conclave began a little under three weeks later.

The Holy Father had died on the day after the feast of St Luke the Evangelist: that is to say on the nineteenth day of October. The remainder of October and the first part of November had been taken up by his funeral and by the almost daily congregations of the College of Cardinals, who had poured into Rome from all across the world to elect his successor. These were private meetings, during which the future of the Church had been discussed. To Lomeli's relief, although the usual split between the progressives and the traditionalists had surfaced occasionally, they had passed off without controversy.

Now, on the feast day of St Herculanus the Martyr – Sunday 7 November – he stood on the threshold of the Sistine Chapel, flanked by the Secretary of the College of Cardinals, Monsignor Raymond O'Malley, and the Master of Papal Liturgical Celebrations, Archbishop Wilhelm Mandorff. The cardinal-electors would be locked into the Vatican that very night. The balloting would begin the following day.

It was shortly after lunchtime and the three prelates were standing just inside the marble and wrought-iron screen that separated the main part of the Sistine Chapel from the vestibule. Together they surveyed the scene. The temporary wooden floor was almost finished. A beige carpet was being nailed down. Television lights were going up, chairs carried in, desks screwed together. Nowhere could one look and not see movement. The teeming activity of Michelangelo's ceiling – all that semi-naked pink-grey flesh stretching and gesturing and bending and carrying – now seemed to Lomeli to have found its clumsy earthly counterpart. At the far end of the Sistine, in the gigantic fresco of Michelangelo's *The Last Judgement,* humanity floated in an azure sky around the Throne of Heaven to an echoing accompaniment of hammering, electric drills and buzz-saws.

'Well, Eminence,' said the Secretary of the College, O'Malley, in his Irish accent. 'I'd say this is a pretty fair vision of hell.'

'Don't be blasphemous, Ray,' replied Lomeli. 'Hell arrives tomorrow, when we bring in the cardinals.'

Archbishop Mandorff laughed slightly too loudly. 'Excellent, Eminence! That is good!'

Lomeli turned to O'Malley. 'He thinks I'm joking.'

O'Malley, who carried a clipboard, was in his late forties: tall, already running to fat, with the bluff red face of a man who had spent his life outdoors – riding to hounds, perhaps – even though he had never done any such thing; it was his Kildare ancestry and a taste for whiskey that had given him his complexion. The Rhinelander Mandorff was older, at sixty, also tall, with a head as smooth and domed and hairless as an egg; he had made his reputation at the University of Eichstätt-Ingolstadt with a treatise on the origins and theological foundations of clerical celibacy.

On either side of the chapel, facing across the long aisle, two dozen plain bare wooden tables had been pushed together to form four rows. Only the table nearest the screen had so far been dressed with cloth, ready for Lomeli's inspection. He stepped into the chapel and ran his hand over the double layers of fabric: a soft crimson felt that reached all the way to the floor, and a thicker, smoother material – beige, to match the carpet – that covered the desktop and its edge, and provided a surface firm enough to write on. It had been set with a Bible, a prayer book, a name card, pens and pencils, a small ballot paper and a long sheet listing the names of all 117 cardinals eligible to vote.

Lomeli picked up the name card: XALXO, SAVERIO. Who was he? He felt a twinge of panic. In the days since the Pope's funeral, he had tried to meet every cardinal and memorise a few personal details. But there were so many new faces – the late Pope had awarded more than sixty red hats, fifteen in the last year alone – that the task had proved beyond him.

'How on earth does one pronounce this? Salso, is it?'

'Khal-koh, Eminence,' said Mandorff. 'He's Indian.'

'Khal-koh. I'm obliged to you, Willi. Thank you.'

Lomeli sat and tested the chair. He was glad to see there was a cushion. And plenty of room to stretch one's legs. He tilted back. Yes, it was comfortable enough. Given the amount of time they were likely to spend locked up in here, it needed to be. He had read the Italian press over breakfast. It was the last time he would see a newspaper until the election was over. The Vatican-watchers were unanimous in predicting a long and divisive Conclave. He prayed it would not be so, and that the Holy Spirit would enter the Sistine early and guide them to a name. But if it failed to materialise – and certainly there had been no sign of it during any of the fourteen congregations – then they could be stuck here for days.

He glanced along the length of the Sistine. It was strange how being seated just a metre above the mosaic floor altered the perspective of the place. In the cavity beneath their feet, the security experts had installed jamming devices to prevent

29

electronic eavesdropping. However, a rival firm of consultants had insisted that such precautions were insufficient. They had claimed that laser beams aimed at the windows set high in the upper gallery could detect vibrations in the glass caused by any words spoken, and that these could be transcribed back into speech. They had recommended that every window should be boarded up. Lomeli had vetoed the proposal. The lack of daylight and the claustrophobia would have been intolerable.

He politely waved away Mandorff's offer of help, pushed himself up from the chair and ventured further into the chapel. The freshly laid carpet smelled sweet, like barley in a threshing room. The workmen stood aside to let him pass; the Secretary of the College and the Master of Papal Liturgical Celebrations followed him. He could still hardly believe it was happening, that he was in charge. It was like a dream.

'You know,' he said, raising his voice to make himself heard above the noise of an electric drill, 'when I was a boy in '58 – when I was still at the seminary in Genoa, in fact – and then again in '63, before I was even ordained, I used to love looking at the pictures of those Conclaves. They had artists' impressions in all the newspapers. I remember how the cardinals used to sit in canopied thrones around the walls during the voting. And when the election was over, one by one they'd pull a lever to collapse their canopies, apart from the cardinal who'd been chosen. Can you imagine that? Old Cardinal Roncalli, who never dreamed of even becoming a cardinal, let alone Pope? And Montini, who was so hated by the old guard there was actually a shouting match in the Sistine Chapel during the voting? Imagine them sitting here in their thrones, and the men who had only a few minutes before been their equals queuing up to bow before them!'

He was aware of O'Malley and Mandorff listening politely. He reproached himself. He was talking like an old man. Nevertheless, the memories moved him. The thrones had been abandoned in 1965 after the Second Vatican Council, like so much else of the Church's old traditions. These days the College of Cardinals was felt to be too large and too multinational for such Renaissance flummery. Still, there was a part of Lomeli that rather hankered after Renaissance flummery, and privately he thought the late Pope had occasionally gone too far in his endless harping on about simplicity and humility. An excess of simplicity, after all, was just another form of ostentation, and pride in one's humility a sin.

He stepped over the electric cables and stood beneath *The Last Judgement* with his hands on his hips. He contemplated the mess. Shavings, sawdust, crates, cartons, strips of underlay. Particles of timber and fabric swirling in the shafts of light. Hammering. Sawing. Drilling. He felt suddenly appalled.

Chaos. Unholy chaos. Like a building site. And in the Sistine Chapel!

This time he had to shout over the racket. 'I assume we *are* going to finish in time?'

'They'll work through the night if they have to,' O'Malley said. 'It will be fine, Eminence, it always is.' He shrugged. 'Italy, you know.'

'Ah yes, Italy! Indeed.' Lomeli stepped down from the altar. To the left was a door, and beyond it the small sacristy known as the Room of Tears. This was where the new Pope would go immediately after his election to be robed. It was a curious little chamber, with a low vaulted ceiling and plain whitewashed walls, almost like a dungeon, crammed with furniture – a table, three chairs, a couch, and the throne that would be carried out for the new pontiff to sit on and receive the obeisance of the cardinal-electors. In the centre was a metal clothes rail on which hung three white papal cassocks wrapped in cellophane – small, medium and large – along with three rochets and three mozzettas. A dozen boxes contained various sizes of papal shoes. Lomeli took out a pair. They were stuffed with tissue paper. He turned them over in his hands. They were slip-ons, made of plain red Morocco leather. He raised them to his nose and sniffed. 'One prepares for every eventuality, but one never knows. For example, Pope John the Twenty-third was too large to fit into the biggest cassock, so they had to button up the front and split the seam at the back – they say he stepped into it arms-first, like a surgeon into his gown, and then the papal tailor sewed him into it.' He replaced the shoes in the box and crossed himself. 'May God bless whoever is called to wear them.'

The three men left the sacristy and strolled back the way they had come, along the carpeted aisle, through the marble screen and down the wooden ramp into the vestibule. Incongruous in one corner, positioned side by side, stood two squat grey metal stoves. Both were about waist-high, one round and one square, each with a copper chimney. The two chimneys had been soldered together to form a single flue. Lomeli eyed it dubiously. It looked very rickety. It rose almost twenty metres, supported by a scaffolding tower, and disappeared through a hole cut in the window. In the round stove they were supposed to burn the voting papers after each ballot, to ensure its secrecy; in the square stove, they released smoke canisters – black to indicate an inconclusive ballot, white when they had a new Pope. The entire apparatus was archaic, absurd, and oddly wonderful.

'The system has been tested?' asked Lomeli.

O'Malley spoke patiently. 'Yes, Eminence. Several times.'

'Of course you would have done that.' He patted the Irishman's arm. 'I'm sorry to fuss.'

They went out across the marbled expanse of the Sala Regia, down the staircase and out into the cobbled car park of the Cortile del Maresciallo. Large wheeled refuse bins overflowed with rubbish. Lomeli said, 'They'll be gone by tomorrow, I trust?'

'Yes, Eminence.'

The trio passed under an archway and into the next courtyard, and the next, and the next – a labyrinth of secret cloisters, with the Sistine always on their left. Lomeli never failed to be disappointed by the dull dun brickwork of the chapel's exterior. Why had every ounce of human genius been poured into that exquisite interior – almost too much genius, in his opinion: it gave one a kind of aesthetic indigestion – and yet seemingly no thought at all had been given to the outside? It looked like a warehouse, or a factory. Or perhaps that was the point. *The treasures of wisdom and knowledge are hidden in God's mystery—*

His thoughts were interrupted by O'Malley, who was walking at his side. 'By the way, Eminence, Archbishop Woźniak wants to have a word.'

'Well I don't think that's possible, do you? The cardinals will begin arriving in an hour.'

'I told him that, but he seemed rather agitated.'

'What's it about?'

'He wouldn't tell me.'

'But really, this is too ridiculous!' He appealed to Mandorff for support. 'The Casa Santa Marta will be sealed off at six. He should have come to me before now. I can't possibly spare the time.'

'It's thoughtless, to say the least.'

'I'll tell him,' said O'Malley.

They walked on, past the saluting Swiss Guards in their sentry boxes and out into the road. They had barely gone a dozen paces before Lomeli's self-reproaches set in. He had spoken too harshly. It was vain of him. It was uncharitable. He was becoming puffed up with his own importance. He would do well to remember that in a few days the Conclave would be over and then no one would be interested in him either. No longer would anyone have to pretend to listen to his stories about canopies and fat Popes. Then he would know what it felt like to be Woźniak, who had lost not only his beloved Holy Father but his position, his home and his prospects, all at the same instant. *Forgive me, God.*

'Actually, that's ungenerous of me,' he said. 'The poor fellow will be worrying about his future. Tell him I'll be at the Casa Santa Marta, meeting the cardinals as they arrive, and I'll try to spare him a few minutes afterwards.'

'Yes, Eminence,' said O'Malley, and made a note on his clipboard.

Before the Casa Santa Marta had been built, more than twenty years earlier, the cardinal-electors were housed for the duration of a Conclave in the Apostolic Palace. The powerful Archbishop of Genoa, Cardinal Siri, a veteran of four Conclaves and the man who had ordained Lomeli a priest in the 1960s, used to complain that it was like being buried alive. Beds were jammed into fifteenth-century offices and reception rooms, with curtains slung between them to provide a rudimentary privacy. Washing facilities for each cardinal consisted of a jug and a basin; sanitation was a commode. It was John Paul II who had decided that such quaint squalor was no longer tolerable on the eve of the twenty-first century and who had ordered the Casa to be built in the south-western corner of the Vatican City at a cost to the Holy See of twenty million dollars.

It reminded Lomeli of a Soviet apartment building: a grey stone rectangle lying on its side, six storeys high. It was arranged over two blocks, each fourteen windows wide, connected by a short central mid-section. In the aerial photographs published in the press that morning it resembled an elongated H, with its northern elevation, Block A, fronting on to the Piazza Santa Marta, and the southern, Block B, overlooking the Vatican wall to the city of Rome. The Casa contained 128 bedrooms with en suite bathrooms, and was run by the blue-habited nuns of the Company of the Daughters of Charity of St Vincent de Paul. In the intervals between papal elections – that is, for the great majority of the time – it was used as a hotel for visiting prelates, and as a semi-permanent hostel for some of the priests working in the bureaucracy of the Curia. The last of these residents had been cleared out of their rooms early in the morning and transferred half a kilometre outside the Vatican to the Domus Romana Sacerdotalis in Via della Traspontina. By the time Cardinal Lomeli entered the building after his visit to the Sistine Chapel, the Casa had taken on a ghostly, abandoned air. He passed through the scanner that had been set up just inside the lobby and collected his key from the sister at the reception desk.

Rooms had been allocated the previous week by lot. Lomeli had drawn one on the second floor of Block A. To reach it he had to pass the late Pope's suite. It had been sealed since the morning after his death, in accordance with the laws of the Holy See, and to Lomeli, whose guilty recreation was detective fiction, it looked disturbingly like one of the crime scenes he had often read about. Red ribbon ran back and forth in a cat's cradle between the door and its frame, fixed in place by blobs of wax bearing the coat of arms of the Cardinal Camerlengo. In the doorway was a large vase of fresh white lilies; they exuded a sickly scent. On the tables either side of them, two dozen votive candles in red glass holders flickered in the wintry gloom. The landing, which had once been so busy as the effective seat of government of the Church, was deserted. Lomeli knelt and took out his rosary. He tried to pray, but his mind kept drifting back to his final conversation with the Holy Father.

You knew my difficulties, he said to the closed door, *yet you refused my resignation. Very well. I understand. You must have had your reasons. Now at least help to provide me with the strength and wisdom to find a way through this trial.*

Behind him he heard the elevator stop and the doors open, but when he glanced over his shoulder, no one was there. The doors closed and the car continued upwards. He put away his beads and struggled to his feet.

His room was halfway along the corridor, on the right. He unlocked the door and opened it on to darkness. He felt around the wall for a switch and turned on the lamp. He was dismayed to discover he had no sitting room, merely a bedroom, with plain white walls, a polished parquet floor and an iron bedstead. But then he thought it was for the best. In the Palace of the Holy Office he had an apartment of four hundred square metres, with plenty of room for a grand piano. It would do him good to be reminded of a simpler life.

He opened the window and tried the shutter, forgetting it had been sealed, like all the others in the building. Every television and radio had been removed. The cardinals were to be entirely sequestered from the world for as long as the election lasted, so that no person and no news could influence their meditation. He wondered what view he would have had if he had been able to open the shutters. St Peter's or the city? He had already lost his bearings.

He checked the closet and saw with satisfaction that his efficient chaplain, Father Zanetti, had already brought over his suitcase from his apartment and had even unpacked it for him. His choir dress was hanging up. His red biretta was on the top shelf, his underwear in the drawers. He counted up the number of socks and smiled. Enough for a week. Zanetti was a pessimist. In the tiny bathroom his toothbrush, razor and shaving brush had been laid out, along with a packet of sleeping pills. On the desk were his breviary and Bible, a bound copy of *Universi Dominici Gregis*, the rules for electing a new Pope, and a much thicker file, prepared by O'Malley, containing the details of every cardinal who was eligible to vote, along with their photograph. Beside it was a leather folder in which was the draft of the homily he would have to deliver the next day when he celebrated the televised Mass in St Peter's Basilica. The mere sight of it was enough to give him stomach cramps, and he had to move quickly to the bathroom. Afterwards he sat on the edge of the bed with his head bowed.

He tried to tell himself that his feelings of inadequacy were simply proof of a proper humility. He was the Cardinal-Bishop of Ostia. Before that he had been the Cardinal-Priest of San Marcello al Corso in Rome. Before that, the titular Archbishop of Aquileia. In all of these positions, however nominal, he had played an active part: had preached sermons and celebrated Mass and heard confessions. But one could be the grandest prince of the Universal Church and still lack the most basic skills of the commonest country priest. If only he had experienced life in an ordinary parish, just for a year or two! Instead, ever since his ordination, his path of service – first as a professor of canon law, then as a diplomat, and finally, briefly, as Secretary of State – had seemed only to lead him away from God rather than towards Him. The higher he had climbed, the further heaven had receded. And now it fell to him, of all unworthy creatures, to guide his fellow cardinals in choosing the man who should hold the Keys of St Peter.

Servus fidelis. A faithful servant. It was on his coat of arms. A prosaic motto for a prosaic man. *A manager . . .*

After a while he went into the bathroom and poured himself a glass of water.

Very well then, he thought. *Manage.*

The doors of the Casa Santa Marta were scheduled to close at six. No one would be admitted after that. 'Come early, Your Eminences,' Lomeli had advised the cardinals at their last congregation, 'and please remember that no communications with the outside world will be permitted after you've checked in. All mobile telephones and computers must be surrendered at the front desk. You will have to pass through a scanner to make sure you have not been forgetful. It would speed up registration considerably if you simply left them behind.'

At five to three, wearing a winter coat over his black cassock, he stood outside the entrance, flanked by his officials. Once again, Monsignor O'Malley, the Secretary of the College, and Archbishop Mandorff, the Master of Papal Liturgical Celebrations, were with him, along with Mandorff's four assistants: two masters of ceremonies, one a monsignor and the other a priest, and two friars of the Order of St Augustine who were attached to the Papal Sacristy. He was also permitted the services of his chaplain, young Father Zanetti. These, and two doctors, on standby in case of medical emergencies, were the sum total of those who would supervise the election of the most powerful spiritual figure on earth.

It was getting cold. Invisible but close in the darkening November sky a helicopter hovered a couple of hundred metres above the ground. The drone of its rotors seemed to come in waves, rising and falling as either it or the wind changed direction. Lomeli scanned the clouds, trying to work out where it was. No doubt it would belong to some television network, dispatched to take aerial pictures of the cardinals arriving at the exterior gates; either that, or it was part of the security forces. He had been briefed about security by the Italian Minister of the Interior, a fresh-faced economist from a well-known Catholic family, who had never worked outside politics and whose hands had shaken as he read through his notes. The threat of terrorism was considered serious and

41

imminent, the Minister had said. Surface-to-air missiles and snipers would be stationed on the roofs of the buildings surrounding the Vatican. Five thousand uniformed police and army personnel would openly patrol the neighbouring streets in a show of strength, while hundreds of plain-clothes officers mingled with the crowds. At the end of the meeting the Minister had asked Lomeli to bless him.

Occasionally above the noise of the helicopter floated the distant sounds of protest: thousands of voices chanting in unison, punctuated by klaxons and drumbeats and whistles. Lomeli tried to distinguish what it was they were complaining about. It was impossible. Supporters of gay marriage and opponents of civil union, pro-divorce advocates and Families for Catholic Unity, women demanding to be ordained as priests and women demanding abortions and contraception, Muslims and anti-Muslims, immigrants and anti-immigrants . . . they merged into a single undifferentiated cacophony of rage. Police sirens cried out somewhere, first one and then another and then a third, as if they were courting one another from opposite ends of the city.

We are an Ark, he thought, surrounded by a rising flood of discord.

Across the piazza, in the nearest corner of the basilica, the melodious clock chimed the four quarter-hours in quick succession; then the great bell of St Peter's tolled three. The anxious security

42

men in their short black coats strutted and turned and fretted like crows.

A few minutes later, the first of the cardinals appeared. They were wearing their everyday long black cassocks with red piping, with wide red silk sashes tied at their waists and red skullcaps on their heads. They climbed the slope from the direction of the Palace of the Holy Office. A member of the Swiss Guard in his plumed helmet walked with them, carrying a halberd. It might have been a scene from the sixteenth century, except for the noise of their wheeled suitcases, clattering over the cobbles.

The prelates came closer. Lomeli squared his shoulders. He recognised two from his briefing book. On the left was the Brazilian Cardinal Sá, Archbishop of São Salvador de Bahia (*aged 60, liberation theologian, a possible Pope, but not this time*), and on the right, the elderly Chilean, Cardinal Contreras, Archbishop Emeritus of Santiago (*aged 77, arch-conservative, one-time confessor of General Augusto Pinochet*). Between them walked a small, dignified figure it took him longer to place: Cardinal Hierra, the Archbishop of Mexico City, of whom Lomeli remembered nothing except his name. He guessed at once that they had been lunching together, doubtless trying to agree on a common candidate. There were nineteen Latin American cardinal-electors, and if they were to vote in a block they would be formidable. But one had only to observe the body

43

language of the Brazilian and the Chilean, the way they refused even to look at one another, to realise that such a common front was impossible. They'd probably struggled even to agree on which restaurant to meet in.

'My brothers,' he said, opening his arms, 'welcome.' Immediately, the Mexican archbishop began complaining in a mixture of Spanish and Italian about his journey across Rome – he showed his arm: the dark fabric was covered in spit – and about their treatment at the entrance to the Vatican, which had scarcely been better. They had been obliged to present their passports, submit to a body search, open their luggage for inspection: 'Are we common criminals, Dean, or what is this?'

Lomeli took the archbishop's gesticulating hand in both of his and clasped it. 'Your Eminence, I hope at least you have had a good lunch – it may be your last for some time – and I am sorry if you felt your treatment was demeaning. But we must do our best to keep this Conclave safe, and I fear a certain inconvenience is the price we shall all have to pay. Father Zanetti will show you to reception.'

And with that, and without letting go of his hand, he gently steered Hierra towards the entrance of the Casa Santa Marta, then released him. Watching them walk away, O'Malley marked their names on his list, then turned to Lomeli and raised his eyebrows, at which Lomeli returned him a look of such reproof that the monsignor's capillaried

44

cheeks turned even redder. He liked the Irishman's sense of humour. But he would not have his cardinals mocked.

In the meantime, another trio had started making its way up the hill. Americans, thought Lomeli, they always stick together: they had even given daily press conferences together until he put a stop to it. He guessed they would have shared a taxi over from the American clergy house, the Villa Stritch. He recognised the Archbishop of Boston, Willard Fitzgerald (*aged 68, preoccupied with pastoral duties, still clearing up the mess of the abuse scandal, good with the media*); Mario Santos SJ, Archbishop of Galveston-Houston (*aged 70, president of the United States Conference of Catholic Bishops, cautious reformer*), and Paul Krasinski (*aged 79, Archbishop Emeritus of Chicago, Prefect Emeritus of the Apostolic Signatura, traditionalist, strong supporter of the Legionaries of Christ*). Like the Latin Americans, the North Americans wielded nineteen votes, and it was widely assumed that Tremblay, as Archbishop Emeritus of Quebec, would pick up most of them. But he wouldn't get Krasinski's vote – the Chicagoan had already endorsed Tedesco, and in language calculatedly insulting to the dead Pope: 'We need a Holy Father who can restore the Church to her proper path after a long period when she has been lost.' He walked with the aid of two sticks and waved one of them at Lomeli. The Swiss Guard carried his big leather suitcase.

'Good afternoon, Dean.' He was gleeful to be back in Rome. 'I bet you never expected to see me again!'

He was the oldest member of the Conclave: another month and he would have reached eighty, the statutory age limit for voting. He also had Parkinson's disease, and there had been doubt until the very last minute whether he would be pronounced fit enough to travel. Well, thought Lomeli grimly, he had made it, and there was nothing that could be done about it.

'On the contrary, Your Eminence, we wouldn't have dared hold a Conclave without you.'

Krasinski squinted at the Casa Santa Marta. 'So then! Where have you put me?'

'I've arranged for you to have a suite on the ground floor.'

'A suite! That's decent of you, Dean. I thought the rooms were distributed by lot?'

Lomeli leaned in. 'I fixed the ballot,' he whispered.

'Ha!' Krasinski struck one of his sticks against the cobbles. 'I wouldn't put it past you Italians to fix the others too!'

He hobbled away. His companions hung back, embarrassed, as if they had been obliged to bring to a family wedding an elderly relative for whose behaviour they could not vouch. Santos shrugged. 'Same old Paul, I'm afraid.'

'Oh, I don't mind him. We've been teasing one another for years.'

And in an odd way Lomeli did feel almost nostalgic for the old brute. They were survivors together. This would be their third papal election. Only a handful of others could say the same. Most of those arriving had never participated in a Conclave before; and if the College chose a young enough man, most would never take part in one again. It was history they were making, and as the afternoon went on and they came up the slope with their suitcases, sometimes singly but mostly in groups of three or four, Lomeli was moved by how many of them were awed by the occasion, even those who tried to put on a show of nonchalance.

What an extraordinary variety of races they represented – what a testament to the breadth of the Universal Church that men born so different should be bound together by their faith in God! From the Eastern ministries, Maronite and Coptic, came the patriarchs of Lebanon, Antioch and Alexandria; from India, the major archbishops of Trivandrum and Ernakulam-Angamaly, and also the Archbishop of Ranchi, Saverio Xalxo, whose name Lomeli took pleasure in pronouncing correctly: 'Cardinal Khal-koh, welcome to the Conclave . . .'

From the Far East came no fewer than thirteen Asian archbishops – Jakarta and Cebu, Bangkok and Manila, Seoul and Tokyo, Ho Chi Minh City and Hong Kong . . . And from Africa another thirteen – Maputo, Kampala, Dar-es-Salaam,

Khartoum, Addis Ababa . . . Lomeli was sure that the Africans would vote as a solid block for Cardinal Adeyemi. Halfway through the afternoon, he noticed the Nigerian strolling across the piazza in the direction of the Palace of the Holy Office. He returned a few minutes later with a group of African cardinals. Presumably he had met them at the gate. As they walked, he pointed out this building and that, in the manner of a proprietor. He brought them over to Lomeli for their official welcome, and Lomeli was struck by how much they deferred to Adeyemi, even the elderly grey-headed eminences like Zucula of Mozambique and the Kenyan, Mwangale, who had been around a lot longer.

But to win, Adeyemni would need to pick up support from beyond Africa and the Third World, and that would be his difficulty. He might win votes in Africa by attacking, as he often did, 'the Satan of global capitalism' and 'the abomination of homosexuality', but he would lose them in America and Europe. And it was still the cardinals of Europe – fifty-six in all – who dominated the Conclave. These were the men Lomeli knew best. Some, like Ugo De Luca, the Archbishop of Genoa, with whom he had studied at the diocesan seminary, had been his friends for half a century. Others he had been meeting at conferences for more than thirty years.

Arm in arm up the hill came the two great liberal theologians of Western Europe, once outcasts but lately awarded their red hats in a show of defiance by the Holy Father: the Belgian, Cardinal Vandroogenbroek (*aged 68, ex-Professor of Theology at Louvain University, advocate of Curial appointments for women, no-hoper*), and the German, Cardinal Löwenstein (*aged 77, Archbishop Emeritus of Rottenburg-Stuttgart, investigated for heresy by the Congregation for the Doctrine of the Faith, 1997*). The Patriarch of Lisbon, Rui Brandão D'Cruz, arrived smoking a cigar, and lingered on the doorstep of the Casa Santa Marta, reluctant to put it out. The Archbishop of Prague, Jan Jandaček, made his way across the piazza still limping as a result of his torture at the hands of the Czech secret police when he was working underground as a young priest in the 1960s. There was the Archbishop Emeritus of Palermo, Calogero Scozzazi, investigated three times for money-laundering but never prosecuted, and the Archbishop of Riga, Gatis Brotzkus, whose family had converted to Catholicism after the war and whose Jewish mother had been murdered by the Nazis. There was the Frenchman, Jean-Baptiste Courtemarche, Archbishop of Bordeaux, once excommunicated as a follower of the heretic Marcel-François Lefebvre, and who had been secretly taped claiming that the Holocaust had never occurred. There was the Spanish Archbishop of Toledo, Modesto Villanueva – at fifty-four the youngest member of the Conclave – an organiser of Catholic Youth, who maintained that the way to God was through the beauty of culture . . .

49

And finally – and broadly speaking it *was* finally – there came that separate and most rarefied species of cardinal, the two dozen members of the Curia, who lived permanently in Rome and who ran the big departments of the Church. They formed in effect their own chapter inside the College, the Order of Cardinal-Deacons. Many, like Lomeli, had grace-and-favour apartments within the walls of the Vatican. Most were Italian. For them it was an easy matter to stroll across the Piazza Santa Marta carrying their suitcases. As a result, they had lingered over their lunches and were among the last to arrive. And although Lomeli greeted them just as warmly as he did the others – they were his neighbours, after all – he couldn't help noticing that they lacked the precious gift of *awe* he had detected in those who had travelled from across the world. Good men though they were, they were somehow knowing; they were blasé. Lomeli had recognised this spiritual disfigurement in himself. He had prayed for the strength to fight it. The late Pope used to rail against it to their faces: 'Be on your guard, my brothers, against developing the vices of all courtiers down the ages – the sins of vanity and intrigue and of malice and gossip.' When Bellini had confided on the day of the Holy Father's death that the Pope had lost his faith in the Church – a revelation so shocking to Lomeli that he had tried ever since to banish it from his mind – it was surely these bureaucrats he had meant.

Yet it was the Pope who had appointed them all. Nobody had made him pick them. For example, there was the Prefect of the Congregation for the Doctrine of the Faith, Cardinal Simo Guttuso. The liberals had had such high hopes for the genial Archbishop of Florence. 'A second Pope John XXIII,' they had called him. But far from granting more autonomy to the bishops, which he had proclaimed as his great cause before he entered the Curia, once installed Guttuso had slowly revealed himself to be every bit as authoritarian as his predecessors, merely lazier. He had become very stout, like a figure from the Renaissance, and walked with difficulty the short distance from his huge apartment in the Palazzo San Carlo to the Casa Santa Marta, which was almost next door. His personal chaplain struggled behind him with his three suitcases.

Lomeli, eyeing the suitcases, said, 'My dear Simo, are you trying to smuggle in your personal chef?'

'Well, Dean, one never knows quite when one will be able to go home, does one?' Guttuso grasped Lomeli's hand in his two fat damp paws and added hoarsely, 'Or even, for that matter, if one *will* be going home.' The phrase hung in the air for several seconds, and Lomeli thought: dear God, he actually believes he might be elected; but then Guttuso winked. 'Ah, Lomeli! Your face! Don't worry, I'm joking. I am one man who is aware of his limitations. Unlike certain of our colleagues . . .' He kissed Lomeli on either cheek and waddled past him. Lomeli watched him pause in the doorway to recover his breath and then disappear into the Casa Santa Marta.

He guessed it had been lucky for Guttuso that the Holy Father had died when he did. Another few months and Lomeli was sure he would have been asked to resign. 'I want a Church that is poor,' the Pope had complained more than once in Lomeli's hearing. 'I want a Church that is closer to the people. Guttuso has a good soul but he has forgotten where he came from.' He had quoted Matthew: 'If you would be perfect, go, sell what you possess and give to the poor, and you will have treasure in heaven; and come, follow me.' Lomeli reckoned the Holy Father had had it in mind to remove almost half the senior men he had appointed. Bill Rudgard, for example, who arrived soon after Guttuso: he might come from New York and look like a Wall Street banker, but he had failed entirely to gain control over the financial management of his department, the Congregation for the Causes of Saints ('Between you, me and the bedpost, I should never have given the job to an American. They are so inno-cent: they have no idea how bribery works. Did you know that the going rate for a beatification is said to be three quarters of a million euros? The only miracle is that anyone pays it . . .').

As for the next man to enter the Casa Santa Marta, Cardinal Tutino, the Prefect of the

Congregation for Bishops, he would surely have gone in the New Year. He had been exposed in the press for spending half a million euros knocking two apartments together to create a place big enough to house the three nuns and the chaplain he felt necessary to serve him. Tutino had been given such a mauling in the media, he looked like the survivor of a physical attack. Someone had leaked his private emails. He was obsessed with finding out who. He moved furtively. He glanced over his shoulder. He found it hard to meet Lomeli's eyes. After only the most cursory of greetings, he slipped into the Casa, ostentatiously carrying his belongings in a cheap plastic holdall.

By five o'clock it was becoming dark. As the sun dipped, the air chilled. Lomeli asked how many of the cardinals had yet to arrive. O'Malley consulted his list. 'Fourteen, Your Eminence.'

'So a hundred and three of our sheep are safely in the pen before nightfall. Rocco,' he said, turning to his priest, 'would you be so kind as to bring me my scarf?'

The helicopter had moved away, but the last of the demonstrators could still be heard. There was a steady, rhythmic beating of drums.

He said, 'I wonder where Cardinal Tedesco has got to?'

O'Malley said, 'Perhaps he isn't coming.'

'That would be too much to hope! Ah, forgive me. That was uncharitable.' He could hardly admonish the Secretary of the College for lacking respect if he didn't show it himself. He must remember to confess his sin.

Father Zanetti returned with his scarf just as Cardinal Tremblay appeared, walking alone from the direction of the Apostolic Palace. Slung over his shoulder was his choir dress in a dry-cleaner's cellophane wrapper. In his right hand he swung a Nike sports bag. It was the image he had projected ever since the Holy Father's funeral: a Pope for the modern age – unpretentious, informal, accessible – even though not one hair of that magnificent silvery helmet beneath his red zucchetto was ever out of place. Lomeli had expected the Canadian's candidacy to fade after the first couple of days. But Tremblay knew how to keep his name before the media. As Camerlengo, he was responsible for the day-to-day running of the Church until a new pontiff was elected. There was not much to do. Nevertheless, he called daily meetings of the cardinals in the Synod Hall and held press conferences afterwards, and soon articles began appearing, quoting 'Vatican sources', saying how much his skilful management had impressed his colleagues. And he had another, more tangible means of ingratiating himself. It was to him, as Prefect of the Congregation for Evangelisation of Peoples, that the cardinals from the developing world, especially the poorer countries, came for funds, not just for their missionary work but for their living expenses in Rome during the time between the Pope's funeral and the Conclave. It was hard not to be impressed. If a man had that strong a sense of destiny, perhaps he had indeed been chosen? Perhaps he had been given a sign, invisible to the rest of them? It was certainly invisible to Lomeli.

'Joe, welcome.'

'Jacopo,' said Tremblay amiably, and lifted his arms with a smile of apology, to show that he couldn't shake hands.

If he wins, Lomeli promised himself as soon as the Canadian had passed, I shall be gone from Rome the very next day.

He knotted his black woollen scarf around his neck and thrust his hands deep into the pockets of his overcoat. He stamped his feet against the cobbles.

Zanetti said, 'We could wait indoors, Your Eminence.'

'No, I'd prefer to get some fresh air while I still can.'

Cardinal Bellini didn't appear until half past five. Lomeli noticed his tall, thin figure moving through the shadows around the edge of the piazza. He was pulling a suitcase with one hand. In the other he carried a thick black briefcase so crammed with books and papers it would not properly close. His head was bowed in meditation. By general agreement, Bellini had emerged as the favourite to succeed to the throne of St Peter. Lomeli wondered what thoughts must be passing through his mind at the prospect. He was far too lofty for gossip or intrigue. The Pope's strictures about the Curia had not applied to him. He had worked so hard as Secretary of State that his officials had been obliged to provide him with a second shift of assistants to come on duty at six every evening and stay with him until the early hours. More than any other member of the College he had the physical and mental capacity to be Pope. And he was a man of prayer. Lomeli had made up his mind to vote for him, although he had been careful not to say so, and Bellini had been too fastidious to ask him. The ex-Secretary was so wrapped up in his thoughts he seemed likely to walk straight past the welcoming party. But at the last minute he remembered where he was, glanced up and wished them all good evening. His face looked more than usually pale and drawn. 'Am I the last?'

'Not quite. How are you, Aldo?'

'Oh, fairly dreadful!' He managed a thin-lipped smile and drew Lomeli aside. 'Well, you've read today's newspapers – how else would you expect me to be? I've twice meditated on the *Spiritual Exercises* of St Ignatius just to try to keep my feet on the ground.'

'Yes, I've seen the press, and if you want my advice, you'd be wise to ignore all these self-appointed "experts". Leave it to God, my friend. If it's His will, it will happen; if not, not.'

'But I'm not merely God's passive instrument, Jacopo. I have some say in the matter. He gave us free will.' He lowered his voice so that the others couldn't hear. 'It's not that I want it, you understand? No sane man could possibly want the papacy.'

'Some of our colleagues seem to.'

'Well then they're fools, or worse. We both saw what it did to the Holy Father. It's a Calvary.'

'Nevertheless, you should prepare yourself. The way things are going, it may well fall to you.'

'But what if I don't want it? What if I know in my heart I'm not worthy?'

'Nonsense. You're more worthy than any of us.'

'I am not.'

'Then tell your supporters not to vote for you. Pass the chalice to someone else.'

A tortured look passed across Bellini's face. 'And let it go to *him*?' He nodded down the hill to where a squat, bulky, almost square figure was marching up the slope towards them, his shape rendered all the more comical by the tall, plumed Swiss Guards flanking him. '*He* has no doubts. He's perfectly ready to undo all the progress we've made these past sixty years. How am I to live with myself if I don't try to stop him?' And without waiting for a reply, he hurried into the Casa Santa Marta, leaving Lomeli to face the Patriarch of Venice.

Cardinal Goffredo Tedesco was the least clerical-looking cleric Lomeli had ever seen. If you showed his picture to someone who didn't know him, they would say he was a retired butcher, perhaps, or a bus driver. He came from a peasant family in Basilicata, right down in the south, the youngest of twelve children – the kind of huge family that used to be so common in Italy but had almost vanished since the end of the Second World War. His nose had been broken in his youth and was bulbous and slightly bent. His hair was too long and roughly parted. He had shaved carelessly. In the fading light he reminded Lomeli of a figure from another century: Gioachino Rossini, perhaps. But the rustic image was an act. He had two degrees in theology, spoke five languages fluently, and had been a protégé of Ratzinger's at the Congregation for the Doctrine of the Faith, where he had been known as the Panzer Cardinal's enforcer. Tedesco had kept well clear of Rome ever since the Pope's funeral, pleading a severe cold. Of course nobody believed him. He scarcely needed any more publicity, and his absence added to his mystique.

'Apologies, Dean. My train was delayed in Venice.'

'Are you well?'

'Oh, not too bad – but is one ever really well at our age?'

'We've missed you, Goffredo.'

'No doubt.' He laughed. 'Alas, it couldn't be helped. But my friends have kept me well informed.

I'll see you later, Dean. No, no, my dear fellow,'
he said to the Swiss Guard, 'give me that,' and so,
a man of the people to the last, he insisted on
carrying his own bag inside.

CHAPTER 3

REVELATIONS

At a quarter to six, the Archbishop Emeritus of Kiev, Vadym Yatsenko, was pushed up the slope in a wheelchair. O'Malley made an exaggerated tick on his clipboard and declared that all 117 cardinals were now safely gathered in.

Relieved and moved, Lomeli bowed his head and closed his eyes. The seven officials of the Conclave immediately followed suit. 'Heavenly Father,' he said, 'Maker of heaven and earth, You have chosen us to be Your people. Help us to give You glory in everything we do. Bless this Conclave and guide it in wisdom, bring us, Your servants, together, and help us to meet one another in love and joy. Father, we praise Your name now and forever. Amen.'

'Amen.'

He turned towards the Casa Santa Marta. Now that all the shutters were locked, not a gleam of light escaped the upper floors. In the darkness it had become a bunker. Only the entrance was illuminated. Behind the thick bulletproof glass, priests and security men moved silently in the yellowish glow like creatures in an aquarium.

Lomeli was almost at the door when someone

touched his arm. Zanetti said, 'Eminence, remember Archbishop Woźniak is waiting to see you.'

'Oh yes – Janusz; I'd forgotten him. He's cutting it a bit fine, isn't he?'

'He knows he has to be gone by six, Eminence.'

'Where is he?'

'I asked him to wait in one of the downstairs meeting rooms.'

Lomeli acknowledged the salute of the Swiss Guard and entered the warmth of the hostel. He followed Zanetti across the lobby, unbuttoning his coat as he walked. After the healthy cold of the piazza, it felt uncomfortably hot. Between the marble pillars, several small groups of cardinals stood talking. He smiled at them as he passed. Who *were* they? His memory was going. When he was a Papal Nuncio, he could remember the names of all his fellow diplomats, and of their wives and even their children. Now every conversation came freighted with the threat of embarrassment.

At the entrance to the meeting room, opposite the chapel, he gave his coat and scarf to Zanetti. 'Would you mind taking these upstairs for me?'

'Do you want me to sit in?'

'No, I'll deal with it.' He put his hand on the doorknob. 'Remind me, what time is vespers?'

'Six thirty, Eminence.'

Lomeli opened the door. Archbishop Woźniak was standing with his back to him at the far end of the room. He appeared to be staring at the bare wall. There was a faint but unmistakable smell of alcohol. Once more Lomeli was obliged to suppress his irritation. As if he didn't have enough to deal with!

'Janusz?' He advanced towards Woźniak, intending to embrace him, but to his alarm, the former Master of the Papal Household sank to his knees and made the sign of the cross.

'Your Eminence, in the name of the Father, and of the Son, and of the Holy Spirit. My last confession was four weeks ago—'

Lomeli stretched out his hand. 'Janusz, Janusz, forgive me, but I simply haven't time to hear your confession. The doors will be closing in a few minutes and you'll have to leave. Just sit down, please, and tell me quickly what is troubling you.' He raised the archbishop to his feet, guided him to a chair and sat down next to him. He gave a smile of encouragement and patted the other man's knee. 'Go on.'

Woźniak's pudgy face was damp with perspiration. Lomeli was close enough to see the smear of dust on his spectacles.

'Your Eminence, I should have come to you before now. But I promised I wouldn't say anything.'

'I understand. Don't worry.' The man seemed to be sweating vodka. What was this myth that it was odourless? His hands shook. He reeked of it. 'Now when you say you promised not to mention it – to whom did you make this promise?'

'Cardinal Tremblay.'

'I see.' Lomeli drew back slightly. After a lifetime

spent listening to secrets, he had developed an instinct for such matters. The vulgar always assumed it was best to try to know everything; in his experience it was often better to know as little as possible. 'Before you go any further, Janusz, I want you to take a moment to ask God if it's right for you to break your promise to Cardinal Tremblay.'

'I have asked Him many times, Your Eminence, and that is why I'm here.' Woźniak's mouth trembled. 'If it's embarrassing for you, though . . .'

'No, no, of course not. But please just give me the straight facts. We have little time.'

'Very well.' The Pole took a breath. 'You remember that on the day the Holy Father died, the last person to have an official appointment with him, at four o'clock, was Cardinal Tremblay?'

'I remember.'

'Well, at that meeting, the Holy Father dismissed Cardinal Tremblay from all his offices in the Church.'

'*What?*'

'He sacked him.'

'Why?'

'For gross misconduct.'

Lomeli couldn't speak at first. 'Really, Archbishop, you could have picked a better time to come and tell me such a thing.'

Woźniak's head drooped. 'I know, Your Eminence, forgive me.'

'In fact you could have come to see me at any time in the past three weeks!'

'I don't blame you for feeling angry, Eminence. But it wasn't until the last day or two that I started hearing all these rumours about Cardinal Tremblay.'

'What rumours?'

'That he might be elected Pope.'

Lomeli paused just long enough to convey his displeasure at such frankness. 'And you see it as your duty to prevent that?'

'I no longer know what my duty is. I've prayed and prayed for guidance, and in the end it seems to me that you should have the facts, and then you can decide whether or not to tell the other cardinals.'

'But what *are* the facts, Janusz? You've given me no facts. Were you present at this meeting between the two of them?'

'No, Eminence. The Holy Father told me about it afterwards, when we had supper together.'

'Did he tell you why he'd dismissed Cardinal Tremblay?'

'No. He said the reasons would become clear soon enough. He was extremely agitated, though – very angry.'

Lomeli contemplated Woźniak. Might he be lying? No. He was a simple soul, plucked from a small town in Poland to be a chaplain and companion for John Paul II in his declining years. Lomeli was sure he was telling the truth. 'Does anyone else know about this, apart from you and Cardinal Tremblay?'

'Monsignor Morales – he was at the meeting between the Holy Father and Cardinal Tremblay.'

Lomeli knew Hector Morales, although not well. He had been one of the Pope's private secretaries. A Uruguayan.

'Listen, Janusz,' he said. 'Are you absolutely certain you've got this right? I can see how upset you are. But, for example, why hasn't Monsignor Morales ever mentioned anything about it? He was there in the apartment with us on the night the Holy Father died. He could have brought it up then. Or he could have told one of the other secretaries.'

'Eminence, you said you wanted the straight facts. These are the straight facts. I've been over them in my mind a thousand times. I found the Holy Father dead. I summoned the doctor. The doctor summoned Cardinal Tremblay. Those are the rules, as you know: "The first member of the Curia to be officially notified in the event of the Pope's death is to be the Camerlengo." Cardinal Tremblay arrived and took control of the situation. Naturally, I was hardly in a position to object, and besides, I was in a state of shock. But then, after about an hour, he drew me aside and asked me if the Holy Father had had anything particular on his mind when we had supper. That's when I should have said something. But I was frightened, Your Eminence. I wasn't supposed to know of these matters. So I just said that he seemed agitated, without going into any details. Afterwards, I saw the cardinal whispering in the corner with Monsignor Morales. My guess is that he was persuading him not to say anything about the meeting.'

'What makes you think that?'

'Because later I did try to mention to the monsignor what the Pope had told me, and he was very firm about it. He said that there had been no dismissal, that the Holy Father had not been his normal self for several weeks, and that for the good of the Church I shouldn't raise the subject again. So I haven't. But it's not right, Eminence. God tells me it's not right.'

'No,' agreed Lomeli, 'it's not right.' His mind was trying to work through the implications. It might easily all be nothing: Woźniak was over-wrought. But then again, if they did elect Tremblay Pope, and some scandal was subsequently discovered, the consequences for the wider Church could be appalling.

There was a loud knock on the door. Lomeli called out, 'Not now!'

The door was thrown open. O'Malley leaned into the room. All his considerable weight was balanced on his right foot, like an ice-skater; his left hand clung to the door frame. 'Your Eminence, Archbishop, I'm very sorry to interrupt, but you are needed urgently.'

'Dear God, what is it now?'

O'Malley glanced briefly at Woźniak. 'I'm sorry, Eminence, I'd prefer not to say. If you could come at once, please?'

He stepped back and gestured in the direction

of the lobby. Reluctantly Lomeli got to his feet. He spoke to Woźniak. 'You'll have to leave the matter with me. But you did the right thing.'

'Thank you. I knew I could always come to you. Would you bless me, Eminence?'

Lomeli laid his hand on the archbishop's head. 'Go in peace to love and serve the Lord.' At the door, he turned. 'And perhaps you would be kind enough to remember me in your prayers tonight, Janusz? I fear I may have greater need of intercession than you.'

In the last few minutes, the lobby had grown more crowded. Cardinals had begun emerging from their rooms, preparing to go to Mass in the hostel's chapel. Tedesco was holding forth to a group at the bottom of the staircase – Lomeli saw him out of the corner of his eye as he strode alongside O'Malley towards the reception desk. A member of the Swiss Guard, his helmet under his arm, was standing at the long polished wooden counter. With him were two security men and Archbishop Mandorff. There was something ominous about the way they were staring straight ahead, not speaking, and it occurred to Lomeli with absolute certainty that a cardinal must have died.

O'Malley said, 'I'm sorry for the mystery, Your Eminence, but I didn't think I could say anything in front of the Archbishop.'

'I know exactly what this is about: you're going to tell me we've lost a cardinal.'

'On the contrary, Dean, we appear to have acquired one.' The Irishman gave a nervous giggle.

'Is that meant to be a joke?'

'No, Eminence.' O'Malley became sombre. 'I mean it literally: another cardinal has just turned up.'

'How is that possible? Did we leave someone off the list?'

'No, his name was never on our list. He says he was created *in pectore*.'

Lomeli felt as if he had walked into an invisible wall. He came briefly to a halt in the middle of the lobby. 'He has to be an impostor, surely?'

'That was my reaction, Eminence. But Archbishop Mandorff has spoken to him. And he thinks not.'

Lomeli hurried over to Mandorff. 'What's this I'm hearing?'

Behind the reception desk, a couple of nuns busied themselves at their computers, pretending not to listen.

'His name is Vincent Benítez, Eminence. He's the Archbishop of Baghdad.'

'Baghdad? I wasn't aware we had an archbishop in such a place. Is he an Iraqi?'

'Hardly! He's a Filipino. The Holy Father appointed him last year.'

'Yes, now I think I do remember.' He had a vague memory of a photograph in a magazine. A Catholic prelate standing in the burnt-out skeleton of a church. Was he really now a cardinal?

Mandorff said, 'You of all people must have been aware of his elevation?'

'I am not. You look surprised.'

'Well, I assumed if he'd been made a cardinal, the Holy Father would have notified the Dean of the College.'

'Not necessarily. If you recall, he completely revised the canon law on *in pectore* appointments shortly before he died.'

Lomeli tried to sound unconcerned, although in truth he felt this latest slight even more acutely than the rest. *In pectore* ('in the heart') was the ancient provision under which a Pope could create a cardinal without revealing his name, even to his closest associates: apart from the beneficiary, God alone would know. In all his years in the Curia, Lomeli had only ever heard of one case of a cardinal created *in pectore*, whose name was never made public, even after the Pope's death. That had been in 2003, under the papacy of John Paul II. To this day no one knew who the man was – the assumption had always been that he was Chinese, and that he had had to remain anonymous to avoid persecution. Presumably the same considerations of safety might well apply to the Church's senior representative in Baghdad. Was that it?

He was aware of Mandorff still staring at him. The German was perspiring freely in the heat. The chandelier gleamed on his watery bald skull. Lomeli said, 'But I'm sure the Holy Father wouldn't have made such a sensitive decision without at least consulting the Secretary of State. Ray, would you be so kind as to find Cardinal

69

Bellini, and ask him to join us?' As O'Malley left, he turned back to Mandorff. 'And you think he's genuinely a cardinal?'

'He has a letter of appointment from the late Pope addressed to the archdiocese of Baghdad, which they kept secret at the Holy Father's request. He has a seal of office. Look for yourself.' He showed the package of documents to Lomeli. 'And he *is* an archbishop, fulfilling a mission in one of the most dangerous places in the world. I cannot think why he would forge his credentials, can you?'

'I suppose not.' The papers certainly looked authentic to Lomeli. He returned them. 'Where is he now?'

'I asked him to wait in the back office.'

Mandorff conducted Lomeli behind the reception desk. Through the glass wall he could see a slender figure sitting on an orange plastic chair in the corner, between a printing machine and boxes of copying paper. He was dressed in a plain black cassock. His head was bare, no skullcap. He was leaning forward with his elbows on his knees, his rosary in his hands, looking down and apparently praying. A lock of dark hair obscured his face.

Mandorff said quietly, as if they were observing a man asleep, 'He arrived at the entrance just as it was closing. His name wasn't on the list, of course, and he isn't dressed as a cardinal, so the Swiss Guard called me. I told them to bring him inside while we had him checked. I behaved correctly, I hope?'

'Of course.'

The Filipino was fingering his rosary, entirely absorbed. Lomeli felt intrusive merely watching. Yet he found it hard to look away. He envied him. It was a long time since he had been able to muster the powers of concentration necessary to shut oneself off from the world. His own head these days was always full of noise. First Tremblay, he thought, now this. He wondered what other shocks awaited him.

Mandorff said, 'No doubt Cardinal Bellini will be able to clear matters up.'

Lomeli looked around to see Bellini approaching with O'Malley. The former Secretary of State wore an expression of uneasy bewilderment.

Lomeli said, 'Aldo, were you aware of this?'

'I wasn't aware the Holy Father had actually gone ahead and done it, no.' He stared wonderingly through the glass at Benítez as if gazing upon some mythical creature. 'And yet there he is . . .'

'So the Pope mentioned it was in his mind?'

'Yes, he raised the possibility a couple of months ago. My advice was strongly against it. Christians have endured enough suffering in that part of the world without inflaming militant Islamic opinion even further. A cardinal in Iraq! The Americans would be appalled. How could we possibly ensure his safety?'

'That is presumably why the Holy Father wanted it kept secret.'

'But people were bound to find out! Everything

leaks eventually, especially from this place – as he knew better than anyone.'

'Well it certainly won't remain a secret now, whatever happens.' Beyond the glass the Filipino silently worked his rosary beads. 'Given that you confirm it was the Pope's intention to make him a cardinal, it's logical to assume his credentials are genuine. Therefore I don't think we have any choice except to admit him.'

He moved to open the door. To his astonishment, Bellini seized his arm. 'Wait, Dean!' he whispered. 'Must we?'

'Why shouldn't we?'

'Are we sure the Holy Father was entirely competent to make this decision?'

'Take great care, my friend. That sounds like heresy.' Lomeli also spoke softly. He didn't want the others to hear. 'It's not for us to decide whether the Holy Father was right or wrong. It's our duty to see that his wishes are honoured.'

'Papal infallibility covers doctrine. It does not extend to appointments.'

'I am well aware of the limits of papal infallibility. But this is a matter of canon law. And on that I am as qualified to judge as you are. Paragraph thirty-nine of the Apostolic Constitution is quite specific: "Should any cardinal-electors arrive *re integra*, that is, before the new pastor of the Church has been elected, they shall be allowed to take part in the election at the stage which it has reached." That man is legally a cardinal.'

He pulled his arm free and opened the door.

Benítez glanced up as he came in and rose slowly to his feet. He was a little below average height, with a fine, handsome face. It was hard to put an age to him. His skin was smooth, his cheekbones sharp, his body thin almost to the point of emaciation. He had a feathery handshake. He appeared utterly exhausted.

Lomeli said, 'Welcome to the Vatican, Archbishop. I'm sorry you've had to wait in here, but we had to make some checks. I do hope you understand. I'm Cardinal Lomeli, Dean of the College.'

'It is I who must apologise to you, Dean, for making such an unorthodox entrance.' He spoke in a quiet, precise voice. 'You are most kind to take me in at all.'

'Never mind. I'm sure there's a good reason for it. This is Cardinal Bellini, whom I think you may know.'

'Cardinal Bellini? I'm afraid not.'

Benítez held out his hand, and for a moment Lomeli thought Bellini might refuse to take it. Eventually he shook it; then he said, 'I'm sorry, Archbishop, but I have to say I think you've made a grave mistake in coming here.'

'And why is that, Your Eminence?'

'Because the position of Christians in the Middle East is perilous enough already, without the provocation of your being made a cardinal and showing yourself in Rome.'

'Naturally I am aware of the risks. That is one

73

of the reasons why I hesitated about coming. But I can assure you I prayed long and hard before undertaking the journey.'

'Well, you've made your choice, and there's an end of the matter. However, now that you're here, I have to tell you I don't see how you can possibly expect to go back to Baghdad.'

'Of course I shall go back, and I shall face the consequences of my faith, like thousands of others.'

Bellini said coldly, 'I doubt neither your courage nor your faith, Archbishop. But your return will have diplomatic repercussions and therefore it won't necessarily be your decision.'

'Nor will it necessarily be yours, Eminence. It will be a decision for the next Pope.'

He was tougher than he looked, thought Lomeli. For once Bellini seemed at a loss for a reply. Lomeli said, 'I think we're getting ahead of ourselves, my brothers. The point is, you have come. Now, to be practical: we need to see if there's a room available for you. Where's your luggage?'

'I have no luggage.'

'What, none at all?'

'I thought it best to go to the airport in Baghdad empty-handed, to disguise my intentions – I am followed by government people wherever I go. I slept overnight in the arrivals lounge in Beirut and landed in Rome two hours ago.'

'Dear me. Let us see what we can do for you.' Lomeli ushered him out of the office and towards the front of the reception desk. 'Monsignor

74

O'Malley is the Secretary of the College of Cardinals. He'll try to get you everything you need. Ray,' he said to O'Malley, 'His Eminence will need toiletries, some clean clothes – and choir dress, of course.'

Benítez said, 'Choir dress?'

'When we go to the Sistine Chapel to vote, we are required to wear our full formal costume. I'm sure there must be a spare set somewhere in the Vatican.'

'When we go to the Sistine Chapel to vote . . .' repeated Benítez. Suddenly he looked stricken. 'Forgive me, Dean, this is quite overwhelming for me. How can I cast my vote with the appropriate seriousness when I don't even know any of the candidates? Cardinal Bellini is right. I should never have come.'

'Nonsense!' Lomeli gripped his arms. They were bone-thin, although yet again he sensed a certain inner wiry strength. 'Listen to me, Your Eminence. You will join us all for dinner tonight. I shall introduce you, and you will talk over a meal to your brother cardinals – some of them at least will be known to you, if only by reputation. You will pray, just like the rest of us. In due course the Holy Spirit will guide us to a name. And it will be a marvellous spiritual experience for us all.'

Vespers had begun in the ground-floor chapel. The sound of plainsong drifted across the lobby. Lomeli felt suddenly very tired. He left O'Malley to look after Benítez and took the elevator up to his room. It was infernally hot up here too. The air-conditioning controls didn't seem to work. For a moment he forgot about the welded shutters and tried to open the window. Defeated, he looked around his cell. The lights were very bright. The whitewashed walls and the polished floor seemed to magnify the glare. He could sense the beginnings of a headache. He turned off the lamps in the bedroom, groped his way to the bathroom and found the cord to turn on the neon strip above the mirror. He half closed the door. Then he lay down on his bed in the bluish gloom, intending to pray. Within a minute he was asleep.

At one point he dreamed he was in the Sistine Chapel and that the Holy Father was praying at the altar, but that every time he tried to approach him, the old man moved away, until finally he walked to the door of the sacristy. He turned and smiled at Lomeli, opened the door to the Room of Tears and plunged from view.

Lomeli woke with a cry, which he stifled quickly by biting on his knuckle. For a few wide-eyed seconds he had no idea where he was. All the familiar objects of his life had vanished. He lay waiting for his heartbeat to steady. After a while he tried to remember what else had been in his dream. There were many, many images, he was sure. He could sense them. But the moment he tried to fix them into thoughts, they shimmered

76

and vanished like burst bubbles. Only the terrible vision of the Holy Father plummeting remained imprinted on his mind.

He heard a pair of male voices talking in English in the corridor. They seemed to be African. There was much fiddling with a key. A door opened and closed. One of the cardinals shuffled off down the passage while the other switched on the light in the next room. The wall was so thin it might have been made of cardboard. Lomeli could hear him moving around, talking to himself – he thought it might be Adeyemi – and then the sound of coughing and hawking, followed by the lavatory flushing.

He looked at his watch. It was almost eight. He had been asleep for over an hour. And yet he felt utterly unrefreshed, as if his time unconscious had been more stressful than his time awake. He thought of all the tasks that lay ahead. *Give me strength, O Lord, to face this trial.* He turned over carefully, sat up, placed his feet on the floor and rocked himself forward several times, building the momentum to stand. This was old age: all these movements one had once taken for granted – the simple act of rising from a bed, for example – that now required a precise sequence of planned manoeuvres. At the third attempt he gained his feet and walked stiffly the short distance to the desk.

He sat down, switched on the reading lamp, and angled it over his brown leather folder. He slid out twelve sheets of A5: thickly woven, cream-coloured, hand-made, watermarked paper that was considered to be of a quality appropriate to the historic occasion. The typeface was large, clear, double-spaced. After he had finished with it, the document would be lodged for all eternity in the Vatican archive.

The sermon was headed *Pro eligendo Romano pontifice* – 'For the election of a Roman pontiff' – and its purpose, in accordance with tradition, was to set out the qualities that would be required of the new Pope. Within living memory, such homilies had swung papal elections. In 1958, Cardinal Antonio Bacci had delivered a liberal's description of the perfect pontiff (*May the new Vicar of Christ form a bridge between all levels of society, between all nations . . .*) that was virtually a word-portrait of Cardinal Roncalli of Venice, who duly became Pope John XXIII. Five years later, the conservatives tried the same tactic in a homily by Monsignor Amleto Tondini (*Doubt should be cast on the enthusiastic applause received by the 'Pope of peace'*), but it only succeeded in provoking such a backlash among the moderates, who thought it in poor taste, that it had helped secure the victory of Cardinal Montini.

Lomeli's address, in contrast, had been carefully constructed to ensure it was neutral to the point of blandness: *Our recent Popes have all been tireless promoters of peace and co-operation at the international level. Let us pray that the future Pope will continue this ceaseless work of charity and love . . .* Nobody could object to that, not even Tedesco,

78

who could sniff out relativism as fast as a trained dog could find a truffle. It was the prospect of the Mass itself that troubled him: his own spiritual capacity. He would be under such scrutiny. The television cameras would be tight on his face.

He put away his speech and went over to the prie-dieu. It was made of simple plain wood, exactly the same as the one the Holy Father had had in his room. He lowered himself to his knees, grasped either side of it, and bowed his head, and in that position he remained for nearly half an hour, until it was time to go down to dinner.

CHAPTER 4

IN PECTORE

The dining hall was the largest room in the Casa Santa Marta. It ran the entire right-hand length of the lobby and was mostly open to it, with a white marble floor and a glassed-in atrium ceiling. The line of potted plants that had once cordoned off the section where the Holy Father took his meals had been removed. Fifteen large round tables had each been set for eight diners, with wine and water bottles in the centre of the white lace tablecloths. By the time Lomeli stepped out of the elevator, the place was full. The din of voices bouncing off the hard surfaces was convivial and anticipatory, like the first night of a business convention. Many of the cardinals had already been served with a drink by the Sisters of St Vincent de Paul.

Lomeli looked around for Benítez and saw him standing alone behind a pillar just outside the dining room. O'Malley had somehow managed to dig out a cassock with the red sash and piping of a cardinal, but it was slightly too large for its new recipient. He seemed lost in it. Lomeli went over. 'Your Eminence, have you settled in? Did Monsignor O'Malley find you a room?'

'Yes, Dean, thank you. On the top floor.' He held out his hand and showed his key with a kind of wonder that he should find himself in such a place. 'It is said to have a marvellous view over the city, but the shutters won't open.'

'That is to prevent your betraying our secrets, or receiving information from the outside world,' said Lomeli; then, noticing Benítez's puzzled expression, he added, 'A joke, Your Eminence. It's the same for all of us. Well, you mustn't just stand on your own all night. This will never do. Come with me.'

'I'm really perfectly happy here, Dean, observing.'

'Nonsense. I'm going to introduce you.'

'Is it necessary? Everyone is talking to someone . . .'

'You are a cardinal now. A certain confidence is demanded.'

He took the Filipino by the arm and propelled him towards the middle of the dining room, nodding affably to the nuns who were waiting to begin serving the meal, squeezing between the tables until he found them a space. He took up a knife and rapped on the side of a wine glass. Quiet fell over the room, apart from the elderly Archbishop Emeritus of Caracas, who continued to talk loudly until his companion waved at him to be quiet and pointed at Lomeli. The Venezuelan peered around and fiddled with his hearing aid. A piercing howl caused those nearest him to wince and hunch their shoulders. He raised his hand in apology.

Lomeli bowed towards him. 'Thank you, Eminence. My brothers,' he said, 'please be seated.'

He waited while they found their places.

'Your Eminences, before we eat, I should like to introduce a new member of our order, whose existence was not known to any of us and who only arrived at the Vatican a few hours ago.' There was a stir of surprise. 'This is a perfectly legitimate procedure, known as a creation *in pectore*. The reason why it had to be done this way is known only to God and to the late Holy Father. But I think we can guess well enough. Our new brother's ministry is a most dangerous one. It has not been an easy journey for him to join us. He prayed long and hard before setting out. All the greater reason therefore for us to welcome him warmly.' He glanced at Bellini, who was staring fixedly at the tablecloth. 'By the Grace of God, a brotherhood of one hundred and seventeen has now become one hundred and eighteen. Welcome to our order, Vincent Benítez, Cardinal Archbishop of Baghdad.'

He turned to Benítez and applauded him. For an embarrassing few seconds his were the only hands clapping. But gradually others joined until it became a warm ovation. Benítez looked around him in wonder at the smiling faces.

When the applause ended, Lomeli gestured to the room. 'Your Eminence, would you care to bless our meal?'

82

Benítez's expression was so alarmed that for an absurd moment it passed through Lomeli's mind that he had never said grace before. But then he muttered, 'Of course, Dean. It would be an honour.' He made the sign of the cross and bowed his head. The cardinals followed suit. Lomeli closed his eyes and waited. For a long time, there was silence. Then, just as Lomeli was beginning to wonder if something had happened to him, Benítez spoke. 'Bless us, O Lord, and these Your gifts, which we are about to receive from Your bounty. Bless, too, all those who cannot share this meal. And help us, O Lord, as we eat and drink, to remember the hungry and the thirsty, the sick and the lonely, and those sisters who prepared this food for us, and who will serve it to us tonight. Through Christ our Lord, Amen.'

'Amen.'

Lomeli crossed himself.

The cardinals raised their heads and unfolded their napkins. The blue-uniformed sisters who had been waiting to serve the meal started coming through from the kitchen carrying soup plates. Lomeli took Benítez by the arm and looked around to see if there was a table where he might receive a friendly welcome.

He led the Filipino over towards his fellow countrymen, Cardinal Mendoza and Cardinal Ramos, the archbishops of Manila and Cotabato respectively. They were sitting at a table with various other cardinals from Asia and Oceania, and both men rose in homage at his approach. Mendoza was especially effusive. He came round from the other side of the table and clasped Benítez's hand. 'I am so proud. *We* are proud. The *whole country* will be proud when it hears of your elevation. Dean, you do know that this man is a legend to us in the diocese of Manila? You know what he did?' He turned back to Benítez. 'How long ago must it be now? Twenty years?'

Benítez said, 'More like thirty, Your Eminence.'

'Thirty!' Mendoza began to reminisce: Tondo and San Andres, Bahala Na and Kuratong Baleleng, Payatas and Bagong Silangan . . . Initially the names meant nothing to Lomeli. But gradually he gathered they were either slum districts where Benítez had served as a priest, or street gangs he had confronted while building rescue missions for their victims, mostly child prostitutes and drug addicts. The missions still existed, and people still spoke of 'the priest with the gentle voice' who had built them. 'It really is such a pleasure for us both to meet you at last,' concluded Mendoza, gesturing to Ramos to include him in the sentiment. Ramos nodded enthusiastically.

'Wait,' said Lomeli. He frowned. He wanted to make sure he had understood correctly. 'Do you three not actually know one another?'

'No, not personally.' The cardinals shook their heads and Benítez added, 'It is many years since I left the Philippines.'

'You mean to say you've been in the Middle East all this time?'

A voice behind him cried out, 'No, Dean – for a long while he was with us, in Africa!'

Eight African cardinals were seated at the neighbouring table. The cardinal who had spoken, the elderly Archbishop Emeritus of Kinshasa, Beaufret Muamba, stood, beckoned Benítez to him, and clasped him to his chest. 'Welcome! Welcome!' He conducted him around the table. One by one the cardinals put down their soup spoons and stood to shake his hand. Watching them, it became apparent to Lomeli that none of these men had ever met Benítez either. They had heard of him, obviously. They even revered him. But his work had been done in remote places, and often outside the traditional structure of the Church. From what Lomeli could pick up – standing nearby, smiling, nodding, and all the while listening keenly, just as he had learnt to do when he was a diplomat – Benítez's ministry in Africa had been like his street work in Manila: active and dangerous. It had involved setting up clinics and shelters for women and girls who had been raped in the continent's civil wars.

The whole business was becoming clearer to him now. Ah yes, he could see exactly why this missionary-priest would have appealed to the Holy Father, who had so often stated his belief that God was most readily encountered in the poorest and most desperate places on earth, not

85

in the comfortable parishes of the First World, and that it took courage to go out and find Him. *If any man would come after me, let him deny himself and take up his cross daily and follow me. For whoever would save his life will lose it; and whoever loses his life for my sake, he will save it* . . . Benítez was precisely the sort of man who would never rise through the layers of Church appointments – who would not even dream of trying to do so – and who would always be awkward socially. How else then was he to be catapulted into the College of Cardinals except by an extraordinary act of patronage? Yes, all of that Lomeli could understand. The only aspect that mystified him was the secrecy. Would it really have been so much more dangerous for Benítez to have been publicly identified as a cardinal than as an archbishop? And why had the Holy Father not taken anyone into his confidence?

Someone behind him politely asked him to move out of the way. The Archbishop of Kampala, Oliver Nakitanda, was holding a spare chair and a handful of cutlery he had retrieved from a neighbouring table, and the cardinals were all shifting round to make room for Benítez to join them. The new Archbishop of Maputo, whose name Lomeli had forgotten, beckoned to one of the sisters to bring an extra serving of soup. Benítez refused a glass of wine.

Lomeli wished him bon appétit and turned to go. Two tables away, Cardinal Adeyemi was

86

holding forth to his dinner companions. The Africans were laughing at one of his famous stories. Even so, the Nigerian seemed distracted, and Lomeli noticed how from time to time he would glance over at Benítez with an expression of puzzled irritation.

Such was the disproportionate number of Italian cardinals in the Conclave, it required more than three tables to seat them. One was occupied by Bellini and his liberal supporters. At the second, Tedesco presided over the traditionalists. The third was filled with cardinals who were either undecided between the two factions or who nursed secret ambitions of their own. At all three tables, Lomeli noted with dismay, a place had been saved for him. It was Tedesco who saw him first. 'Dean!' He indicated he should join them with a firmness that made refusal impossible.

They had finished their soup and had moved on to antipasti. Lomeli sat down opposite the Patriarch of Venice and accepted half a glass of wine. For the sake of politeness, he also took a little ham and mozzarella, even though he had no appetite. Around the table were the conservative arch-bishops – Agrigento, Florence, Palermo, Perugia – and Tutino, the disgraced Prefect of the Congregation for Bishops, who had always been considered a liberal but who no doubt hoped that a Tedesco pontificate might rescue his career.

Tedesco had a curious way of eating. He would

87

hold his plate in his left hand and empty it with great rapidity using a fork in his right. At the same time, he would glance frequently from side to side, as if fearful that someone might be about to steal his food. Lomeli presumed it was the result of coming from a large and hungry family.

'So, Dean,' said Tedesco, through a full mouth, 'your homily is prepared?'

'It is.'

'And it will be in Latin, I hope?'

'It will be in Italian, Goffredo – as you well know.'

The other cardinals had broken off their private conversations and were all listening. One never knew what Tedesco might say.

'Such a pity! If *I* were delivering it, I would insist on Latin.'

'But then no one would understand it, Your Eminence. And that would be a tragedy.'

Tedesco was the only one who laughed. 'Yes, well, I confess that my Latin is poor, but I would inflict it on you all nonetheless, simply to make a point. Because what I would try to say, in my simple peasant Latin, is this: that change almost invariably produces the opposite effect to the improvement it is intended to bring about, and that we should bear that in mind when we come to make our choice of Pope. The abandonment of Latin, for example . . .' He wiped the grease from his thick lips with his napkin and inspected it. For a moment he seemed distracted, but then he resumed. 'Look around this dining room,

88

Dean. Observe how unconsciously, how instinctively, we have arranged ourselves according to our native languages. We Italians are here – closest to the kitchens, very sensibly. The Spanish-speakers are sitting there. The English-speakers are over towards the reception. Yet when you and I were boys, Dean, and the Tridentine Mass was still the liturgy of the entire world, the cardinals at a Conclave were able to converse with one another in Latin. But then in 1962, the liberals insisted we should get rid of a dead language in order to make communication easier, and now what do we see? They have only succeeded in making communication harder!'

'That may be true of the narrow instance of a Conclave. The same hardly applies to the mission of the Universal Church.'

'The Universal Church? But how can a thing be considered universal if it speaks fifty different languages? Language is vital. Because from language, over time, arises thought, and from thought arises philosophy and culture. It has been sixty years since the Second Vatican Council, but already what it means to be a Catholic in Europe is no longer the same as what it means to be a Catholic in Africa, or Asia, or South America. We have become a confederation, at best. Look around the room, Dean – look at the way language divides us over even such a simple meal as this, and tell me there is not truth in what I say.'

Lomeli refused to respond. He thought the other

89

man's reasoning was preposterous. But he was determined to be neutral. He was not going to be drawn into an argument. Besides, one could never tell whether Tedesco was teasing or being serious. 'All I can say is that if those are your views, Goffredo, you will find my homily a grave disappointment.'

'The abandonment of Latin,' persisted Tedesco, 'will lead eventually to the abandonment of Rome. Mark my words.'

'Oh come now – this is too much, even for you!'

'I am perfectly serious, Dean. Men will soon be asking openly: why Rome? They've already started to whisper it. There's no rule in doctrine or Scripture that says the Pope must preside in Rome. He could set up the Throne of St Peter anywhere on earth. Our mysterious new cardinal is from the Philippines, I believe?'

'Yes, you know he is.'

'So now we have three cardinal-electors from that country, which has – what? – eighty-four million Catholics. In Italy we have fifty-seven million – the great majority of whom never take Communion in any case – and yet we have *twenty-six* cardinal-electors! You think this anomaly will continue for much longer? If you do, you are a fool.' He threw down his napkin. 'Now I have spoken too harshly, and I apologise. But I fear this Conclave may be our last chance to preserve our Mother the Church. Another ten years like the last ten – another Holy

Father like the last one – and she will cease to exist as we know her.'

'So in effect what you are saying is that the next Pope must be Italian.'

'Yes, I am! Why not? We haven't had an Italian Pope for more than forty years. There's never been such an interregnum in all of history. We have to recover the papacy, Dean, to save the Roman Church. Surely all Italians can agree on that?'

'We Italians might well agree on that, Your Eminence. But as we can never agree on anything else, I suspect the odds may be stacked against us. Well, now I must circulate among our colleagues. Good evening to you.'

And with that Lomeli rose, bowed to the cardinals, and went to sit on Bellini's table.

'We won't ask you to tell us how much you enjoyed breaking bread with the Patriarch of Venice. Your face tells us all we need to know.'

The former Secretary of State was sitting with his praetorian guard: Sabbadin, the Archbishop of Milan; Landolfi of Turin; Dell'Acqua of Bologna; and a couple of members of the Curia – Santini, who was not only Prefect of the Congregation for Catholic Education but also Senior Cardinal-Deacon, which meant that he would be the one who proclaimed the name of the new Pope from the balcony of St Peter's; and Cardinal Panzavecchia, who ran the Pontifical Council for Culture.

'I will give him this, at least,' replied Lomeli,

taking another glass of wine to calm his anger. 'He plainly has no intention of tempering his views to win votes.'

'He never has. I rather admire him for that.'

Sabbadin, who had a reputation for cynicism, and who was the nearest Bellini had to a campaign manager, said, 'It was shrewd of him to keep away from Rome until today. With Tedesco, less is always more. One outspoken newspaper interview could have finished him. Instead, he will do well tomorrow, I think.'

'Define "well",' said Lomeli.

Sabbadin looked over at Tedesco. His head rocked slightly from side to side, like a farmer appraising a beast at market. 'I should say he's worth fifteen votes in the first ballot.'

'And your man?'

Bellini covered his ears. 'Don't tell me! I don't want to know.'

'Between twenty and twenty-five. Certainly ahead on the first ballot. It's tomorrow night that the serious work will start. Somehow we have to get him to a two-thirds majority. That requires seventy-nine votes.'

A look of agony passed across Bellini's long pale face. Lomeli thought he looked more than ever like a martyred saint. 'Please let's not talk of it. I won't utter a word of entreaty to win even one vote. If our colleagues don't know me by now, after all these years, there's nothing I can say in the space of a single evening that will convince them.'

They fell silent as the nuns moved around the table, serving the main course of veal scallopini. The meat looked rubbery, the sauce congealed. If anything forces this Conclave to a swift conclusion, thought Lomeli, it will be the food. After the sisters had set down the last plate, Landolfi – who at sixty-two was the youngest present – said in his usual deferential manner, 'You don't have to say anything, Eminence. Naturally you must leave that to us. But if we have to tell the uncommitted what you stand for, how would you like us to answer?'

Bellini nodded towards Tedesco. 'Tell them I stand for everything he does not. His beliefs are sincere, but they are sincere nonsense. We are never returning to the days of Latin liturgy, and priests celebrating Mass with their backs to the congregation, and families of ten children because Mamma and Papà know no better. It was an ugly, repressive time, and we should be joyful that it has passed. Tell them that I stand for respecting other faiths, and for tolerating differing views within our own Church. Tell them I believe the bishops should have greater powers and that women should play more of a role within the Curia—'

'Wait,' Sabbadin interrupted him. 'Really?' He made a face and sucked his teeth. 'I think we should keep off the subject of women entirely. It will only give Tedesco an opening for mischief. He'll say you secretly favour female ordination – which you don't.'

Perhaps it was Lomeli's imagination, but there

seemed to be the tiniest flicker of hesitation before Bellini said, 'I accept that the issue of female ordination is closed for my lifetime – and probably for several lifetimes to come.'

'No, Aldo,' replied Sabbadin firmly, 'it is closed for *all* time. It has been decreed on papal authority: the principle of an exclusively male priesthood is founded on the written word of God—'

'"Set forth infallibly by the ordinary and universal magisterium" – yes, I know the ruling. Not perhaps the wisest of St John Paul's many declarations, but there it is. No, of course I am not proposing female ordination. But there is nothing to stop us bringing women into the Curia at the highest levels. The work is administrative, not sacerdotal. The late Holy Father often spoke of it.'

'True, but he never actually *did* it. How can a woman instruct a bishop, let alone *select* a bishop, when she isn't even allowed to celebrate Communion? The College will see it as ordination by the back door.'

Bellini prodded his piece of veal a couple of times and then laid down his fork. He rested his elbows on the table, leaned forward and looked at each of them in turn. 'Listen to me, my brothers, please. Let me be absolutely clear. I do not seek the papacy. I dread it. Therefore I have no intention of concealing my views or pretending to be anything other than I am. I urge you – I plead with you – not to canvass on my behalf. Not a word. Is that understood? Now, I am afraid I have lost my appetite, and if you will excuse me, I shall retire to my room.'

They watched him go, his stork-like figure bobbing stiffly between the tables and across the lobby until he disappeared upstairs. Sabbadin took off his spectacles, breathed on the lenses, polished them with his napkin, and then put them back on. He opened a small black notebook. 'Well, my friends,' he said, 'you heard him. Now I suggest we divide the task. Rocco,' he said to Dell'Acqua, 'your English is the best: you talk to the North Americans, and to our colleagues from Britain and Ireland. Which of us has good Spanish?' Panzavecchia raised his hand. 'Excellent. The South Americans can be your responsibility. I shall speak to all the Italians who are frightened of Tedesco – that is, most of them. Gianmarco,' he said to Santini, 'presumably your work at the Congregation for Education means you know a lot of the Africans – will you deal with them? Needless to say, we avoid all mention of women in the Curia . . .'

Lomeli cut his veal into tiny pieces and ate them one at a time. He listened as Sabbadin went round the table. The Archbishop of Milan's father had been a prominent Christian Democrat senator; he had learnt how to count votes in the cradle. Lomeli guessed he would be Secretary of State in a Bellini pontificate. When he had finished doling out assignments, he shut his notebook, poured himself a glass of wine and sat back with a satisfied expression.

Lomeli looked up from his plate. 'I take it then you don't believe our friend is sincere when he says he doesn't want to be Pope.'

'Oh, he's perfectly sincere – that's one of the reasons I support him. The men who are dangerous – the men who must be stopped – are the ones who actively desire it.'

Lomeli had kept an eye out all evening for Tremblay, but it wasn't until the end of the meal, when the cardinals were queuing for coffee in the lobby, that he had the chance to approach him. The Canadian was standing in the corner holding a cup and saucer and listening to the Archbishop of Colombo, Asanka Rajapakse, by common consent one of the great bores of the Conclave. Tremblay's eyes were fixed upon him. He was leaning towards him and nodding intently. Occasionally Lomeli heard him murmur, 'Absolutely . . . absolutely . . .' He waited nearby. He sensed that Tremblay was aware of his presence but was ignoring it, hoping he would give up and move away. But Lomeli was determined, and in the end it was Rajapakse, whose eyes kept darting to him, who reluctantly interrupted his own monologue and said, 'I think the dean wishes to speak with you.'

Tremblay turned and grinned. 'Jacopo, hello!' he cried. 'This has been a lovely evening.' His teeth were an unnaturally brilliant white. Lomeli suspected he had had them polished for the occasion.

'I wonder if I might borrow you for a moment, Joe?' he said.

'Yes, of course.' Tremblay turned to Rajapakse. 'Perhaps we could continue our conversation later?' The Sri Lankan nodded to both men and moved away. Tremblay seemed sorry to see him go, and when he returned his attention to Lomeli, there was a trace of irritation in his voice. 'What is this about?'

'Could we talk somewhere more private? Your room, perhaps?'

Tremblay's brilliant teeth vanished. His mouth turned down. Lomeli thought he might refuse. 'Well I suppose so, if we must. But briefly, if you don't mind. There are still some colleagues I need to speak to.'

His room was on the first floor. He led Lomeli up the stairs and along the passage. He walked quickly, as if anxious to get the thing over with. It was a suite, exactly the same as the Holy Father's. All the lights – the overhead chandelier, the bedside and desk lamps, even the lights in the bathroom – had been left burning. It seemed antiseptic, gleaming like an operating theatre, entirely bare of possessions, apart from a can of hairspray on the nightstand. Tremblay closed the door. He didn't invite Lomeli to sit. 'What is this about?'

'It concerns your final meeting with the Holy Father.'

'What about it?'

'I've been told it was difficult. Was it?'

97

Tremblay rubbed his forehead and frowned, as if making a great effort of memory. 'No, not that I recall.'

'Well, to be more specific, I have been told that the Holy Father demanded your resignation from all your offices.'

'Ah!' His expression cleared. 'That piece of nonsense! This has come from Archbishop Woźniak, I presume?'

'That I can't say.'

'Poor Woźniak. You know how it is?' Tremblay's hand wobbled an imaginary glass in mid-air. 'We must make sure he receives proper treatment when all this is over.'

'So there's no truth in the allegation that at the meeting you were dismissed?'

'None whatsoever! How utterly absurd! Ask Monsignor Morales. He was present.'

'I would if I could, but obviously I can't at the moment, as we're sequestered.'

'I can assure you he'll only confirm what I'm telling you.'

'No doubt. But still, it seems rather curious. Can you think of any reason why such a story should be circulating?'

'I should have thought that was obvious, Dean. My name has been mentioned as a possible future Pope – a ludicrous suggestion, I need hardly add, but you must have heard the same rumours – and someone wants to blacken my name with false slurs.'

'And you think that person is Woźniak?'

'Who else could it be? I know for a fact he went to Morales with some story about what the Holy Father was alleged to have said to him – I know that because Morales told me. I might say he's never dared speak directly to *me* about it.'

'And you ascribe this entirely to a malicious plot to discredit you?'

'I fear that's what it comes to. It's very sad.' Tremblay put his hands together. 'I shall mention the archbishop in my prayers tonight, and ask God to help him through his difficulties. Now, if you'll excuse me, I would like to go back downstairs.'

He made a move towards the door. Lomeli blocked his way.

'Just one last question, if I may, simply to put my mind at rest: could you tell me what it was that you discussed with the Holy Father in that final meeting?'

Outrage came as easily to Tremblay as piety and smiles. His tone became metallic. 'No, Dean, I cannot. And to be truthful, I am shocked that you should expect me to disclose a private conversation – a very precious and private conversation, given that those were the last words I ever exchanged with the Holy Father.'

Lomeli pressed his hand to his heart and bowed his head slightly in apology. 'I quite understand. Forgive me.'

The Canadian was lying, of course. They both

knew it. Lomeli stood aside. Tremblay opened the door. In silence they walked back together along the corridor and at the staircase went their separate ways, the Canadian down to the lobby to resume his conversations, the dean wearily up another flight to his room and his doubts.

CHAPTER 5

PRO ELIGENDO ROMANO PONTIFICE

That night he lay in bed in the darkness with the rosary of the Blessed Virgin around his neck and his arms folded crosswise on his chest. It was a posture he had first adopted in puberty to avoid the temptations of the body. The objective was to maintain it until morning. Now, nearly sixty years later, when such temptations were no longer a danger, he continued out of habit to sleep like this – like an effigy on a tomb.

Celibacy had not made him feel neutered or frustrated, as the secular word generally imagined a priest must be, but rather powerful and fulfilled. He had imagined himself a warrior within a knightly caste: a lonely and untouchable hero, above the common run. *If anyone comes to me and does not hate his own father and mother and wife and children and brothers and sisters, yes, and even his own life, he cannot be my disciple.* He was not entirely naïve. He had known what it was to desire, and to be desired, both by women and by men. And yet he had never succumbed to physical attraction. He had gloried in his solitariness. It was only when he was diagnosed

101

with prostate cancer that he had begun to brood on what he had missed. Because what was he nowadays? No longer a shining knight: just another impotent old fellow, no more heroic than the average patient in a nursing home. Sometimes he wondered what had been the point of it all. The night-time pang was no longer of lust; it was of regret.

In the next-door room, he could hear the African cardinal snoring. The thin partition wall seemed to vibrate like a membrane with each stertorous breath. He was sure it was Adeyemi. No one else could be so loud, even in his sleep. He tried counting the snores in the hope that the repetition would lull him to sleep. When he reached five hundred, he gave up.

He wished he could have opened the shutters for some fresh air. He felt claustrophobic. The great bell of St Peter's had ceased tolling at midnight. In the sealed chamber, the dark early-morning hours were long and trackless.

He turned on his bedside lamp and read a few pages from Guardini's *Meditations Before Mass*.

If someone were to ask me what the liturgical life begins with, I should answer: with learning stillness . . . That attentive stillness in which God's word can take root. This must be established before the service begins, if possible in the silence on the way to church, still better in a brief period of composure the evening before.

But how was such stillness to be achieved? That was the question to which Guardini offered no answer, and in place of stillness, as the night wore on, the noise in Lomeli's mind became even shriller than usual. *He saved others; himself he cannot save* – the jeer of the scribes and elders at the foot of the cross. The paradox at the heart of the Gospel. The priest who celebrates Mass and yet is unable to achieve Communion himself.

He pictured a great shaft of cacophonous darkness, filled with taunting voices thundering down upon him from heaven. A divine revelation of doubt.

At one point in his despair he picked up the *Meditations* and flung it at the wall. It bounced off it with a thump. The snoring ceased for a minute, and then resumed.

At 6.30 a.m., the alarm sounded throughout the Casa Santa Marta – a clanging seminary bell. Lomeli opened his eyes. He was curled up on his side. He felt groggy, raw. He had no idea how long he had been asleep, only that it couldn't have been for more than an hour or two. The sudden remembrance of all he had to do in the coming day passed over him like a wave of nausea, and for a while he lay unable to move. Normally his waking routine was to meditate for fifteen minutes then rise and say his morning prayers. But on this occasion, when at last he managed to summon the will to put his feet to the floor, he went directly into the bathroom and ran a shower as hot as he could bear. The water scourged his back and shoulders. He twisted and turned beneath it and cried out in pain. Afterwards he rubbed away the moisture on the mirror and surveyed with disgust his raw and scalded skin. *My body is clay, my good fame a vapour, my end is ashes.*

He felt too tense to breakfast with the others. He stayed in his room, rehearsing his homily and attempting to pray, and left it until the very last minute to go downstairs.

The lobby was a red sea of cardinals robing for the short procession to St Peter's. The officials of the Conclave, led by Archbishop Mandorff and Monsignor O'Malley, had been allowed back into the hostel to assist; Father Zanetti was waiting at the foot of the stairs to help Lomeli dress. They went into the same waiting room opposite the chapel in which he had met Woźniak the night before. When Zanetti asked him how he had slept, he replied, 'Very soundly, thank you,' and hoped the young priest would not notice the dark circles beneath his eyes and the way his hands shook when he handed him his sermon for safe keeping. He ducked his head into the opening of the thick red chasuble that had been worn by successive deans of the College over the past twenty years and held out his arms as Zanetti fussed around him like a tailor, straightening and adjusting it. The mantle felt heavy on his shoulders. He prayed silently: *Lord, who hast said, My yoke is easy and*

My burden is light, grant that I may so bear it as to attain Thy grace. Amen.

Zanetti stood in front of him and reached up to place upon his head the tall mitre of white watered silk. The priest stepped back a pace to check it was correctly aligned, squinted, came forward again and altered it by a millimetre, then walked behind Lomeli and tugged down the ribbons at the back and smoothed them. It felt alarmingly precarious. Finally he gave him the crozier. Lomeli lifted the golden shepherd's crook a couple of times in his left hand, testing the weight. *You are not a shepherd*, a familiar voice whispered in his head. *You are a manager.* He had a sudden urge to give it back, to tear off the vestments, to confess himself a fraud and disappear. He smiled and nodded. 'It feels good,' he said. 'Thank you.'

Just before 10 a.m., the cardinals began moving off from the Casa Santa Marta, walking out of the plate-glass doors in pairs, in order of seniority, checked off by O'Malley on his clipboard. Lomeli, resting on the crozier, waited with Zanetti and Mandorff beside the reception desk. They had been joined by Mandorff's deputy, the Dean of the Master of Papal Ceremonies, a cheerful, tubby Italian monsignor named Epifano, who would be his chief assistant during the Mass. Lomeli spoke to no one, looked at no one. He was still trying vainly to clear a space in his mind for God. *Eternal Trinity, I intend by Your grace to celebrate Mass to Your glory, and for the benefit of all, both living and dead, for whom Christ died, and to apply the ministerial fruit for the choosing of a new Pope . . .*

At last they stepped out into the blank November morning. The double file of scarlet-robed cardinals stretched ahead of him across the cobbles towards the Arch of the Bells, where they disappeared into the basilica. Again the helicopter hovered somewhere nearby; again the faint sounds of demonstrators carried on the cold air. Lomeli tried to shut out all distractions, but it was impossible. Every twenty paces stood security men who bowed their heads as he passed and blessed them. He walked with his supporters beneath the arch, across the piazza dedicated to the early martyrs, along the portico of the basilica, through the massive bronze door and into the brilliant illumination of St Peter's, lit for the television cameras, where a congregation of twenty thousand was waiting. He could hear the chanting of the choir beneath the dome and the vast echoing rustle of the multitude. The procession halted. He kept his eyes fixed straight ahead, willing stillness, conscious of the immense throng standing close-packed all around him – nuns and priests and lay clergy, staring at him, whispering, smiling.

Eternal Trinity, I intend by Your grace to celebrate Mass to Your glory . . .

After a couple of minutes, they moved on again, up the wide central aisle of the nave. He glanced from side to side, leaning on the crozier with his left hand, motioning vaguely with his right, conferring his blessing upon the blur of faces. He glimpsed himself on a giant TV screen – an erect, elaborately costumed, expressionless figure, walking as if in a trance. Who was this puppet, this hollow man? He felt entirely disembodied, as though he were floating alongside himself.

At the end of the aisle, where the apse gave on to the cupola of the dome, they had to pause beside Bernini's statue of St Longinus, close to where the choir was singing, and wait while the last few pairs of cardinals filed up the steps to kiss the central altar and descended again. Only when this elaborate manoeuvre had been completed was Lomeli himself cleared to walk around to the rear of the altar. He bowed towards it. Epifano stepped forward and took away the crozier and gave it to an altar boy. Then he lifted the mitre from Lomeli's head, folded it, and handed it to a second acolyte. Out of habit, Lomeli touched his skullcap to check it was in place.

Together he and Epifano climbed the seven wide carpeted steps to the altar. Lomeli bowed again and kissed the white cloth. He straightened and rolled back the sleeves of his chasuble as if he were about to wash his hands. He took the silver thurible of burning coals and incense from its bearer and swung it by its chain over the altar – seven times on this side, and then, walking round, a separate censing on each of the other three. The sweet-smelling smoke evoked feelings beyond memory. Out of the corner of his eye he saw dark-suited figures moving his throne into position. He gave back the thurible, bowed again, and allowed himself to be conducted round to the front of the altar. An altar boy held up the missal, opened to the correct page; another extended a microphone on a pole.

Once, in his youth, Lomeli had enjoyed a modest fame for the richness of his baritone. But it had become thin with age, like a fine wine left too long. He clasped his hands, closed his eyes for a moment, took a breath, and intoned in a wavering plainsong, amplified around the basilica:

'*In nomine Patris et Filii et Spiritus Sancti . . .*'

And from the colossal congregation arose the murmured sung response:

'*Amen.*'

He raised his hands in benediction and chanted again, extending the three syllables into half a dozen:

'*Pa-a-x vob-i-is.*'

And they responded:

'*Et cum spiritu tuo.*'

He had begun.

Afterwards, no one watching a tape of the Mass would have been able to guess at the inner turmoil of its celebrant, or at least not until he came to deliver his homily. True, his hands shook occasionally during the Penitential Act, but no more than was to be expected in a man of seventy-five. True also that once or twice he seemed unsure of what

108

was required of him, for instance before the Evangelium, when he had to spoon incense on to the burning coals inside the thurible. However, for the most part his performance was assured. Jacopo Lomeli of the diocese of Genoa had risen to the highest levels in the councils of the Roman Church for the very qualities he showed that day: impassivity, gravity, coolness, dignity, steadiness.

The first reading was in English, delivered by an American Jesuit priest, and taken from the prophet Isaiah (*The spirit of the Lord has been given to me*). The second was proclaimed in Spanish by a woman prominent in the Focolare Movement, and came from St Paul's Letter to the Ephesians, describing how God created the Church (*The body grows until it has built itself up, in love*). Her voice was monotonous. Lomeli sat on his throne and tried to concentrate by translating the familiar words in his mind.

To some, his gift was that they should be apostles; to some, prophets; to some, evangelists; to some, pastors and teachers . . .

Before him in a semicircle was arrayed the full College of Cardinals: both halves of it – those who were entitled to participate in the Conclave and those, roughly the same number, who were over eighty and therefore no longer eligible to vote. (Pope Paul VI had introduced the age limit fifty years before, and the constant turnover had greatly enhanced the power of the Holy Father to shape the Conclave in his own image.) How bitterly some of these decrepit fellows resented their loss of authority! How jealous they were of the younger men! Lomeli could almost see their scowls from where he sat.

. . . so that the saints together make a unity in the work of service, building up the body of Christ . . .

His eyes travelled along the four widely spaced rows of seats. Wise faces, bored faces, faces suffused with religious ecstasy; one cardinal asleep. They looked as he imagined the togaed Senate of ancient Rome might have looked in the days of the old republic. Here and there he registered the leading contenders – Bellini, Tedesco, Adeyemi, Tremblay – sitting far apart from one another, each preoccupied with his own thoughts, and it struck him what an imperfect, arbitrary, man-made instrument the Conclave was. It had no basis in Holy Scripture whatsoever. There was nothing in the reading to say that God had created cardinals. Where did they fit into St Paul's picture of His Church as a living body?

. . . If we live by the truth and in love, we shall grow in all ways into Christ, who is the head by whom the whole body is fitted and joined together, every joint adding its own strength . . .

The reading ended. The Gospel was acclaimed. Lomeli sat motionless on his throne. He felt he had just been granted an insight into something, but he was not sure what. The smouldering thurible was produced before him, along with a dish of incense and a tiny silver ladle. Epifano had to prompt him, guiding his hand as he sprinkled the incense on to the coals. After the fuming censer had been taken away, his assistant gestured to him to stand, and as he reached up to remove Lomeli's mitre, he peered anxiously into his face and whispered, 'Are you well, Eminence?'

'Yes, I'm fine.'

'The time has almost come for your homily.'

'I understand.'

He made an effort to compose himself during the chanting of the Gospel of St John (*I chose you, and I commissioned you to bear fruit*). And then very quickly the Evangelium was over. Epifano took away his crozier. He was supposed to sit while his mitre was replaced. But he forgot, which meant that Epifano, who had short arms, had to stretch awkwardly to put it back on his head. An altar boy handed him the pages of his script, threaded together by a red ribbon in the top left-hand corner. The microphone was thrust in front of him. The acolytes withdrew.

Suddenly he was facing the dead eyes of the television cameras and the great magnitude of the congregation, too huge to take in, roughly arranged in blocks of colour: the black of the nuns and the laity in the distance, just inside the bronze doors; the white of the priests halfway up the nave; the purple of the bishops at the top of the aisle; the scarlet of the cardinals at his feet, beneath the dome. An anticipatory silence fell over the basilica.

He looked down at his text. He had spent hours that morning going over it. Yet now it appeared entirely unfamiliar to him. He stared at it until he was conscious of a slight stirring of unease around him and realised he had better make a start.

'Dear Brothers and Sisters in Christ . . .'

To begin with he read automatically. 'At this moment of great responsibility in the history of the Holy Church of Christ . . .'

The words issued from his mouth, went forth into nothingness, and seemed to expire halfway along the nave and drop inert from mid-air. Only when he mentioned the late Holy Father, 'whose brilliant pontificate was a gift from God', was there a gradual welling-up of applause that started among the laity at the far end of the basilica and rolled towards the altar until finally it was taken up with diminished enthusiasm by the cardinals. He was obliged to stop until it subsided.

'Now we must ask our Lord to send us a new Holy Father through the pastoral solicitude of the cardinal fathers. And in this hour we must remember first of all the faith and the promise of Jesus Christ, when He said to the one He had chosen: "You are Peter, and on this rock I will build my church, and the powers of death shall not prevail against it. I will give you the keys of the kingdom of heaven."

'To this very day the symbol of papal authority remains a pair of keys. But to whom are these keys to be entrusted? It is the most solemn and sacred responsibility that any of us will ever be called upon to exercise in our entire lives, and we must pray to God for that loving assistance He always reserves for His Holy Church and ask Him to guide us to the right choice.'

Lomeli turned over to the next page and scanned it briefly. Platitude followed platitude, seamlessly interlocked. He flicked over to the third page, and the fourth. They were no better. On impulse he turned around and placed the homily on the seat of his throne, then turned back to the microphone.

'But you know all that.' There was some laughter. Beneath him he could see the cardinals turning to one another in alarm. 'Let me speak from the heart for a moment.' He paused to arrange his thoughts. He felt entirely calm.

'About thirty years after Jesus entrusted the keys of His Church to St Peter, St Paul the Apostle came here to Rome. He had been preaching around the Mediterranean, laying the foundations of our Mother the Church, and when he came to this city he was thrown into prison, because the authorities were frightened of him – as far as they were concerned, he was a revolutionary. And like a revolutionary, he continued to organise, even from his cell. In the year AD 62 or 63, he sent one of his ministers, Tychicus, back to Ephesus, where he'd lived for three years, to deliver that remarkable letter to the faithful, part of which we listened to just now.

'Let us contemplate what we've just heard. Paul tells the Ephesians – who were, let us remember, a mixture of Gentiles and Jews – that God's gift to the Church is its variety: some are created by Him to be apostles, some prophets, some evangelists, some pastors and others teachers, who "together make a unity in the work of service, building up the body of Christ". They *make a unity in the work of service*. These are different people – one may suppose strong people, with forceful personalities, unafraid of persecution – serving the Church in their different ways: it is the work of service that brings them together and makes the Church. God could, after all, have created a single archetype to serve Him. Instead, He created what a naturalist might call a whole ecosystem of mystics and dreamers and practical builders – managers, even – with different strengths and impulses, and from these He fashioned the body of Christ.'

The basilica was entirely still apart from a lone cameraman circling the base of the altar, filming him. Lomeli's mind was fully engaged. Never had he been more sure of exactly what he wanted to say.

'In the second part of the reading, we heard Paul reinforcing this image of the Church as a living body. "If we live by the truth and in love," he says, "we shall grow *in all ways* into Christ, who is the head by whom the whole body is joined and fitted together." Hands are hands, just as feet are feet, and they serve the Lord in their different ways. In other words, we should have no fear of diversity, because it is this variety that gives our Church its strength. And then, says Paul, when we have achieved completeness in truth and love, "we shall not be children any longer, or tossed one way and another and carried along by every wind of doctrine, at the mercy of all the tricks men play and their cleverness in deceit".

'I take this idea of the body and the head to be a beautiful metaphor for collective wisdom: of a religious community working together to grow into Christ. To work together, and grow together, we must be tolerant, because all of the body's limbs are needed. No one person or faction should seek to dominate another. "Be subject to one another out of reverence for Christ," Paul urges the faithful elsewhere in that same letter.

'My brothers and sisters, in the course of a long life in the service of our Mother the Church, let me tell you that the one sin I have come to fear more than any other is certainty. Certainty is the great enemy of unity. Certainty is the deadly enemy of tolerance. Even Christ was not certain at the end. *"Eli, Eli, lama sabachtani?"* He cried out in His agony at the ninth hour on the cross. "My God, my God, why have you forsaken me?" Our faith is a living thing precisely *because* it walks hand in hand with doubt. If there was only certainty, and if there was no doubt, there would be no mystery, and therefore no need for faith.

'Let us pray that the Lord will grant us a Pope who doubts, and by his doubts continues to make the Catholic faith a living thing that may inspire the whole world. Let Him grant us a Pope who sins, and asks forgiveness, and carries on. We ask this of the Lord, through the intercession of Mary most holy, Queen of the Apostles, and of all the martyrs and saints, who through the course of history made this Church of Rome glorious through the ages. Amen.'

He retrieved from his seat the homily he had not delivered and handed it to Monsignor Epifano, who took it from him with a quizzical look, as if he were not sure exactly what he was supposed to do with it. It had not been delivered, so was it now to go to the Vatican archive or not? Then he sat. By tradition there now followed a silence of one and a half minutes so that the meaning of the sermon could be absorbed. Only the occasional cough disturbed the immense hush. He could not gauge the reaction. Perhaps they were all in a state of shock. If they were, then so be it. He felt closer to God than he had for many months – closer perhaps than he had ever felt before in his life. He closed his eyes and prayed. *O Lord, I hope my words have served Your purpose, and I thank You for granting me the courage to say what was in my heart, and the mental and physical strength to deliver it.*

When the period of reflection was over, an altar boy produced the microphone again, and Lomeli rose and chanted the first line of the Credo – '*Credo in unum deum.*' His voice was firmer than before. He felt a great surge of spiritual energy, and the power stayed with him, so that in every stage of the Eucharist that followed he was aware of the presence of the Holy Spirit. Those long sung passages of Latin, the prospect of which had filled him with trepidation – the Universal Prayer, the Offertory Chant, the Preface and the Sanctus and the Eucharistic Prayer and the Rite of Communion – every word and every note of them seemed alive with the presence of Christ. He went down to the nave to offer Communion to selected ordinary members of the congregation, while around and behind him the cardinals queued to go up to the altar. Even as he placed the wafers on the tongues of the kneeling communicants, he was half aware of the looks he was receiving from his colleagues. He sensed astonishment. Lomeli – the smooth, the reliable, the competent Lomeli; Lomeli the lawyer; Lomeli the diplomat – had done something they had never expected. He had said something interesting. He had not expected it of himself, either.

At 11.52 a.m., he intoned the Concluding Rites, '*Benedicat vos omnipotens Deus,*' and made the sign of the cross three times, to the north, to the east and to the south: '*Pater . . . et Filius . . . et Spiritus Sanctus.*'

'*Amen.*'

117

'Go forth, the Mass is ended.'

'Thanks be to God.'

He stood at the altar with his hands clasped on his chest while the choir and the congregation sang the Antiphona Mariana. As the cardinals processed in pairs back up the nave and out of the basilica, he scrutinised them dispassionately. He knew he would not be alone in thinking that the next time they returned, one of them would be Pope.

CHAPTER 6

SISTINE CHAPEL

L omeli, along with his attendants, arrived back at the hostel a few minutes after the other cardinals. They were being divested in the lobby, and almost at once he sensed a change in their attitude towards him. For a start, nobody came over to speak to him, and when he gave his crozier and mitre to Father Zanetti, he noticed how the young priest avoided meeting his gaze. Even Monsignor O'Malley, who offered to help him remove his chasuble, seemed subdued. Lomeli was expecting him at the very least to make one of his usual overfamiliar jokes. Instead he merely said, 'Would Your Eminence care to pray while the vestments are removed?'

'I think I've prayed enough for one morning, Ray, don't you?' He bowed his head and allowed the chasuble to be pulled away. It was a relief to have the weight off his shoulders. He rotated his neck to ease the tension in his muscles. He smoothed his hair and checked his zuchetta was properly in place then glanced around the lobby. The schedule permitted the cardinals a long lunch break – two and a half hours, which they could spend as they wished until a fleet of six minibuses arrived at the Casa Santa Marta to ferry them to the vote. Some were already making their way upstairs to rest and meditate in their rooms.

O'Malley said, 'The press office have been calling.'

'Really?'

'The media have noticed the presence of a cardinal who doesn't appear on any official list. Some of the better-informed have already identified him as Archbishop Benítez. The press people want to know how they should handle it.'

'Tell them to confirm it, and have them explain the circumstances.' He could see Benítez standing over by the reception desk, in conversation with the other two cardinals from the Philippines. He was wearing his zuchetta at a sideways angle, like a schoolboy's cap. 'I suppose we'll also need to put out some biographical details. You must have access to his file at the Congregation for Bishops?'

'Yes, Eminence.'

'Could you pull something together, and let me have a copy? I wouldn't mind knowing a little more about our new colleague myself.'

'Yes, Eminence.' O'Malley was scribbling on his clipboard. 'Also, the press office want to release the text of your homily.'

'I don't have a copy, I'm afraid.'

'It doesn't matter. We can always make a transcript from the tape.' He made another note.

Lomeli was still waiting for him to pass some

comment on his sermon. 'Is there anything else you have to say to me?'

'I think that's all I need to bother you with at the moment, Eminence. Do you have any other instructions?'

'Actually, there is one thing.' Lomeli hesitated. 'A delicate matter. Do you know who I mean by Monsignor Morales? He was in the Holy Father's private office.'

'I don't know him personally; I know *of* him.'

'Is there any chance you might be able to have a word with him, in confidence? It needs to be done today – I'm sure he must be in Rome.'

'*Today?* That won't be easy, Eminence . . .'

'Yes, I know. I'm sorry. Perhaps you could do it while we're voting?' He lowered his voice so that none of the cardinals disrobing around them could hear. 'Use my authority. Say that as dean I need to know what happened in the final meeting between the Holy Father and Cardinal Tremblay: did anything occur that might render Cardinal Tremblay unfit to assume the papacy?' The normally unflappable O'Malley gaped at him. 'I'm sorry to land you with such a sensitive mission. Obviously I'd do it myself, but I'm now officially forbidden to make contact with anyone outside the Conclave. I need hardly add that you mustn't breathe a word to a soul.'

'Of course not.'

'Bless you.' He patted O'Malley's arm. He couldn't suppress his curiosity any longer. 'Well,

Ray, I notice you've said nothing about my homily. You're not usually so tactful. Was it really as bad as all that?'

'Far from it, Your Eminence. It was extremely well said, although I expect it will have raised a few eyebrows over at the Congregation for the Doctrine of the Faith. But tell me: was it really extempore?'

'Yes, as a matter of fact, it was.' He was taken aback by the implication that his spontaneity might have been an act.

'I only ask because you may find that it's had a considerable effect.'

'Well – that's to the good, surely?'

'Absolutely. Although I have heard murmurings that you are trying to pick the new Pope.'

Lomeli's first reaction was to laugh. 'You are not serious!' Until that moment it had not occurred to him that his words might be interpreted as an attempt to manipulate the voting one way or another. He had spoken simply as the Holy Spirit had moved him. Unfortunately, he couldn't now remember the exact phrases he had used. That was the peril of speaking without a prepared text, which was why he had never done it before.

'I only report what I've heard, Eminence.'

'But that is absurd! What did I call for? Three things: unity; tolerance; humility. Are colleagues now suggesting we need a Pope who is schismatic, intolerant and arrogant?' O'Malley bowed his head in deference, and Lomeli realised he had raised his voice. A couple of cardinals had turned to look at him. 'I'm sorry, Ray. Excuse me. I think I'll go to my room for an hour. I'm feeling rather drained.'

All he had ever desired in this contest was to be neutral. Neutrality had been the leitmotif of his career. When the traditionalists had taken control of the Congregation for the Doctrine of the Faith in the nineties, he had kept his head down and got on with his work as Papal Nuncio in the United States. Twenty years later, when the late Holy Father had decided to clear out the old guard and had asked him to step down as Secretary of State, he had nevertheless served him loyally in the lesser role of Dean. *Servus fidelis*: all that mattered was the Church. He had meant what he said that morning. He had seen at first hand the damage that could be done by inflexible certainty in matters of faith.

Now, though, as he made his way across the lobby to the elevator, he found to his dismay that although he was receiving some friendly acknow-ledgement – the occasional pat on the back, a few smiles – this came entirely from the liberal faction. At least as many cardinals who were listed in Lomeli's file as traditionalists frowned or turned their heads away from him. Archbishop Dell'Acqua of Bologna, who had been at Bellini's table the night before, called out, loudly enough for the whole room to hear, 'Well said, Dean!' But Cardinal Gambino, the Archbishop of Perugia, who was one of Tedesco's strongest supporters, ostentatiously

123

wagged his finger at him in silent reproof. To cap it all, when the elevator doors opened, there stood Tedesco himself, red-faced and doubtless on his way to an early lunch, accompanied by the Archbishop Emeritus of Chicago, Paul Krasinski, who was leaning on his stick. Lomeli stepped aside to let them out.

As he passed, Tedesco said sharply, 'My goodness, that was a novel interpretation of Ephesians, Dean – to portray St Paul as an Apostle of Doubt! I've never heard that one before!' He swung round, determined to have an argument. 'Did he not also write to the Corinthians, "For if the trumpet give forth an uncertain note, who shall prepare himself to the battle?"'

Lomeli pressed the button for the second floor. 'Perhaps it would have been more palatable to you in Latin, Patriarch?' The doors closed, cutting off Tedesco's reply.

He was halfway along the corridor to his room before he realised he had locked his key inside. A childish self-pity welled within him. Did he have to think of everything? Shouldn't Father Zanetti be looking after him just a little better? There was nothing for it except to turn around, descend the stairs and explain his foolishness to the nun behind the reception desk. She disappeared into the office and returned with Sister Agnes of the Daughters of Charity of St Vincent de Paul, a tiny Frenchwoman in her late sixties. Her face was sharp and fine, her eyes a crystalline blue. One

124

of her distant aristocratic forebears had been a member of the order during the French Revolution and had been guillotined in the marketplace for refusing to swear an oath to the new regime. Sister Agnes was reputed to be the only person of whom the late Holy Father had been afraid, and perhaps for that reason he had often sought out her company. 'Agnes,' he used to say, 'will always tell me the truth.'

After Lomeli had repeated his apologies, she tut-tutted and gave him her pass key.

'All I can say, Your Eminence, is that I hope you take better care of the Keys of St Peter than you do of the keys to your room!'

By now most of the cardinals had drifted away from the lobby, either to go to their quarters to rest or meditate, or to have lunch in the dining hall. Unlike dinner, lunch was self-service. The clatter of plates and cutlery, the smell of hot food, the warm drone of conversation – all were tempting to Lomeli. But looking at the queue, he guessed that his sermon would be the main topic of conversation. It would be wiser to let it speak for itself.

At the bend in the stairs, he encountered Bellini on his way down. The former Secretary of State was alone, and as he drew level with Lomeli he said quietly, 'I never knew you were so ambitious.'

For a moment Lomeli wasn't sure he had heard correctly. 'What an extraordinary thing to say!'

'I didn't mean any offence, but you must agree

that you have . . . how should one put it? Stepped out of the shadows, shall we say?'

'And how exactly is one to remain in the shadows if one has to celebrate a televised Mass in St Peter's for two hours?'

'Oh now you're being disingenuous, Jacopo.' Bellini's mouth twisted into an awful smile. 'You know what I'm talking about. And to think that only a little while ago you tried to resign! But now . . .?' He shrugged, and the smile twisted again. 'Who knows how things may turn out?'

Lomeli felt almost faint, as if he were suffering an attack of vertigo. 'Aldo, this conversation is very distressing to me. You cannot seriously believe I have the slightest desire, or the remotest chance, of becoming Pope?'

'My dear friend, every man in this building has a chance, at least in theory. And every cardinal has entertained the fantasy, if nothing else, that one day he might be elected, and has selected the name by which he would like his papacy to be known.'

'Well *I* haven't . . .'

'Deny it if you like, but go away and search your heart and then tell me it isn't so. And now, if you'll excuse me, I have promised the Archbishop of Milan that I will go down to the dining room and attempt to make conversation with some of our colleagues.'

After he had gone, Lomeli stood motionless on the stairs. Bellini was obviously under the most tremendous strain, otherwise he would not have spoken to him in such terms. But when he reached his room, and let himself in, and lay on his bed attempting to rest, he found he could not get the accusation out of his mind. Was there really, deep within his soul, a devil of ambition he had refused to acknowledge all these years? He tried to make an honest audit of his conscience, and at the end of it his conclusion was that Bellini was wrong, as far as he could tell.

But then another possibility occurred to him – one that, however absurd, was much more alarming. He was almost afraid to examine it:

What if God had a plan for him?

Could that explain why he had been seized by that extraordinary impulse in St Peter's? Were those few sentences, which he now found so hard to remember, not actually his at all, but a manifestation of the Holy Spirit working through him?

He tried to pray. But God, who had felt so close only a few minutes before, had vanished again, and his pleas for guidance seemed to vanish into the ether.

It was just before 2 p.m. when Lomeli finally roused himself from his bed. He undressed to his underwear and socks, opened his closet and laid out the various elements of his choir dress on the counterpane. As he removed each item from its cellophane wrapping, it exuded the sweet chemical aroma of dry-cleaning fluid – a scent that always

127

reminded him of his years in the Nuncio's residence in New York, when all his laundry was done at a place on East 72nd Street. For a moment he closed his eyes and heard once more the ceaseless soft horns of the distant Manhattan traffic.

Every garment had been made to measure by Gammarelli, papal outfitters since 1798, in their famous shop behind the Pantheon, and he took his time in dressing, meditating on the sacred nature of each element in an effort to heighten his spiritual awareness.

He slipped his arms into the scarlet woollen cassock and fastened the thirty-three buttons that ran from his neck to his ankles – one button for each year of Christ's life. Around his waist he tied the red watered-silk sash of the cincture, or fascia, designed to remind him of his vow of chastity, and checked to make sure its tasselled end hung to a point midway up his left calf. Then he pulled over his head the thin white linen rochet – the symbol, along with the mozzetta, of his judicial authority. The bottom two-thirds and the cuffs were of white lace with a floral pattern. He tied the tapes in a bow at his neck and tugged the rochet down so that it extended to just below his knees. Finally he put on his mozzetta, an elbow-length nine-buttoned scarlet cape.

He picked up his pectoral cross from the nightstand and kissed it. John Paul II had presented him in person with the cross to mark his recall from New York to Rome to serve as Secretary for

Relations with Foreign States. The Pope's Parkinsonism had been terribly advanced by then; his hands had shaken so much as he tried to hand it over, it had dropped on the floor. Lomeli unclipped the gold chain and replaced it with a cord of red and gold silk. He murmured the customary prayer for protection (*Munire digneris me . . .*) and hung the cross round his neck so that it lay next to his heart. Then he sat on the edge of the bed, worked his feet into a pair of well-worn black leather brogues and tied the laces. Only one item remained: his biretta of scarlet silk, which he placed over his skullcap.

On the back of the bathroom door was a full-length mirror. He switched on the stuttering light and checked himself in the bluish glow: front first, then his left side, then his right. His profile had become beaky with age. He thought he looked like some elderly moulting bird. Sister Anjelica, who kept house for him, was always telling him he was too thin, that he should eat more. Hanging up in his apartment were vestments he had first worn as a young priest more than forty years ago and which still fitted him perfectly. He smoothed his hands over his stomach. He felt hungry. He had missed both breakfast and lunch. Let it be so, he thought. The pangs of hunger would serve as a useful mortification of the flesh, a constant tiny reminder throughout the first round of voting of the vast agony of Christ's sacrifice.

★   ★   ★

At 2.30 p.m., the cardinals began boarding the fleet of white minibuses that had been queuing all afternoon in the rain outside the Casa Santa Marta.

The atmosphere had become much more sombre in the time since lunch. Lomeli remembered it had been exactly the same at the last Conclave. It wasn't until the moment for voting arrived that one felt the full weight of the responsibility. Only Tedesco seemed immune to it. He was leaning against a pillar, humming to himself and smiling at everyone as they passed. Lomeli wondered what had happened to improve his mood. Perhaps he was indulging in some kind of gamesmanship to disconcert his opponents. With the Patriarch of Venice, all things were possible. It made him uneasy.

Monsignor O'Malley, in his role of Secretary of the College, stood in the centre of the lobby holding his clipboard. He called out their names like a tour guide. They filed out to the buses in silence, in reverse order of seniority: first the cardinals from the Curia, who made up the Order of Deacons; then the cardinal-priests, who mostly comprised the archbishops from around the world; and finally the cardinal-bishops, of whom Lomeli was one, and who also included the three Eastern patriarchs.

Lomeli, as Dean, was the last to leave, immediately behind Bellini. They made eye contact briefly as they hoisted the skirts of their choir dress to

130

climb up on to the bus, but Lomeli didn't attempt to speak. He could tell that Bellini's mind had elevated itself to some higher plane and was no longer registering – as Lomeli's did – all those trivial details that crowded out the presence of God: the boil on the back of their driver's neck, for example, or the scrape of the windscreen wipers, or the awful slovenly creases in the mozzetta of the Patriarch of Alexandria . . .

Lomeli made his way to a seat on the right, halfway down, away from the others. He took off his biretta and placed it in his lap. O'Malley sat beside the driver. He turned to check that everyone was on board. The doors closed with a hiss of compressed air and the coach pulled away, its tyres drumming over the cobbles of the piazza.

Flecks of rain, dislodged by the motion of the bus, streamed diagonally across the thick glass, veiling the view of St Peter's. Beyond the windows on the other side of the vehicle, Lomeli could see security men with umbrellas patrolling the Vatican Gardens. The coach drove slowly around the Via delle Fondamenta, passed under an arch and then came to a halt in the Cortile della Sentinella. Through the misty windscreen the brake lights of the buses up ahead glowed red like votive candles. Officers of the Swiss Guard sheltered in their sentry box, the plumes of their helmets bedraggled by the rain. The bus inched forward through the next two courtyards and turned sharp right into the Cortile del Maresciallo, pulling up directly opposite the entrance to the staircase. Lomeli was pleased to see the bins of rubbish had been removed, then irritated by his pleasure – it was another trivial detail to disrupt his meditation. The coach door opened, letting in a gust of chilly damp air. He replaced his biretta. As he climbed out, two more members of the Swiss Guard saluted. Instinctively he glanced up, past the high brick facade, to the narrow patch of grey sky. He felt the drizzle on his face. For an instant he had an incongruous mental image of a prisoner in an exercise yard, and then he was through the door and climbing the long flight of grey marble steps that led to the Sistine Chapel.

According to the Apostolic Constitution, the Conclave was required to assemble first in the Pauline Chapel, next door to the Sistine, 'at a suitable hour in the afternoon'. The Pauline was the private chapel of the Holy Father, heavily marbled, gloomier and more intimate than the Sistine. By the time Lomeli arrived, the cardinals were already seated in their pews and the television lights had been switched on. Monsignor Epifano was waiting beside the door, holding the dean's scarlet silk stole, which he draped carefully around Lomeli's neck, and together they walked towards the altar, between Michelangelo's frescos of St Peter and St Paul. Peter, on the right of the aisle, was depicted being crucified upside down. His head was twisted in such a way that he seemed to stare out in angry accusation at whoever had the temerity to look at him. Lomeli felt the saint's scorching eyes on his back all the way to the altar steps.

At the microphone, he turned to face the cardinals. They stood. Epifano held up before him the slim volume containing the stipulated rituals, open at section two, 'The Approach to the Conclave'. Lomeli made the sign of the cross.

'*In nomine Patris et Filii et Spiritus Sancti.*'

'*Amen.*'

'Venerable brothers in the College, having completed the sacred acts this morning, now we enter into the Conclave in order to elect our new Pope . . .'

His amplified voice filled the small chapel. But unlike the great Mass in the basilica, this time he felt no emotion, no spiritual presence. The words were words only: an incantation without magic.

'The entire Church, which is joined to us in common prayer, begs the immediate grace of the Holy Spirit that a worthy pastor for the whole flock of Christ may be elected by us.

'May the Lord direct our steps in the way of truth so that with the intercession of the Blessed Virgin Mary, Saints Peter and Paul and all the saints, we may act in a way that is truly pleasing to them.'

Epifano closed the book and removed it. The processional cross by the door was lifted by one of the trio of masters of ceremonies, the two others

133

held aloft lighted candles, and the choir began to file out of the chapel singing the Litany of the Saints. Lomeli stood facing the Conclave with his hands clasped, his eyes closed, his head bowed, apparently in prayer. He hoped the television cameras had cut away from him by now, and that the close-ups hadn't betrayed his lack of grace. The chanting of the saints' names grew fainter as the choir processed across the Sala Regia towards the Sistine. He heard the cardinals' shoes shuffling down the marble aisle to follow them.

After a while Epifano whispered, 'Eminence, we should go.'

He looked up to find the chapel had almost emptied. Leaving the altar and passing St Peter's crucifixion for a second time, he tried to keep his gaze fixed on the door ahead. But the force of the painting was irresistible. *And you?* the eyes of the martyred saint seemed to demand. *In what way are you worthy to choose my successor?*

In the Sala Regia, a line of Swiss Guards stood to attention. Lomeli and Epifano joined the end of the procession. The cardinals were intoning their response – '*Ora pro nobis*' – to the chanting of each saint's name. They passed into the vestibule of the Sistine Chapel. Here they were obliged to halt while those queuing ahead of them were shown to their places. To Lomeli's left were the twin stoves in which the ballot papers were to be burnt; in front of him the long, narrow back of Bellini. He wanted to tap him on the shoulder, lean forward, wish him good luck. But the TV cameras were everywhere; he didn't dare risk it. Besides, he was sure Bellini was in communion with God.

A minute later they processed up the temporary wooden ramp, through the screen and on to the raised floor of the chapel. The organ was playing. The choir was still chanting the names of the saints: '*Sancte Antoni . . . Sancte Benedicte . . .*' Most of the cardinals were standing at their places behind the long rows of desks. Bellini was the last to be conducted to his seat. When the aisle was cleared, Lomeli walked along the beige carpet to the table where the Bible had been set up for the swearing of the oath. He took off his biretta and handed it to Epifano.

The choir began to sing the Veni Creator Spiritus:

> Come, creator spirit,
> Visit the hearts of your people,
> Fill with celestial grace
> The hearts you have made . . .

When the hymn was over, Lomeli advanced towards the altar. It was wide and narrow, flush to the wall, like a double hearth. Above it, *The Last Judgement* filled his vision. He must have seen it a thousand times yet he had never experienced its power as he did in those few seconds. He felt almost as if he was being sucked into it. When he mounted the step, he found himself at eye level with the damned being dragged down to hell, and

135

he had to take a moment to steady himself before he turned and faced the Conclave.

Epifano held the book up for him. He intoned the prayer – '*Ecclesiae tuae, Domine, rector et custos*' – and then began to administer the oath. The cardinals, following the text in their order of service, read out the words along with him:

' "We, the cardinal-electors present in this election of the Supreme Pontiff, promise, pledge and swear, as individuals and as a group, to observe faithfully and scrupulously the prescriptions contained in the Apostolic Constitution . . .

' "We likewise promise, pledge and swear that whichever of us by divine disposition is elected Roman pontiff will commit himself faithfully to carrying out the Petrine Primacy of Pastor of the Universal Church . . .

' "We promise and swear to observe with the greatest fidelity and with all persons, clerical or lay, secrecy regarding everything that in any way relates to the election of the Roman pontiff and regarding what occurs in the place of the election . . ." '

Lomeli walked back down the aisle to the table where the Bible was propped up. 'And I, Jacopo Baldassare, Cardinal Lomeli, do so promise, pledge and swear.' He placed his palm on the open page. 'So help me God and these Holy Gospels which I touch with my hand.'

Once he had finished, he took his seat at the end of the long desk nearest the altar. In the next seat was the Patriarch of Lebanon; one place further along was Bellini. Lomeli could do nothing now except watch as the cardinals queued in the aisle and stepped forward one after another to swear the short oath. He had a perfect view of every face. In a few days' time, the television producers would be able to spool through their tapes of the ceremony and find the new Pope at exactly this moment, placing his hand on the Gospel, and then his elevation would seem inevitable: it always did. Roncalli, Montini, Wojtyła, even poor little awkward Luciani, who had died after barely a month in office: viewed down the long majestic gallery of hindsight, each one shone with the aura of destiny.

As he scrutinised the parade of cardinals, he tried to imagine every individual clothed in pontifical white. Sá, Contreras, Hierra, Fitzgerald, Santos, De Luca, Löwenstein, Jandaček, Brotzkus, Villanueva, Nakitanda, Sabbadin, Santini – it could be any of these men. It didn't have to be one of the front-runners. There was an old saying: 'He who enters the Conclave a Pope leaves it a cardinal.' Nobody had tipped the late Holy Father before the last election, and yet he had achieved a two-thirds majority on the fourth ballot. *O Lord, let our choice fall on a worthy candidate, and may You so guide us in our deliberations that our Conclave is neither long nor divisive but an emblem of the unity of Your Church. Amen.*

It took more than half an hour for the entire

137

college to swear their oaths. Then Archbishop Mandorff, as Master of Papal Liturgical Celebrations, stepped up to the microphone erected on its stand beneath *The Last Judgement.* In his quiet, precise voice, stressing all four syllables distinctly, he intoned the official formula, '*Extra omnes.*'

The television lights were switched off, and the four masters of ceremonies, the priests and officials, the choristers, the security men, the television cameramen, the official photographer, one solitary nun and the commandant of the Swiss Guard in his white-plumed helmet all left their positions and made their way out of the chapel.

Mandorff waited until the last of them had gone, then he walked down the carpeted aisle to the big double doors. It was 4.46 p.m. precisely. The outside world's last view of the Conclave was of his solemn bald head, and then the doors were closed from the inside and the television transmission ended.

CHAPTER 7

THE FIRST BALLOT

L ater, when the experts who were paid to analyse the Conclave tried to breach the wall of secrecy and piece together exactly what had happened, their sources were all agreed on this: that the divisions started the moment Mandorff closed the doors.

Only two men who were not cardinal-electors now remained in the Sistine Chapel. Mandorff was one; the other was the Vatican's oldest resident, Cardinal Vittorio Scavizzi, the ninety-four-year-old Vicar General Emeritus of Rome.

Scavizzi had been chosen by the College soon after the Holy Father's funeral to deliver what was described in the Apostolic Constitution as 'the second meditation'. This was stipulated to take place in private immediately before the first ballot; its function was to remind the Conclave one last time of their heavy responsibility 'to act with the right intention for the good of the Universal Church'. Traditionally it was given by one of the cardinals who had passed the age of eighty and was therefore ineligible to vote – a sop, in other words, to the old guard.

Lomeli could not remember how they had ended up choosing Scavizzi. There had been so much else for him to worry about, he had not paid the decision much attention. He suspected the original proposal might have come from Tutino – this was before it was discovered that the Prefect of the Congregation for Bishops, who was under investigation for his wretched apartment extension, was planning to switch his support to Tedesco. Now, as Lomeli watched the elderly cleric being helped towards the microphone by Archbishop Mandorff – his shrivelled body listing to one side, his notes clutched fiercely in his arthritic hand, his narrow eyes bright with resolve – he had a sudden premonition of trouble.

Scavizzi grabbed the microphone and pulled it towards him. Amplified thumps ricocheted off the Sistine's walls. He held his pages up very close to his eyes. For a few seconds nothing happened, and then gradually from the rasp of his laboured breathing words began to emerge.

'Cardinal brothers, at this moment of great responsibility, let us listen with special attention to what the Lord says to us in His own words. When I heard the dean of this order, in his homily this morning, use St Paul's Letter to the Ephesians as an argument for doubt, I felt I could not believe my ears. Doubt! Is that what we are short of in the modern world? *Doubt?*'

There was a slight noise from the body of the chapel – a murmuring, a general intake of breath,

140

a shifting of positions in seats. Lomeli could hear his own pulse in his eardrums.

'I implore you even at this late hour to listen to what St Paul actually says: that we need unity in our faith and in our knowledge of Christ in order not to be children "tossed one way and another and carried along by every wind of doctrine".

'This is a boat in a storm he is talking about, my brothers. This is the Barque of St Peter, our Holy Catholic Church, which, as never before in its history, is "at the mercy of all the tricks men play and their cleverness in practising deceit". The winds and the waves our ship is battling go by many different names – atheism, nationalism, agnosticism, Marxism, liberalism, individualism, feminism, capitalism – but every one of these "isms" seeks to divert us from our true course.

'Your task, cardinal-electors, is to choose a new captain who will ignore the doubters among us and hold the rudder fast. Every day, some new "ism" arises. But not all ideas are of equal value. Not every opinion can be given due weight. Once we succumb to "the dictatorship of relativism", as it has been properly called, and attempt to survive by accommodating ourselves to every passing sect and fad of modernism, our ship is lost. We do not need a Church that will move *with* the world but a Church that will *move* the world.

'Let us pray to God that the Holy Spirit enters these deliberations and directs you to a pastor who will put an end to the drifting of recent times – a pastor who will guide us once again to knowledge of Christ, to His love and to true joy. Amen.'

Scavizzi let go of the microphone. An explosion of amplification rang around the chapel. He gave a wobbly bow to the altar, then took Mandorff's arm. Leaning heavily on the archbishop, he limped slowly down the aisle, watched in complete silence by every pair of eyes in the chapel. The old man looked at no one, not even at Tedesco, who was seated in the front row almost opposite Lomeli. Now Lomeli knew why the Patriarch of Venice had been in such a good humour. He had known what was coming. It was possible even that he had written it.

Scavizzi and Mandorff passed out of sight behind the screen. In the stunned hush it was easy to hear their footsteps on the marble floor of the vestibule, the Sistine's doors opening and closing, and a key turning in the lock.

Conclave. From the Latin, *con clavis*: 'with a key'. Since the thirteenth century, this was how the Church had ensured its cardinals would come to a decision. They would not be released from the chapel, except for meals and to sleep, until they had chosen a Pope.

Finally, the cardinal-electors were alone.

Lomeli rose and walked to the microphone. He moved slowly, trying to think how best to contain the damage that had just been done. The personal nature of the attack had stung him, naturally. But that concerned him less than the wider threat it posed to his mission, which was above all to maintain the unity of the Church. He sensed the need to slow things down, to let the shock of what had happened dissipate, to give the argument for tolerance a chance to percolate back to the surface of the cardinals' minds.

He faced the Conclave just as the great bell of St Peter's began tolling five o'clock. He glanced up at the windows. The sky was dark. He waited until the reverberations of the last strike had died away.

'Cardinal brothers, after that stimulating meditation . . .' he paused, and there was some sympathetic laughter, 'we can now proceed to the first ballot. However, according to the Apostolic Constitution, voting may be delayed if a member of the Conclave has any objections. Does anyone wish to postpone the voting until tomorrow? I appreciate it has been an exceptionally long day, and we may wish to reflect further on what we have just heard.'

There was a pause, and then Krasinski used his stick to push himself up on to his feet. 'The eyes of the world are on the Sistine chimney, cardinal brothers. In my view it would look odd, to say the least, if we stopped for the night. I believe we should vote.'

He lowered himself carefully back into his seat. Lomeli glanced at Bellini. His face remained impassive. Nobody else spoke.

'Very well,' said Lomeli. 'We shall vote.' He returned to his place and collected his rule book and ballot paper, then went back to the microphone. 'Dear brothers, you will find in front of you one of these.' He held up the ballot paper, and waited while the cardinals opened their red leather folders. 'You can see that it has "I elect as Supreme Pontiff" written in Latin in the top half, and the bottom half is blank: that is where you should write the name of your chosen candidate. Please make sure no one can see your vote, and be sure to put down one name only, otherwise your ballot will be null and void. And please write legibly, and in a way that ensures your handwriting cannot be identified.

'Now, if you would all turn to Chapter Five, paragraph sixty-six of the Apostolic Constitution, you will see the procedure that has to be followed.'

When they had opened their rule books, he read the paragraph aloud, just to make sure they all understood:

' "Each cardinal-elector, in order of precedence, having completed and folded his ballot, holds it up so that it can be seen and carries it to the altar, at which the scrutineers stand and upon which there is placed a receptacle, covered by a plate, for receiving the ballots. Having reached the altar, the cardinal-elector says aloud the words of the following oath: *I call as my witness Christ the Lord, who will be my judge, that my vote is given to the one who before God I think should be elected.* He then places the ballot on the plate, with which he drops it into the receptacle. Having done this, he bows to the altar and returns to his place."

'Is that clear to everyone? Very good. Scrutineers, would you take your positions, please?'

The three men who would count the ballots had been chosen by lot the previous week. They were the Archbishop of Vilnius, Cardinal Lukša; the Prefect for the Congregation of Clergy, Cardinal Mercurio; and the Archbishop of Westminster, Cardinal Newby. They rose from their places in different parts of the chapel and made their way to the altar. Lomeli went back to his chair and picked up the pen that had been provided by the College. He shielded his ballot paper with his arm, like a candidate in an examination who doesn't want his answer to be seen by his neighbour, and wrote in capital letters: BELLINI. He folded it, stood, held it aloft and walked to the altar.

'I call as my witness Christ the Lord, who will be my judge, that my vote is given to the one who before God I think should be elected.'

On the altar was a large ornate urn, bigger than a normal altar vessel, covered by a plain silver chalice, which served as its lid. Watched intently by the scrutineers, he put his ballot paper on the chalice, lifted it with both hands and tipped his vote into the urn. Replacing the chalice, he bowed to the altar and resumed his seat.

The three patriarchs of the Eastern Churches were the next to go up, followed by Bellini. He

145

recited the oath with a sigh in his voice, and when he returned to his place he put his hand to his brow and appeared to sink into deep thought. Lomeli, too tense for prayer or meditation, once again observed the cardinals as they passed him. Tedesco seemed uncharacteristically nervous. He fumbled the tipping of his ballot into the urn so that it fell briefly on to the altar and he had to retrieve it and then drop it in by hand. Lomeli wondered if he had voted for himself – certainly Tremblay might have done so: there was nothing in the rules to say one couldn't. The oath was simply to vote for the person one thought should be elected. The Canadian approached the altar with reverentially downcast eyes, then raised them to *The Last Judgement*, apparently transported, and made an exaggerated sign of the cross. Another man who had faith in his own abilities was Adeyemi, who swore the oath with his trademark boom. He had made his name as Archbishop of Lagos when the Holy Father had first toured Africa: he had organised a Mass attended by a congregation of more than four million. The Pope had joked in his homily that Joshua Adeyemi was the only man in the Church who could have conducted the service without the need for amplification.

And then there was Benítez, of whom Lomeli had lost track since the previous night. One could at least be certain that *he* would not be voting for himself. The choir dress that had been found for him was too long. His rochet hung almost to the ground and he nearly tripped over it as he reached the altar. When he had finished voting and turned to go back to his seat, he gave Lomeli a wry glance. Lomeli nodded and smiled encouragement in return. The Filipino had an attractive quality, he thought, not easy to define: an inner grace. Now that he was becoming better known, he might go far.

The voting went on for more than an hour. When it began, there had been a few whispered conversations. But by the time the scrutineers had cast their own ballots, and the last man to vote – Bill Rudgard, the Junior Cardinal-Deacon – had returned to his seat, the silence seemed to have become endless and absolute, like the infinity of space. God has entered the room, thought Lomeli. We are sequestered under lock and key at the point where time and eternity meet.

Cardinal Lukša lifted the urn and displayed it to the Conclave, as if he were about to bless the sacrament. He shook it several times to mix up the ballots. Then he offered it to Cardinal Newby, who, without unfolding the voting papers, extracted them one by one, counting them out loud, and transferred them to a second urn standing on the altar.

At the end, the Englishman announced, in his thickly accented Italian, 'One hundred and eighteen votes have been cast.'

He and Cardinal Mercurio went into the Room

of Tears, the sacristy to the left of the altar where the three different sizes of papal vestments were hanging, and emerged almost at once carrying between them a small table, which they set up in front of the altar. Cardinal Lukša covered it with a white cloth and placed the urn containing the votes in the centre. Newby and Mercurio returned to the sacristy and fetched three chairs. Newby unclipped the microphone from its stand and carried it over to the table.

'My brothers,' he said, 'we shall proceed to count the first ballot.'

And now, at last, emerging from its trance, the Conclave stirred. In the folder in front of them, every elector had been issued with a list, arranged alphabetically, of the cardinals eligible to vote. Lomeli was glad to see it had been reprinted overnight to include Benítez. He picked up his pen.

Lukša extracted the first ballot paper from the urn, unfolded it, and made a note of the name. He passed it to Mercurio, who studied it in turn and also recorded it. Then Mercurio handed it to Newby, who used a silver needle to pierce the vote through the word 'elect' and thread it on to a length of red silk cord. He leaned into the microphone. He had the easy, confident voice of a public-school-and-Oxford man. 'The first vote is cast for Cardinal Tedesco.'

Each time a vote was announced, Lomeli put a tick against the candidate's name. At first it was impossible to get a sense of who was ahead. Thirty-four cardinals – more than a quarter of the Conclave – received at least one vote: it was said afterwards to be a record. Men voted for themselves, or for a friend, or a fellow countryman. Quite early on, Lomeli heard his own name read out, and awarded himself a tick on his list. He was touched that someone should have considered him worthy of the supreme honour; he wondered who it was. But when it happened several times more, he began to feel alarmed. In such a crowded field, anything more than half a dozen votes would be enough, at least in theory, to put one in contention.

He kept his head down, concentrating on his tally. Even so, he was aware of cardinals occasionally staring at him across the aisle. The race was slow and close, the distribution of support bizarrely random, so that one of the front-runners might get two or three votes in a row, and then receive none of the succeeding twenty. Still, after about eighty or so ballots had been read out, it was clear which cardinals had the potential strength to emerge as Pope, and as predicted they were Tedesco, Bellini, Tremblay and Adeyemi. When a hundred votes had been counted, there was still nothing between them. But then at the end, something strange happened. Bellini's vote stalled, and the final few names read out must have felt like hammer blows to him: Tedesco, Lomeli, Adeyemi, Adeyemi, Tremblay, and last of all – amazingly – Benítez.

As the scrutineers conferred and checked the totals, whispered conversations broke out all around the chapel. Lomeli ran his pen down his list, adding up the votes. He scribbled the figures beside each name:

Tedesco 22
Adeyemi 19
Bellini 18
Tremblay 16
Lomeli 5
Others 38

The size of his own vote dismayed him. Assuming he had drawn away support from Bellini, he might well have cost him first place, and with it the sense of inevitability that might have carried him to victory. Indeed, the more he studied the figures, the more disappointing for Bellini they looked. Hadn't Sabbadin, his campaign manager, predicted at dinner that he was certain to be in the lead after the first ballot, with up to twenty-five votes, and that Tedesco would receive no more than fifteen? Yet Bellini had come in third, behind Adeyemi – no one had envisaged that – and even Tremblay was only two votes behind him. One thing was certain, Lomeli concluded: no candidate was anywhere near the seventy-nine votes it would take to win the election.

He was only half listening as Newby read out the official results: they merely confirmed what he had already worked out for himself. Instead he was flicking through the Apostolic Constitution to paragraph seventy-four. No modern Conclave had lasted beyond three days, but that didn't mean it might not happen. Under the rules they were obliged to keep on balloting until they found a candidate who could command a two-thirds majority, if necessary for as many as thirty ballots, extending over twelve days. Only at the end of that time would they be permitted to use a different system, whereby a simple majority would be sufficient to elect a new Pope.

Twelve days – an appalling prospect!

Newby had finished giving the results. He held up the red silk cord on which all the ballot papers were threaded. He knotted the two ends together and looked towards the dean.

Lomeli rose from his place and took the microphone. From the altar step he could see Tedesco studying the voting figures, Bellini staring into nothing, Adeyemi and Tremblay talking quietly to the men sitting next to them.

'My brother cardinals, that concludes the first ballot. No candidate having achieved the necessary majority, we shall now adjourn for the evening and resume voting in the morning. Will you please remain in your places until the officials are allowed back into the chapel. And may I remind Your Eminences that you are forbidden to take any written record of the voting out of the Sistine. Your notes will be collected from you, and burnt along with the ballot papers. There will be buses outside to take you back to the Casa Santa Marta. I would ask you humbly not to discuss this afternoon's vote in the hearing of the drivers. Thank you for your patience. I now invite the Junior Cardinal-Deacon to ask for us to be released.'

Rudgard stood and walked to the back of the chapel. They could hear him knocking on the doors and calling for them to be opened – '*Aprite le porte! Aprite le porte!*' – like a prisoner summoning his guard. A few moments later he returned accompanied by Archbishop Mandorff, Monsignor O'Malley and the other masters of ceremonies. The priests were carrying paper sacks and went up and down the rows of desks collecting the voting tallies. Some of the cardinals were reluctant to hand them over, and had to be persuaded to put them in the sacks. Others hung on to them for a last few seconds. No doubt they were trying to memorise the figures, Lomeli thought. Or perhaps they were simply savouring the only record there would ever be of the day they received a vote to be Pope.

Most of the cardinals did not go downstairs to the buses immediately but gathered in the vestibule to watch the ballot papers and notes being burnt. It was something after all even for a Prince of the Church to be able to say that he had witnessed such a spectacle.

Even now, the process of checking the votes had

still not quite ended. Three cardinals, known as revisers, also chosen by ballot before the Conclave, were required to recount the tallies. The rules were centuries old and indicated how little the Fathers of the Church had trusted one another: it would require a conspiracy of at least six men to rig the election. When the revising was done, O'Malley squatted on his haunches, opened the round stove and stuffed it with the paper sacks and the threaded ballot papers. He struck a match, lit a firelighter and placed it carefully inside. Lomeli found it odd to see him doing something so practical. There was a soft *wumph* of combustion, and within seconds the material was ablaze. O'Malley closed the iron door. The second stove, the square one, contained a mixture of potassium perchlorate, anthracene and sulphur in a cartridge that ignited when a switch was pressed. At 7.42 p.m., the temporary metal chimney jutting above the roof of the Sistine, picked out in the November darkness by a search-light, began to gush jet-black smoke.

As the members of the Conclave filed out of the chapel, Lomeli drew O'Malley aside. They stood in a corner of the vestibule. Lomeli had his back to the stoves. 'Did you speak to Morales?'
'Only on the telephone, Your Eminence.'
'And?'
O'Malley put his finger to his lips and glanced over Lomeli's shoulder. Tremblay was passing, sharing a joke with a group of cardinals from the

United States. His bland face was cheerful. After the North Americans had strolled out into the Sala Regia, O'Malley said, 'Monsignor Morales was emphatic that he knows of no reason why Cardinal Tremblay should not be Pope.'

Lomeli nodded slowly. He had not expected much else. 'Thank you at least for asking him.'

A sly look came into O'Malley's eyes. 'However, will you forgive me, Your Eminence, if I say that I did not entirely believe the good monsignor?'

Lomeli stared at him. When there wasn't a Conclave, the Irishman was Secretary of the Congregation for Bishops. He had access to the files on five thousand senior clerics. He was said to have a nose for discovering secrets. 'Why do you say that?'

'Because when I tried to press him regarding the meeting between the Holy Father and Cardinal Tremblay, he went out of his way to assure me it was entirely routine. My Spanish isn't perfect, but I have to say he was so emphatic, he rather aroused my suspicions. So I implied – I didn't specifically state it as a *fact*, I hope – let us say I *hinted* in my inadequate Spanish that you might have seen a document that contradicted that. And he said you were not to worry about the document: *"El informe ha sido retirada."*'

'*El informe*? A report? He said there was a report?'

'"The report has been withdrawn" – those were his exact words.'

'A report on what? Withdrawn when?'

154

'That I don't know, Eminence.'

Lomeli was silent, considering this. He rubbed his eyes. It had been a long day, and he was hungry. Was he to be worried that a report had been compiled, or reassured that it might no longer exist? And did it matter much in any case, given that Tremblay was only in fourth place? Suddenly he threw up his hands: he couldn't deal with it now, not while he was sequestered in the Conclave. 'It's probably nothing. Let's leave it there. I know I can rely on your discretion.'

The two prelates walked across the Sala Regia. A security man watched them from beneath a fresco of the Battle of Lepanto. He turned his body away slightly, and whispered something, into either his sleeve or his lapel. Lomeli wondered what it was they were always talking about in such urgent tones. He said, 'Is anything happening in the outside world that I ought to be aware of?'

'Not really. The main story in the international media is the Conclave.'

'No leaks, I trust?'

'None. The reporters interview one another.' They began to descend the stairs. There were a great many steps – thirty or forty – lit on either side by electric lamps shaped like candles; some of the older cardinals found their steepness a challenge. 'I should add there is great interest in Cardinal Benítez. We have put out a biographical note, as you requested. I have also included a background note for you, in confidence. He really

155

has enjoyed the most remarkable series of promotions of any bishop in the Church.' O'Malley pulled an envelope from beneath his vestments and handed it to Lomeli. '*La Repubblica* believes his dramatic arrival is all part of the late Holy Father's secret plan.'

Lomeli laughed. 'I would be delighted if there was a plan – secret or otherwise! But I sense that the only one with a plan for this Conclave is God, and so far He seems to be determined to keep it to Himself.'

CHAPTER 8

MOMENTUM

L omeli rode back to the hostel in silence, his cheek pressed against the cold window of the bus. The swish of the tyres on the wet cobbles as they passed through the successive courtyards was oddly comforting. Above the Vatican Gardens the lights of a passenger jet descended towards Fiumicino airport. He promised himself that the next morning he would walk to the Sistine, whether it was raining or not. This airless seclusion was not merely unhealthy: it was unconducive to spiritual reflection.

When they reached the Casa Santa Marta, he strode past the gossiping cardinals and went straight to his room. The nuns had been in to clean while the Conclave was voting. His vestments had been neatly hung in the closet, the sheets on his bed turned down. He took off his mozzetta and rochet and draped them over the back of the chair, then knelt at the prie-dieu. He gave thanks to God for helping him perform his duties throughout the day. He even risked a little humour. *And thank you, O Lord, for speaking to us through the voting in the Conclave, and I pray that soon You*

157

will give us the wisdom to understand what it is You are trying to say.

From the adjoining room emanated muffled voices occasionally punctuated by laughter. Lomeli glanced at the wall. He was sure now that his neighbour must be Adeyemi. No other member of the Conclave had a voice so deep. It sounded as if he was having a meeting with his supporters. There was another burst of hilarity. Lomeli's mouth tightened in disapproval. If Adeyemi truly sensed the papacy might be closing in on him, he ought to be lying prone on his bed in the darkness in silent terror, not relishing the prospect. But then he rebuked himself for his priggishness. The first black Pope would be a tremendous thing for the world. Who could blame a man if he felt exhilarated at the prospect of being the vehicle of such a manifestation of the Divine Will?

He remembered the envelope O'Malley had given him. Slowly he raised himself on his creaking knees, sat at his desk and tore open the envelope. Two sheets of paper. One was the biographical note released by the Vatican press office:

Cardinal Vincent Benítez

Cardinal Benítez is 67 years old. He was born in Manila, Philippines. He studied at the San Carlos Seminary and was ordained in 1978 by the Archbishop of Manila, His Eminence Cardinal Jaime Sin. His first ministry was at the church of Santo Niño de Tondo and afterwards at Our Lady of the Abandoned Parish (Santa Ana). Well known for his work in the poorest areas of Manila, he established eight shelters for homeless girls, the Project of the Blessed Santa Margherita de Cortona. In 1996, following the assassination of the former Archbishop of Bukavu, Christopher Munzihirwa, Fr Benítez, at his own request, was transferred to the Democratic Republic of the Congo, where he undertook missionary work. He subsequently set up a Catholic hospital in Bukavu to assist female victims of the genocidal sexual violence perpetrated during the First and Second Congo Wars. In 2017 he was created monsignor. In 2018 he was appointed Archbishop of Baghdad, Iraq. He was admitted to the College of Cardinals earlier this year by the late Holy Father, *in pectore*.

Lomeli read it through twice just to make sure he wasn't missing anything. The Archdiocese of Baghdad was tiny – if he remembered rightly, these days it numbered barely more than two thousand souls – but even so, Benítez appeared to have gone straight from missionary to archbishop with no intervening stage. He had never heard of such a meteoric promotion. He turned to O'Malley's accompanying handwritten note:

159

Eminence,

From Cardinal Benítez's file in the dicas-
tery, it would appear that the late Holy
Father first met him during his African
tour in 2017. He was sufficiently impressed
by his work to create him monsignor.
When the Baghdad archdiocese fell vacant,
the Holy Father rejected the three suggested
nominations put forward by the Congregation
for Bishops and insisted on appointing Fr
Benítez. In January this year, following minor
injuries sustained in a car-bomb attack,
Archbishop Benítez offered his resignation
on medical grounds, but withdrew it after a
private meeting in the Vatican with the Holy
Father. Otherwise, the file is *remarkably*
scanty.
RO'M

Lomeli sat back in his chair. He had a habit of
biting the side of his right forefinger when he was
thinking. So Benítez was in delicate health, or had
been, as the result of a terrorist incident in Iraq?
Perhaps that accounted for his fragile appearance.
All in all, his ministry had been served in some
terrible places: such a life was bound to take its
toll. What was certain was that the man represented the best that the Christian faith had to
offer. Lomeli resolved to keep a discreet eye on
him, and to mention him in his prayers.

A bell rang, to announce that dinner was served. It was 8.30 p.m.

'Let us face facts. We did not do as well as we had hoped.' The Archbishop of Milan, Sabbadin, his rimless lenses glinting in the light of the chandeliers, looked around the table at the Italian cardinals who formed the core of Bellini's support. Lomeli was seated opposite him.

This was the night when the real business of the Conclave started to be done. Although in theory the papal constitution forbade the cardinal-electors from entering into 'any form of pact, agreement, promise or commitment' on pain of excommunication, this had now become an election, and hence a matter of arithmetic: who could get to seventy-nine votes? Tedesco, his authority enhanced by coming top in the first ballot, was telling a funny story to a table of South American cardinals, and dabbing his eyes with his napkin at his own hilarity. Tremblay was listening earnestly to the views of the South-East Asians. Adeyemi, worryingly for his rivals, had been invited to join the conservative archbishops of Eastern Europe – Wrocław, Riga, Lviv, Zagreb – who wanted to test his views on social issues. Even Bellini seemed to making an effort: he had been parked by Sabbadin on a table of North Americans and was describing his ambition to give greater autonomy to the bishops. The nuns who were serving the food could hardly help overhearing the state of play, and

161

afterwards several of them were to prove useful sources for reporters trying to piece together the inside story of the Conclave: one even preserved a napkin on which a cardinal had jotted the voting figures of the first-round leaders.

'Does that mean we cannot win?' continued Sabbadin. Again he sought to look each man in the eye, and Lomeli thought unkindly how rattled he looked: his hopes of becoming Secretary of State under a Bellini papacy had taken a knock. 'Of course we can still win! All that can be said for certain after today's vote is that the next Pope will be one of four men: Bellini, Tedesco, Adeyemi or Tremblay.'

Dell'Acqua, the Archbishop of Bologna, interrupted. 'Aren't you forgetting our friend the dean here? He received five votes.'

'With the greatest respect to Jacopo, it would be unprecedented for a candidate with so little support on the first ballot to emerge as a serious contender.'

But Dell'Acqua refused to let the subject drop. 'What about Wojtyła in the second Conclave of '78? He received only a scattering of votes in the first round yet went on to be elected on the eighth ballot.'

Sabbadin fluttered his hand irritably. 'All right, so it's happened once in a century. But let's not distract ourselves – our dean does not exactly have the ambition of a Karol Wojtyła. Unless, that is, there's something he's not telling us?'

162

Lomeli looked at his plate. The main course was chicken wrapped in Parma ham. It was overcooked and dry but they were eating it nonetheless. He knew that Sabbadin blamed him for taking votes off Bellini. In the circumstances, he felt he should make an announcement. 'My position is an embarrassment to me. If I find out who my supporters are, I shall plead with them to vote for someone else. And if they ask me who I'll be voting for, I shall tell them Bellini.'

Landolfi, the Archbishop of Turin, said, 'Aren't you supposed to be neutral?'

'Well, I can't be seen to campaign for him, if that's what you're implying. But if I'm asked my view, I feel I have a right to express it. Bellini is unquestionably the best-qualified man to govern the Universal Church.'

'Listen to that,' urged Sabbadin. 'If the dean's five votes come to us, that takes us to twenty-three. All those hopeless candidates who have received one or two nominations today will fall away tomorrow. That means another thirty-eight votes are about to become available. We simply have to pick up most of them.'

'Simply?' repeated Dell'Acqua. His tone was mocking. 'I'm afraid there's nothing simple about it, Your Eminence!'

Nobody could say anything to that. Sabbadin flushed pink and they resumed their melancholy chewing in silence.

★　　★　　★

163

If that force which the secular call momentum and the religious believe is the Holy Spirit was with any of the candidates that night, it was with Adeyemi. His rivals seemed to sense it. For example, when the cardinals rose for coffee and the Patriarch of Lisbon, Rui Brandão D'Cruz, went out into the enclosed courtyard to smoke his evening cigar, Lomeli noticed how Tremblay immediately hurried after him, presumably to canvass his support. Tedesco and Bellini moved from table to table. But the Nigerian simply went and stood coolly in the corner of the lobby and left it to his supporters to bring over potential voters who wanted to have a word with him. Soon a small queue began to form.

Lomeli, leaning against the reception desk, sipping coffee, watched him as he held court. If he were a white man, he thought, Adeyemi would be condemned by the liberals as more reactionary even than Tedesco. But the fact that he was black made them reluctant to criticise his views. His fulminations against homosexuality, for example, they could excuse as merely an expression of his African cultural heritage. Lomeli was beginning to sense that he had underestimated Adeyemi. Perhaps he was indeed the candidate to unite the Church. He certainly had the largeness of personality required to fill St Peter's Throne.

He was staring too openly, he realised. He ought to mingle with the others. But he didn't much want to talk to anyone. He wandered around the lobby, holding his cup and saucer like a shield in front of him, smiling and bowing slightly to those cardinals who approached him, but all the time keeping moving. Just around the corner, next to the door to the chapel, he spotted Benítez at the centre of a group of cardinals. They were listening intently to what he was saying. He wondered what the Filipino was telling them. Benítez glanced over their shoulders and noticed Lomeli looking in his direction. He excused himself, and came over.

'Good evening, Your Eminence.'

'And good evening to you.' Lomeli put his hand on Benítez's shoulder and gazed at him with concern. 'How is your health bearing up?'

'My health is excellent, thank you.'

He seemed to tense slightly at the question, and Lomeli remembered that he had only been told in confidence of his offer to resign on medical grounds. He said, 'I'm sorry, that wasn't intended to be intrusive. I meant have you recovered from your journey?'

'Entirely, thank you. I slept very well.'

'That's wonderful. It's a privilege to have you with us.' He patted the Filipino's shoulder and swiftly withdrew his hand. He sipped his coffee. 'And I noticed in the Sistine that you found someone to vote for.'

'Indeed I did, Dean.' Benítez smiled shyly. 'I voted for you.'

165

Lomeli rattled his cup against its saucer in surprise. 'Oh, good heavens!'

'Forgive me. Am I not supposed to say?'

'No, no, it's not that. I'm honoured. But really I'm not a serious candidate.'

'With respect, Your Eminence, isn't that for your colleagues to decide?'

'Of course it is. But I fear that if you knew me better, you would appreciate that I'm in no way worthy to be Pope.'

'Any man who is truly worthy must consider himself unworthy. Isn't that the point you were making in your homily? That without doubt there can be no faith? It resonated with my own experience. The scenes I witnessed in Africa especially would make any man sceptical of God's mercy.'

'My dear Vincent – may I call you Vincent? – I beg you, in the next ballot, give your vote to one of our brothers who has a realistic chance of winning. Bellini would be my choice.'

Benítez shook his head. 'Bellini seems to me – what was the phrase the Holy Father once used to me to describe him? – "brilliant but neurotic". I'm sorry, Dean. I shall vote for you.'

'Even if I plead with you not to? You received a vote yourself this afternoon, didn't you?'

'I did. It was absurd!'

'Then imagine how you would feel if I insisted on voting for you, and by some miracle you won.'

'It would be a disaster for the Church.'

'Yes, well that is how it would be if I became Pope. Will you at least think about what I'm asking?'

Benítez promised that he would.

After his conversation with Benítez, Lomeli was sufficiently troubled to try to seek out the main contenders. He found Tedesco alone in the lobby, lying back in one of the crimson armchairs, his plump and dimpled hands folded across his capacious stomach, his feet up on a coffee table. They were surprisingly dainty for a man of his girth, shod in scuffed and shapeless orthopaedic shoes. Lomeli said, 'I just wanted to tell you that I'm doing all in my power to withdraw my name from the second ballot.'

Tedesco regarded him through half-open eyes. 'And why would you do that?'

'Because I don't wish to compromise my neutrality as dean.'

'You rather did that this morning, didn't you?'

'I'm sorry if you took it that way.'

'Ah, don't worry about it. As far as I'm concerned, I hope you continue as a candidate. I want to see the issues aired: I thought Scavizzi answered you well enough in his meditation. Besides . . .' he wiggled his little feet happily and closed his eyes, 'you're splitting the liberal vote!'

Lomeli studied him for a moment. One had to smile. He was as cunning as a peasant selling a pig at market. Forty votes, that was all the Patriarch of Venice needed: forty votes, and he would have the blocking third he needed to prevent the election of a detested 'progressive'. He would drag the Conclave out for days if he had to. All the more urgency, then, for Lomeli to extricate himself from the embarrassing position in which he was now placed.

'I wish you a good night's sleep, Patriarch.'

'Goodnight, Dean.'

Before the evening was over, he had managed to speak in turn to each of the other three leading candidates, and to each he repeated his pledge to withdraw. 'Mention it to anyone who brings up my name, I implore you. Tell them to come and see me if they doubt my sincerity. All I wish is to serve the Conclave and to help it arrive at the right decision. I can't do that if I'm seen as a contender myself.'

Tremblay frowned and rubbed his chin. 'Forgive me, Dean, but if we do that, won't we simply make you look like a paragon of modesty? If one was being Machiavellian about it, one could almost say it was a clever move to swing votes.'

It was such an insulting response, Lomeli was tempted to raise the issue of the so-called withdrawn report into the Camerlengo's activities. But what was the point? He would only deny it. Instead he said politely, 'Well that is the situation, Your Eminence, and I shall leave you to handle it as you see fit.'

Next he talked to Adeyemi, who was statesman-like. 'I consider that a principled position, Dean,

168

exactly as I would have expected from you. I shall tell my supporters to spread the word.'

'And you certainly have plenty of supporters, I think.' Adeyemi looked at him blankly. Lomeli smiled. 'Forgive me: I couldn't help overhearing the meeting in your room earlier this evening. We're next-door neighbours. The walls are very thin.'

'Ah, yes!' Adeyemi's expression cleared. 'There was a certain exuberance after the first ballot. Perhaps it wasn't very seemly. It won't happen again.'

Lomeli intercepted Bellini just as he was about to go upstairs to bed and told him what he had told the others. He added, 'I feel very wretched that my meagre tally may have come at your expense.'

'Don't be. I'm relieved. There seems to be a general feeling that the chalice is slipping away from me. If that is the case – and I pray that it is – I can only hope that it passes to you.' Bellini threaded his arm through Lomeli's, and together the two old friends began to climb the stairs.

Lomeli said, 'You are the only one of us with the holiness and the intellect to be Pope.'

'No, that's kind of you, but I fret too much, and we cannot have a Pope who frets. You will have to be careful, though, Jacopo. I'm serious: if my position weakens further, much of my support will probably switch to you.'

'No, no, no, that would be a disaster!'

'Think about it. Our fellow countrymen are desperate to have an Italian Pope, but at the same time most of them can't abide the thought of Tedesco. If I fade, that leaves you as the only viable candidate for them to rally behind.'

Lomeli stopped, mid-step. 'What an appalling thought! That must not be allowed to happen!' When they resumed climbing he said, 'Perhaps Adeyemi will turn out to be the answer. He certainly has the wind behind him.'

'Adeyemi? A man who has more or less said that all homosexuals should be sent to prison in this world and to hell in the next? He is not the answer to anything!'

They reached the second floor. The candles flickering outside the Holy Father's apartment cast a red glow across the landing. The two most senior cardinals in the electoral college stood for a moment contemplating the sealed door.

'What was going through his head in those final weeks, I wonder?' Bellini said, almost to himself.

'Don't ask me. I didn't see him at all for the last month.'

'Ah, I wish you had! He was strange. Unreachable. Secretive. I believe he sensed his death was approaching and his mind was full of curious ideas. I feel his presence very strongly, don't you?'

'I do indeed. I still speak to him. I often sense he is watching us.'

'I'm quite certain of it. Well, this is where we part. I am on the third floor.' Bellini studied his key. 'Room 301. I must be directly above the Holy Father. Perhaps his spirit radiates through the

170

floor? That would explain why I am so restless. Be sure that you sleep well, Jacopo. Who knows where we'll be this time tomorrow?'

And then, to Lomeli's surprise, Bellini kissed him lightly on either cheek before turning away and continuing on up the staircase.

Lomeli called after him: 'Goodnight.'

Without turning round, Bellini raised his hand in response.

After he had gone, Lomeli stood for another minute, staring at the closed door with its barrier of wax and ribbons. He was remembering his conversation with Benítez. Could it really be true that the Holy Father had known the Filipino well enough, and trusted him enough, to criticise his own Secretary of State? Yet the remark had the ring of authenticity. 'Brilliant but neurotic': he could almost hear the old man saying it.

Lomeli's sleep that night was also restless. For the first time in many years he dreamt of his mother – a widow for forty years, who used to complain that he was cold towards her – and when he woke in the early hours, her plaintive voice still seemed to be whining in his ears. But then, after a minute or two, he realised the voice he could hear was real. There *was* a woman nearby.

A woman?

He rolled on to his side and groped for his watch. It was almost 3 a.m.

The female voice came again: urgent, accusatory,

almost hysterical. And then a deep male response: gentle, soothing, placatory.

Lomeli threw off his bedclothes and turned on the light. The unoiled springs of the iron bedstead creaked loudly as he put his feet to the floor. He tiptoed cautiously across the room and put his ear to the wall. The voices had fallen silent. He sensed that on the other side of the plasterboard partition they too were listening. For several minutes he held the same position, until he began to feel foolish. Surely his suspicions were absurd? But then he heard Adeyemi's unmistakable voice – even the cardinal's whispers had resonance – followed by the click of a door closing. He moved quickly to his own door and flung it open, just in time to see a flash of the blue uniform of the Daughters of Charity of St Vincent de Paul disappearing around the corner.

Later, it would be obvious to Lomeli what he should have done next. He should have dressed immediately and knocked on Adeyemi's door. It might still have been possible, at that early moment, before positions were fixed and when the episode was undeniable, to have a frank conversation about what had just happened. Instead, the dean climbed back into his bed, drew the sheet up to his chin, and contemplated the possibilities.

The best explanation – that is to say, the least damaging from his point of view – was that the nun was troubled, that she had concealed herself after the other sisters had left the building at midnight and had come to Adeyemi to seek guidance. Many of the nuns in the Casa Santa Marta were African, and it was entirely possible she had known the cardinal from his years in Nigeria. Obviously Adeyemi was guilty of a serious indiscretion in admitting her to his room unchaperoned in the middle of the night, but an indiscretion was not necessarily a sin. After that came a range of other explanations, from nearly all of which Lomeli's imagination recoiled. In a literal sense, he had trained himself not to deal with such thoughts. A passage in Pope John XXIII's *Journal of a Soul* had been his guiding text ever since his tormenting days and nights as a young priest:

As for women, and everything to do with them, never a word, never; it was as if there were no women in the world. This absolute silence, even between close friends, about everything to do with women was one of the most profound and lasting lessons of my early years in the priesthood.

This was the core of the hard mental discipline that had enabled Lomeli to remain celibate for more than sixty years. *Don't even think about them!* The mere idea of going next door and talking man to man with Adeyemi about a woman was a concept that lay entirely outside the dean's closed intellectual system. Therefore he resolved to forget

173

about the whole incident. If Adeyemi chose to confide in him, naturally he would listen, in the spirit of a confessor. Otherwise he would act as if it had never happened.

He reached over and switched off the light.

CHAPTER 9

THE SECOND BALLOT

At 6.30 a.m., the bell rang for morning Mass. Lomeli woke with an impending sense of doom somewhere at the back of his mind, as if his anxieties were all coiled together ready to spring out at him the moment he was fully awake. He went into the bathroom and tried to banish them with another scalding shower. But when he stood at the mirror to shave, they were still there, lurking behind him.

He dried himself and put on his robe, knelt at the prie-dieu and recited his rosary, then prayed for Christ's wisdom and guidance throughout the trials that the day would bring. As he dressed, his fingers shook. He paused and told himself to be calm. There was a set prayer for every garment – cassock, cincture, rochet, mozzetta, zuchetta – and he recited them as he put on each item. 'Protect me, O Lord, with the girdle of faith,' he whispered as he knotted the cincture around his waist, 'and extinguish the fire of lust so that chastity may abide in me, year after year.' But he did so mechanically, with no more feeling than if he were giving out a telephone number.

Just before he left the room, he caught sight of himself in the mirror wearing his choir dress. The chasm between the figure he appeared to be and the man he knew he was had never seemed so wide.

He walked with a group of other cardinals down the stairs to the ground-floor chapel. It was housed in an annexe attached to the main building: an antiseptic modernist design with a vaulted ceiling of white wooden beams and glass, suspended above a cream and gold polished marble floor. The effect was too much like an airport lounge for Lomeli's taste, yet the Holy Father, amazingly, had preferred it to the Pauline. One entire side consisted of thick plate glass, behind which ran the old Vatican wall, spotlit with potted shrubs at its base. It was impossible to see the sky from this angle, or even to tell whether it was yet dawn.

Two weeks earlier, Tremblay had come to see Lomeli and offered to take charge of celebrating the morning Masses in the Casa Santa Marta, and Lomeli, burdened with the prospect of the *Missa pro eligendo Romano Pontifice*, had been grateful to accept. Now he rather regretted it. He saw that he had given the Canadian the perfect opportunity to remind the Conclave of his skill at performing the liturgy. He sang well. He looked like a cleric in some Hollywood romantic movie: Spencer Tracy came to mind. His gestures were dramatic enough to suggest he was infused with the divine spirit, yet not so theatrical that they seemed false or egocentric. When Lomeli queued to receive Communion and knelt before the cardinal, the sacrilegious thought occurred to him that just this one service might have been worth three or four votes to the Canadian.

Adeyemi was the last to receive the host. He very carefully did not glance at Lomeli or anyone else as he returned to his seat. He seemed entirely self-possessed, grave, remote, aware. By lunchtime he would probably know whether he was likely to be Pope.

After the blessing, a few of the cardinals remained behind to pray, but most headed straight to the dining hall for breakfast. Adeyemi joined his usual table of African cardinals. Lomeli took a place between the archbishops of Hong Kong and Cebu. They tried to make polite conversation, but the silences soon became longer and more frequent, and when the others went up to collect their food from the buffet, Lomeli stayed where he was.

He watched the nuns as they moved between the tables serving coffee. To his shame, he realised he had never bothered to take any notice of them until now. Their average age, he guessed, was around fifty. They were of all races, but without exception short of stature, as if Sister Agnes had been determined not to recruit anyone taller than herself. Most wore spectacles. Everything about them – their blue habits and headdresses, their modest demeanour, their downcast eyes, their silence – might have been designed to efface them from

177

notice, let alone prevent them becoming objects of desire. He presumed they were under orders not to speak: when one nun poured coffee for Adeyemi, he did not even turn to look at her. Yet the late Holy Father used to make a point of eating with a group of these sisters at least once a week – another manifestation of his humility that made the Curia mutter with disapproval.

Just before nine o'clock, Lomeli pushed away his untouched plate, rose and announced to the table that it was time to return to the Sistine Chapel. His move began a general exodus towards the lobby. O'Malley was already in position by the reception desk, clipboard in hand.

'Good morning, Your Eminence.'

'Good morning, Ray.'

'Did Your Eminence sleep well?'

'Perfectly, thank you. If it isn't raining, I think I'll walk.'

He waited while one of the Swiss Guards unlocked the door, and then stepped out into the daylight. The air was cool and damp. After the heat of the Casa Santa Marta, the slight breeze on his face was a tonic. A line of minibuses with their engines running coiled around the edge of the piazza, each watched by an individual plainclothes security man. Lomeli's departure on foot provoked a flurry of whispering into sleeves, and as he set off in the direction of the Vatican Gardens, he was aware of being followed by a bodyguard of his own.

Normally this part of the Vatican would have been busy with officials from the Curia arriving for work or moving between appointments; cars with their 'SCV' licence plates would be thrumming over the cobbles. But the area had been cleared for the duration of the Conclave. Even the Palazzo San Carlo, where the foolish Cardinal Tutino had created his vast apartment, looked abandoned. It was as if some terrible calamity had befallen the Church, wiping out all the religious and leaving no one alive except security men, swarming over the deserted city like black dung beetles. In the gardens they stood grouped behind the trees and scrutinised Lomeli as he passed. One patrolled the path with an Alsatian on a short leash, checking the flower beds for bombs.

On a whim, Lomeli turned off the road and climbed a flight of steps, past a fountain, to a lawn. He lifted the hem of his cassock to protect it from the damp. The grass was spongy beneath his feet, oozing moisture. From here he had a view across the trees to the low hills of Rome, grey in the pale November light. To think that whoever was elected Pope would never be able to wander around the city at will, could never browse in a bookstore or sit outside a café, but would remain a prisoner here! Even Ratzinger, who resigned, could not escape but ended his days cooped up in a converted convent in the gardens, a ghostly presence. Lomeli prayed yet again that he might be spared such a fate.

Behind him a detonation of radio static disturbed his meditation. It was followed by an unintelligible electronic jabber. He muttered under his breath, 'Oh, do go *away!*'

As he turned around, the security man stepped abruptly out of sight behind a statue of Apollo. Really, it was almost comical, this clumsy attempt at invisibility. He could see, looking down to the road, that several other cardinals had followed his example and had chosen to walk. Further back, alone, was Adeyemi. Lomeli descended the steps rapidly, hoping to avoid him, but the Nigerian quickened his pace and caught him up.

'Good morning, Dean.'

'Good morning, Joshua.'

They stood back to let one of the minibuses drive by, then walked on, past the western elevation of St Peter's, towards the Apostolic Palace. Lomeli sensed that he was expected to speak first. But he had learnt long ago not to babble into a silence. He did not wish to refer to what he had seen, had no desire to be the keeper of anyone's conscience except his own. Eventually it was Adeyemi, once they had acknowledged the salutes of the Swiss Guards at the entrance to the first courtyard, who was obliged to make the opening move. 'There's something I feel I have to tell you. You won't think it improper, I hope?'

Lomeli said guardedly, 'That would depend on what it is.'

Adeyemi pursed his lips and nodded, as if this confirmed something he'd already guessed. 'I just want you to know that I very much agreed with what you said in your homily yesterday.'

Lomeli glanced at him in surprise. 'I wasn't expecting that!'

'I hope that perhaps I am a subtler man than you may think. We are all tested in our faith, Dean. We all lapse. But the Christian faith is above all a message of forgiveness. I believe that was the crux of what you were saying?'

'Forgiveness, yes. But also tolerance.'

'Exactly. Tolerance. I trust that when this election is over, your moderating voice will be heard in the very highest counsels of the Church. It certainly will be if I have anything to do with it. *The very highest counsels*,' he repeated with heavy emphasis. 'I hope you understand what I'm saying. Will you excuse me, Dean?'

He lengthened his stride, as if eager to get away, and hurried forward to catch up with the cardinals who were walking ahead of them. He clamped his arms around the shoulders of both and hugged them to him, leaving Lomeli to trail behind, wondering if he had imagined things, or if he had just been offered, in return for his silence, his old job back as Secretary of State.

They assembled in the Sistine Chapel in the same places as before. The doors were locked. Lomeli stood in front of the altar and read out in turn

181

the name of every cardinal. Each man answered, 'Present.'

'Let us pray.'

The cardinals stood.

'O Father, so that we may guide and watch over Your Church, give to us, Your servants, the blessings of intelligence, truth and peace, so that we may strive to know Your will, and serve You with total dedication. For Christ our Lord . . .'

'Amen.'

The cardinals sat.

'My brothers, we will now proceed to the second ballot. Scrutineers, if you would take your positions, please?'

Lukša, Mercurio and Newby rose from behind their desks and made their way to the front of the chapel.

Lomeli returned to his seat and took out his ballot paper. When the scrutineers were ready, he uncapped his pen, shielded what he was doing, and once again wrote in capital letters: BELLINI. He folded the ballot, stood, held it up high so that the entire Conclave could see, and walked to the altar. Above him in *The Last Judgement*, all the hosts of heaven swarmed while the damned sank into the abyss.

'I call as my witness Christ the Lord, who will be my judge, that my vote is given to the one who before God I think should be elected.'

He placed his vote on the chalice and tipped it into the urn.

★   ★   ★

In 1978, Karol Wojtyła brought a Marxist journal into the Conclave that elected him Pope, and sat reading it calmly during the long hours it took for a total of eight ballots to be cast. However, as Pope John Paul II, he did not accord the same distraction to his successors. All electors were forbidden by his revised rules of 1996 to bring any reading material into the Sistine Chapel. A Bible was placed on the desk in front of every cardinal so that they could consult the Scriptures for inspiration. Their sole task was to meditate on the choice before them.

Lomeli studied the frescos and the ceiling, flicked through the New Testament, observed the candidates as they paraded past him to vote, closed his eyes, prayed. In the end, according to his wristwatch, it took sixty-eight minutes for all the votes to be cast. Shortly before 10.45 a.m., Cardinal Rudgard, the last man to vote, returned to his seat at the back of the chapel and Cardinal Lukša lifted the filled urn of ballots and showed it to the Conclave. Then the scrutineers followed the same ritual as before. Cardinal Newby transferred the folded ballot papers to the second urn, counting each one out loud until he reached 118. After that, he and Cardinal Mercurio set up the table and three chairs in front of the altar. Lukša covered it in a cloth and placed upon it the urn. The three men sat. Lukša thrust his hand into the ornate silver vessel, as if drawing a raffle ticket for some diocesan fund-raiser, and pulled out the first ballot paper. He unfolded it, read it, made a note, and handed it on to Mercurio.

Lomeli took up his pen. Newby pierced the ballot with his needle and thread and ducked his head to the microphone. His atrocious Italian filled the Sistine: 'The first vote cast in the second ballot is for Cardinal Lomeli.'

For an appalling few seconds Lomeli had a vision of his colleagues secretly colluding behind his back overnight to draft him, and of his being borne to the papacy on a tide of compromise votes before he had time to gather his wits to prevent it. But the next name read out was Adeyemi's, then Tedesco's, then Adeyemi's again, and there followed a blessedly long period when Lomeli wasn't mentioned at all. His hand moved up and down the list of cardinals, adding a tick each time a vote was declared, and soon he could see that he was trailing in fifth place. By the time Newby read out the final name – 'Cardinal Tremblay' – Lomeli had gathered a total of nine votes, almost double what he had received in the first ballot, which was not at all what he had hoped for but was still enough to keep him safe. It was Adeyemi who had come storming through to take first place:

Adeyemi 35
Tedesco 29
Bellini 19
Tremblay 18

Lomeli 9
Others 8

Thus, out of the fog of human ambition, did the will of God begin to emerge. As always in the second ballot, the no-hopers had fallen away, and the Nigerian had picked up sixteen of their votes: a phenomenal endorsement. And Tedesco would be pleased, Lomeli thought, to have added a further seven to his first-ballot total. Meanwhile Bellini and Tremblay had hardly moved: not a bad result for the Canadian, perhaps, but a disaster surely for the former Secretary of State, who probably would have needed to poll in the high twenties to keep his candidacy alive.

It was only as he checked his calculations for a second time that Lomeli noticed another small surprise – a footnote, as it were – that he had missed in his concentration on the main story. Benítez had also increased his support, from one vote to two.

CHAPTER 10

THE THIRD BALLOT

After Newby had read out the results, and the three cardinal-revisers had checked them, Lomeli rose and approached the altar. He took the microphone from Newby. The Sistine seemed to be emitting a low-level hum. Along all four rows of desks the cardinals were comparing lists and whispering to their neighbours.

From the altar step he could see the four main contenders. Bellini, as a cardinal-bishop, was closest to him, on the right-hand side of the chapel as Lomeli looked at it: he was studying the figures and tapping his forefinger against his lips, an isolated figure. A little further down, on the other side of the aisle, Tedesco was tilting back in his chair to listen to the Archbishop Emeritus of Palermo, Scozzazi, who was in the row behind him and was leaning over his desk to tell him something. A few places further on from Tedesco, Tremblay was twisting his torso from side to side to stretch his muscles, like a sportsman between rounds. Opposite him, Adeyemi was staring straight ahead, so utterly immobile he might have been a figure carved in ebony, oblivious to the glances he was attracting from all sides of the Sistine.

Lomeli tapped the microphone. It echoed off the frescos like a drumbeat. At once the murmuring ceased. 'My brothers, in accordance with the Apostolic Constitution, we will not stop to burn the ballot papers at this point, but instead proceed immediately to the next vote. Let us pray.'

For the third time, Lomeli voted for Bellini. He was settled in his own mind that he would not desert him, even though one could see – almost literally physically see – the authority draining from the former favourite as he walked stiffly up to the altar, recited the oath in a flat voice and cast his ballot. He turned to go back to his seat, a husk. It was one thing to dread becoming Pope; it was another altogether to confront the sudden reality that it was never going to happen – that after years of being regarded as the heir apparent, your peers had looked you over and God had guided their choice elsewhere. Lomeli wondered if he would ever recover. As Bellini passed behind him to get to his seat, he gave him a consoling pat on the back, but the former Secretary of State seemed not to notice.

While the cardinals voted, Lomeli passed his time in contemplation of the ceiling panels nearest to him. The prophet Jeremiah lost in misery. The anti-Semite Haman denounced and slain. The prophet Jonah about to be swallowed

187

by a giant eel. The turmoil of it struck him for the first time; the violence; the force. He craned his neck to examine God separating light and darkness. The creation of the sun and planets. God dividing water from the earth. Without noticing, he allowed himself to become lost in the painting. *And there will be signs in sun and moon and stars, and upon the earth distress of nations in great perplexity at the roaring of the sea and the waves, men fainting with fear and with foreboding of what is coming on the world; for the powers of the heavens will be shaken* . . . He felt a sudden intimation of disaster, so profound that he shuddered, and when he looked around he realised that an hour had passed and the scrutineers were preparing to count the ballots.

'Adeyemi . . . Adeyemi . . . Adeyemi . . .'

Every second vote seemed to be for the cardinal from Nigeria, and as the last few ballots were read out, Lomeli said a prayer for him.

'Adeyemi . . .' Newby threaded the paper on to his scarlet ribbon. 'My brothers, that concludes the voting in the third ballot.'

There was a collective exhalation around the chapel. Quickly Lomeli counted the forest of ticks he had placed against Adeyemi's name. He made it fifty-seven. *Fifty-seven!* He couldn't resist leaning forward and peering down the row of desks to where Adeyemi was sitting. Almost half the Conclave was doing the same. Another three votes

188

and he would have a straight majority; another twenty-one and he would be Pope.

The first black Pope.

Adeyemi's massive head was bent forward on to his chest. In his right hand he was grasping his pectoral cross. He was praying.

In the first ballot, thirty-four cardinals had received at least one vote. Now there were only six who registered support:

Adeyemi 57
Tedesco 32
Tremblay 12
Bellini 10
Lomeli 5
Benítez 2

Adeyemi would be elected pontiff before the day was out. Lomeli was sure of it. The prophecy was written in the numbers. Even if Tedesco somehow managed to reach forty on the next ballot and deny him a two-thirds majority, the blocking minority would crumble quickly in the following round. Few cardinals would wish to risk a schism in the Church by obstructing such a dramatic manifestation of the Divine Will. Nor, to be practical about it, would they wish to make an enemy of the incoming Pope, especially one with as powerful a personality as Joshua Adeyemi.

Once the voting papers had been checked by the

revisers, Lomeli returned to the altar step and addressed the Conclave. 'My brothers, that concludes the third ballot. We shall now adjourn for luncheon. Voting will resume at two thirty. Kindly remain in your places while the officials are readmitted, and remember not to discuss our proceedings until you are back inside the Casa Santa Marta. Would the Junior Cardinal-Deacon please ask for the doors to be unlocked?'

The members of the Conclave surrendered their voting papers to the masters of ceremonies. Afterwards, making animated conversation, they filed across the vestibule of the Sistine, out into the marbled grandeur of the Sala Regia and down the staircase to the buses. Already it was noticeable how they deferred to Adeyemi, who seemed to have developed an invisible protective shield around him. Even his closest supporters kept their distance. He walked alone.

The cardinals were eager to get back to the Casa Santa Marta. Few now lingered to watch the burning of the ballots. O'Malley stuffed the paper sacks into one furnace and released the chemicals from the other. The fumes mingled and rose up the copper flue. At 12.37 p.m., black smoke began to issue from the Sistine Chapel chimney. Observing it, the Vatican experts on the main television news channels continued confidently to predict a victory for Bellini.

★   ★   ★

190

Lomeli left the Sistine soon after the smoke was released, at roughly a quarter to one. In the courtyard, the security men were holding the last minibus for him. He declined the offer of help and climbed up on to it unaided to find Bellini among the passengers, sitting near the front with his usual squad of supporters – Sabbadin, Landolfi, Dell'Acqua, Santini, Panzavecchia. He had done himself no favours, Lomeli thought, by trying to win over a worldwide electorate with a clique of Italians. As the rear seats were occupied, Lomeli was obliged to sit with them. The bus pulled away. Conscious of the driver's eyes examining them in the rear-view mirror, the cardinals didn't speak at first. But then Sabbadin, turning round in his place, said to Lomeli, with deceptive pleasantness, 'I noticed, Dean, that you spent nearly an hour this morning examining Michelangelo's ceiling.'

'I did – and what a ferocious work it is, when one has time to study it. So much disaster bearing down upon us – executions, killings, the Flood. One detail I hadn't noticed before is God's expression when He separates light from darkness: it is pure murder.'

'Of course, the most appropriate episode for us to have contemplated this morning would have been the story of the Gadarene swine. What a pity the master never got around to painting *that*.'

'Now, now, Giulio,' warned Bellini, glancing at the driver. 'Remember where we are.'

But Sabbadin could not contain his bitterness.

His only concession was to drop his voice to a hiss, so that they all had to lean in to hear him. 'Seriously, have we taken leave of our senses? Can't we see we're stampeding over a cliff? What am I to tell them in Milan when they start to discover our new Pope's social views?'

Lomeli whispered, 'Don't forget there will also be great excitement at the prospect of the first African pontiff.'

'Oh yes! Very good! A Pope who will permit tribal dancing in the middle of the Mass but will not countenance Communion for the divorced!'

'Enough!' Bellini made a cutting gesture with his hand to signal that the conversation was over. Lomeli had never seen him so angry. 'We must all accept the collective wisdom of the Conclave. This isn't one of your father's political caucuses, Giulio – God doesn't do re-counts.' He stared out of the window and didn't speak again for the remainder of the short journey. Sabbadin sat back, arms folded, furious in his frustration and disappointment. In the rear-view mirror, the driver's eyes were wide with curiosity.

It took less than five minutes to drive from the Sistine Chapel to the Casa Santa Marta. Lomeli calculated later therefore that it must have been roughly 12.50 p.m. when they disembarked outside the hostel. They were the last to arrive. Perhaps half the cardinals were already seated, and another thirty were queuing with their trays; the remainder must have gone up to their rooms. The nuns were moving between the tables, serving wine. There was an atmosphere of unsuppressed excitement: permitted to talk openly, the cardinals swapped their opinions of the extraordinary result. As he joined the end of the line, Lomeli was surprised to see Adeyemi sitting at the same table he had occupied at breakfast, with the same contingent of African cardinals: if he had been in the Nigerian's position, he would have been in the chapel, away from this hubbub, deep in prayer.

He had reached the counter and was helping himself to a little *riso tonnato* when he heard the sound of raised voices behind him, followed by the crash of a tray hitting the marble floor, glass shattering, and then a woman's scream. (Or was scream the right word? Perhaps cry would be better: a woman's cry.) He swivelled round to see what was happening. Other cardinals were rising from their seats to do the same; they obscured his view. A nun, her hands clasped to her head, ran across the dining room and into the kitchen. Two sisters hurried after her. Lomeli turned to the cardinal nearest him – it was the young Spaniard, Villanueva. 'What happened? Did you see?'

'She dropped a bottle of wine, I think.'

Whatever it was, the incident seemed to be over. The cardinals who had stood resumed their seats. The drone of conversation slowly started up again. Lomeli turned back to the counter to collect his food. Holding his tray, he looked around for a place where he could sit. A nun

193

came out of the kitchen carrying a bucket and a mop and went towards the Africans' table, at which point Lomeli noticed that Adeyemi was no longer there. In a moment of terrible clarity, he knew what must have happened. But still – how he reproached himself for this afterwards! – *still* his instinct was to ignore it. The discretion and self-discipline of a lifetime guided his feet towards the nearest empty chair, and then commanded his body to sit, his mouth to smile a greeting at his neighbours, his hands to unfold a napkin, while in his ears all he could hear was a noise like a waterfall.

So it was that the Archbishop of Bordeaux, Courtemarche – who had questioned the historical evidence for the Holocaust, and whom Lomeli had always shunned – suddenly found himself sitting next to the Dean of the College. Mistaking it for an official overture, he began to make a plea on behalf of the Society of St Pius X. Lomeli listened without hearing. A nun, her gaze modestly averted, came and stood at his shoulder to offer him wine. He looked up to refuse, and for a fraction of a second she looked back at him – a terrible, accusing look: it made his mouth go dry.

'. . . the Immaculate Heart of Mary . . .' Courtemarche was saying, '. . . the intention of heaven declared at Fatima . . .'

Behind the nun, three of the African archbishops who had been sitting with Adeyemi – Nakitanda, Mwangale and Zucula – were approaching Lomeli's table. The youngest, Nakitanda of Kampala, seemed to be their spokesman. 'Could we request a word with you, Dean?'

'Of course.' He nodded to Courtemarche. 'Excuse me.'

He followed the trio into a corner of the lobby. 'What just happened?' he asked.

Zucula shook his head mournfully. 'Our brother is troubled.'

Nakitanda said, 'One of the nuns serving our table started talking to Joshua. He tried to ignore her at first. She dropped the tray and shouted something. He got up and left.'

'What did she say?'

'We don't know, unfortunately. She was speaking in a Nigerian dialect.'

'Yoruba,' Mwangale said. 'It was Yoruba. Adeyemi's dialect.'

'And where is Cardinal Adeyemi now?'

'We don't know, Dean,' said Nakitanda, 'but clearly something is wrong and he has to tell us what it is. And we need to hear from the sister before we go back to the Sistine to vote. What exactly is her complaint against him?'

Zucula seized Lomeli's arm. For such a seemingly frail man, his grip was fierce. 'We have waited a long time for an African Pope, Jacopo, and if God wills it to be Joshua, I am happy. But he must be pure in heart and conscience – a truly holy man. Anything short of that would be a disaster for all of us.'

195

'I understand. Let me see what I can do.' Lomeli looked at his watch. It was three minutes past one.

To reach the kitchen from the lobby, Lomeli had to walk all the way across the dining room. The cardinals had been observing his conversation with the Africans, and he was conscious of his progress being followed by dozens of pairs of eyes – of men leaning across to whisper to one another, of forks poised in mid-air. He pushed open the door. It was many years since he had been inside a kitchen, and never one as busy as this. He looked around in bewilderment at the nuns who were preparing the food. The sisters closest to him bowed their heads.

'Your Eminence . . .'

'Your Eminence . . .'

'Bless you, my children. Tell me, where is the sister who had the accident just now?'

An Italian nun said, 'She is with Sister Agnes, Your Eminence.'

'Would you be kind enough to take me to her?'

'Of course, Eminence. Please.' She indicated the door that led back out to the dining room.

Lomeli shied away from it. 'Is there a rear exit we can take?'

'Yes, Eminence.'

'Show me, child.'

He followed her through a storeroom and into a service passage.

'What is the name of the sister, do you know?'

'No, Eminence. She is new.'

The nun knocked timidly on the glass door of

196

an office. Lomeli recognised it as the place where he had first met Benítez, only now the blinds had been lowered for privacy and it was impossible to see inside. After a few moments he knocked himself, more loudly. He heard the sound of someone moving, and then the door was opened a crack by Sister Agnes.

'Your Eminence?'

'Good afternoon, Sister. I need to speak with the nun who dropped her tray just now.'

'She is safe with me, Your Eminence. I am dealing with the situation.'

'I am sure you are, Sister Agnes. But I must see her myself.'

'I hardly think a dropped tray should concern the Dean of the College of Cardinals.'

'Even so. If I may?' He gripped the door handle.

'It's really nothing I can't deal with . . .'

He pushed gently at the door, and after one last attempt at resistance, she yielded.

The nun was sitting on the same chair Benítez had occupied, next to the photocopier. She stood as he entered. He had an impression of a woman of about fifty – short, plump, bespectacled, timid: identical to the others. But it was always so hard to see beyond the uniform and the headdress to the person, especially when that person was staring at the floor.

'Sit down, child,' he said gently. 'My name is Cardinal Lomeli. We're all worried about you. How are you feeling?'

Sister Agnes said, 'She's feeling much better, Eminence.'

'Could you tell me your name?'

'Her name is Shanumi. She can't understand a word you're saying – she doesn't speak any Italian, poor creature.'

'English?' he asked the nun. 'Do you speak English?' She nodded. She still hadn't looked at him. 'Good. So do I. I lived in the United States for some years. Please, do sit down.'

'Eminence, I really do think it would be better if I—'

Without turning to look at her, Lomeli said firmly, 'Would you be so good as to leave us now, Sister Agnes?' And only when she dared to protest again did he at last swing round and give her a look of such freezing authority that even she, before whom three Popes and at least one African warlord had quailed, bowed her head and backed out of the room, closing the door behind her.

Lomeli drew up a chair and sat opposite the nun, so close to her that their knees were almost touching. Such intimacy was hard for him. *O God,* he prayed, *give me the strength and the wisdom to help this poor woman and to find out what I need to know, so that I may fulfil my duty to You.* He said, 'Sister Shanumi, I want you to understand, first of all, that you're not in any sort of trouble. The fact of the matter is, I have a responsibility before God and to the Mother Church, which we both of us try to serve as best we are able, to make

198

sure that the decisions we take here are the right ones. Now, it's important that you tell me anything that is in your heart and that is troubling you in so far as it relates to Cardinal Adeyemi. Can you do that for me?'

She shook her head.

'Even if I give you my absolute assurance it will go no further than this room?'

A pause, followed by another shake of the head.

It was then that he had an inspiration. Afterwards he would always believe that God had come to his aid. 'Would you like me to hear your confession?'

CHAPTER 11

THE FOURTH BALLOT

Roughly an hour later, and only twenty minutes before the minibuses were due to leave for the Sistine for the start of the fourth ballot, Lomeli went in search of Adeyemi. He checked in all parts of the lobby first, and then in the chapel. Half a dozen cardinals were on their knees with their backs to him. He hurried up to the altar to get a look at their faces. None was the Nigerian's. He left, took the elevator to the second floor and strode quickly down the corridor to the room next to his.

He knocked loudly. 'Joshua? Joshua? It's Lomeli!' He knocked again. He was about to give up, but then he heard footsteps and the door was opened.

Adeyemi, still in full choir dress, was drying his face with a towel. He said, 'I shall be ready in a moment, Dean.'

He left the door open and disappeared into the bathroom; after a brief hesitation, Lomeli stepped over the threshold and closed the door after him. The shuttered room smelled strongly of the cardinal's aftershave. On the desk was a framed black-and-white picture of Adeyemi as a young seminarian, standing outside a Catholic mission with a proud-looking older woman wearing a hat – his mother, presumably, or perhaps an aunt. The bed was rumpled, as if the cardinal had been lying on it. There was the sound of a lavatory flushing, and Adeyemi emerged, buttoning the lower part of his cassock. He acted as if he was surprised that Lomeli was in the room rather than the corridor. 'Shouldn't we be leaving?'

'In a moment.'

'That sounds ominous.' Adeyemi bent to look in the mirror. He planted his zuchetta firmly on his head and adjusted it so that it was straight. 'If this is about the incident downstairs, I have no desire to talk about it.' He flicked invisible dust from the shoulders of his mozzetta. He jutted out his chin. He adjusted his pectoral cross. Lomeli maintained his silence, watching him. Finally Adeyemi said quietly, 'I am the victim of a disgraceful plot to ruin my reputation, Jacopo. Someone brought that woman here and staged this entire melodrama solely to prevent my election as Pope. How did she come to be in the Casa Santa Marta in the first place? She'd never left Nigeria before.'

'With respect, Joshua, the issue of how she came to be here is secondary to the issue of your relationship with her.'

Adeyemi threw up his arms in exasperation. 'But I have no relationship with her! I hadn't set eyes on her for thirty years – not until last night, when she turned up outside my room! I didn't even recognise her. Surely you can see what's happening here?'

'The circumstances are curious, I grant you, but let's put that aside for now. It's the condition of your soul that concerns me more.'

'My soul?' Adeyemi spun on the ball of his foot. He brought his face up very close to Lomeli's. His breath was sweet-smelling. 'My soul is full of love for God and His Church. I sensed the presence of the Holy Spirit this morning – you must have felt it too – and I am ready to take on this burden. Does a single lapse thirty years ago disqualify me? Or does it make me stronger? Allow me to quote your own homily from yesterday: "Let God grant us a Pope who sins, and asks forgiveness, and carries on."'

'And have you asked forgiveness? Have you confessed your sin?'

'Yes! Yes, I confessed my sin at the time, and my bishop moved me to a different parish, and I never lapsed again. Such relationships were not uncommon in those days. Celibacy has always been culturally alien in Africa – you know that.'

'And the child?'

'The child?' Adeyemi flinched, faltered. 'The child was brought up in a Christian household, and to this day he has no idea who his father is – if indeed it is me. That is the child.'

He recovered his equilibrium sufficiently to glare at Lomeli, and for one moment longer the edifice remained in place – defiant, wounded, magnificent:

he would have made a tremendous figurehead for the Church, Lomeli thought. Then something seemed to give way and he sat down abruptly on the edge of his bed and clasped his hands on the top of his head. He reminded Lomeli of a photograph he had once seen of a prisoner poised on the edge of a pit waiting his turn to be shot.

What an appalling mess it all was! Lomeli could not recall a more exquisitely painful hour in his life than the one he had just spent listening to the confession of Sister Shanumi. By her account, she had not even been a novitiate when the thing began but a mere postulant, a child, whereas Adeyemi had been the community's priest. If it had not been statutory rape, it had not been far off it. What sin therefore did *she* have to confess? Where was her guilt? And yet carrying the burden of it had been the ruin of her life. Worst of all for Lomeli had been the moment when she had produced the photograph, folded up to the size of a postage stamp. It showed a boy of six or seven in a sleeveless Aertex shirt, grinning at the camera: a good Catholic school photograph, with a crucifix on the wall behind him. The creases where she had folded and refolded it over the past quarter-century had cracked the glossy surface so deeply it looked as if he were staring out from behind a latticework of bars.

The Church had arranged the adoption. After the birth she had wanted nothing from Adeyemi except some sort of acknowledgement of what had happened, but he had been transferred to a parish in Lagos and her letters had all been returned unopened. Seeing him in the Casa Santa Marta, she had not been able to help herself. That was why she had visited him in his room. He had told her they must forget about the whole thing. And when he had refused in the dining room even to look at her, and when one of the other sisters had whispered that he was about to be elected Pope, she had been unable to control herself any longer. She was guilty of so many sins, she insisted, she barely knew where to begin – lust, anger, pride, deceit.

She had sunk to her knees and made the Act of Contrition: 'O my God, I am heartily sorry for having offended You, and I detest all my sins, because I dread the loss of heaven and the pains of hell. But most of all because I have offended You, my God, who are all good and deserving of all my love. I firmly resolve, with the help of Your grace, to confess my sins, to do penance and to amend my life. Amen.'

Lomeli had raised her to her feet and absolved her. 'It is not you who has sinned, my child, it is the Church.' He made the sign of the cross. 'Give thanks to the Lord, for He is good.'

'For His mercy endures forever.'

After a while, Adeyemi said in a low voice, 'We were both very young.'

'No, Your Eminence, *she* was young; you were thirty.'

'You want to destroy my reputation so that you can be Pope!'

'Don't be absurd. Even the thought of it is unworthy of you.'

Adeyemi's shoulders had begun to shake with sobs. Lomeli sat down on the bed next to him. 'Compose yourself, Joshua,' he said kindly. 'The only reason I know any of this is because I heard the poor woman's confession, and she won't ever speak of it in public, I'm sure, if only to protect the boy. As for me, I'm bound by the vows of the confessional never to repeat what I've heard.'

Adeyemi gave him a sideways look. His eyes were glistening. Even now, he could not quite accept his dream was over. 'Are you saying I still have a hope?'

'No, none whatever.' Lomeli was appalled. He managed to control himself and went on in a more reasonable tone, 'After such a public scene, I'm afraid there are bound to be rumours. You know what the Curia is like.'

'Yes, but rumours are not the same as facts.'

'In this case they are. You know as well as I do that if there is one thing that terrifies our colleagues above all others, it is the thought of yet more sexual scandals.'

'So that is it? I can never be Pope?'

'Your Eminence, you cannot be *anything*.'

Adeyemi seemed unable to raise his gaze from the floor. 'What shall I do, Jacopo?'

'You are a good man. You will find some way to atone. God will know if you are truly penitent, and He will decide what is to happen to you.'

'And the Conclave?'

'Leave them to me.'

They sat without speaking. Lomeli could not bear to imagine his agony. *God forgive me for what I have had to do.* Eventually Adeyemi said, 'Would you pray with me for a moment?'

'Of course.'

And so the two men got down on their knees under the electric light in the sealed room that was sweet with the scent of aftershave – got down easily in Adeyemi's case, stiffly in Lomeli's – and prayed together side by side.

Lomeli would have liked to have walked to the Sistine again – to have inhaled some cool fresh air and turned his face to the mild November sun. But it was too late for that. By the time he reached the lobby, the cardinals were already boarding the minibuses, and Nakitanda was waiting for him by the reception desk.

'Well?'

'He will have to resign all his offices.'

Nakitanda's head dropped in dismay. 'Oh no!'

'Not immediately – I hope we may avoid a humiliation – but certainly in a year or so. I'll leave it up to you to decide what you tell the others. I have spoken to both parties and I am bound by vows. I cannot say any more.'

On the minibus he sat at the very back with his eyes closed, his biretta on the seat next to him to discourage company. Every part of this business sickened him, but one aspect in particular had started to niggle away in his mind. It was the first thing Adeyemi had brought up: the timing. According to Sister Shanumi, her work in Nigeria for the past twenty years had been at the Iwaro Oko community in Ondo province, helping women suffering from HIV/AIDs.

'Were you happy there?'

'Very much so, Your Eminence.'

'Your work must have been somewhat different from what you have to do here, I would imagine?'

'Oh yes. There I was a nurse. Here I am a maid.'

'So what made you want to come to Rome?'

'I never wanted to come to Rome!'

Quite how she had ended up in the Casa Santa Marta was still a mystery to her. One day in September she had been called in to see the sister in charge of their community and informed that an email had been received from the office of the Superioress General in Paris, requesting her immediate transfer to the order's mission in Rome. There had been great excitement among the other sisters at such an honour. Some even believed that the Holy Father himself must be responsible for the invitation.

'How extraordinary. Had you ever met the Pope?'

'Of course not, Your Eminence!' It was the only time she laughed – at the absurdity of the idea. 'I saw him once, when he made his tour of Africa, but I was just one of millions. For me, he was a white dot in the distance.'

'So at what point were you asked to come to Rome?'

'Six weeks ago, Eminence. I was given three weeks to prepare myself, and then I caught the plane.'

'And when you got here, did you have a chance to speak to the Holy Father?'

'No, Eminence.' She crossed herself. 'He died the day after I arrived. May his soul be at peace.'

'I don't understand why you agreed to come. Why would you leave your home in Africa and travel all this way?'

Her answer pierced him almost more than anything else she said: 'Because I thought it might be Cardinal Adeyemi who had sent for me.'

One had to hand it to Adeyemi. The Nigerian cardinal comported himself with the same dignity and gravity he had shown at the end of the third ballot. No one watching him as he entered the Sistine Chapel could have guessed from his appearance that his manifest sense of destiny had been in any way disrupted, let alone that he was ruined. He ignored the men around him and sat at his desk calmly reading the Bible while the roll call was taken. When his name was read out he responded firmly: 'Present.'

At 2.45 p.m., the doors were locked and Lomeli for the fourth time led the prayers. Yet again he wrote Bellini's name on his ballot paper and stepped up to the altar to tip it into the urn.

'I call as my witness Christ the Lord, who will be my judge, that my vote is given to the one who before God I think should be elected.'

He settled back into his seat to wait.

The first thirty cardinals who voted were the most senior members of the Conclave – the patriarchs, the cardinal-bishops, the cardinal-priests of longest standing. Scrutinising their impassive faces as they rose from their desks one after another at the front of the chapel, it was impossible for Lomeli to guess what was going through their minds. Suddenly he was seized by an anxiety that perhaps he hadn't done enough. What if they had no idea of the gravity of Adeyemi's sin and were voting for him in ignorance? But after a quarter of an hour, the cardinals seated around Adeyemi in the central section of the Sistine began to file up to vote. To a man, on their way back from casting their ballots, they averted their eyes from the Nigerian. They were like members of a jury filing into a courtroom to deliver their verdict, unable to look at the accused they were about to condemn. Observing them, Lomeli began to feel a little calmer. When it came to Adeyemi's turn to vote, he walked with a solemn tread to the urn and recited the oath with the same absolute assurance as before. He passed Lomeli without a glance.

At 3.51 p.m., the voting was concluded and the scrutineers took over. One hundred and eighteen ballots having been certified as cast, they set up their table and the ritual of the count began.

'The first ballot cast is for Cardinal Lomeli . . .'

Oh no, God, he prayed, *not again; let this pass from me.* It had been Adeyemi's taunt that he was motivated by personal ambition. It wasn't true – he was certain of it. But now as he marked down the results he couldn't help noticing his own tally beginning to tick back up again, not to a dangerous level, but still to a point that was a little too high for comfort. He leaned forward slightly and peered down the row of desks to where Adeyemi was sitting. Unlike the men around him, he was not even bothering to write down the votes but was simply staring at the opposite wall. Once Newby had read out the last ballot, Lomeli added up the totals:

Tedesco 36
Adeyemi 25
Tremblay 23
Bellini 18
Lomeli 11
Benítez 5

He placed the list of results on the desk and studied it, his elbows on the table propping up his head, his knuckles pressed to his temples. Adeyemi had lost more than half his support since they paused for lunch – a staggering haemorrhage: thirty-two votes – of which Tremblay had picked up eleven, Bellini eight, himself six, Tedesco four and Benítez three. Clearly Nakitanda had spread the word, and enough cardinals had either witnessed the scene in the dining hall or heard about it afterwards for them to have taken serious fright.

As the Conclave absorbed this new reality, there was a general outbreak of conversation all around the Sistine. Lomeli could tell from their faces what they were saying. To think that if they hadn't broken for lunch, Adeyemi might by now be Pope! Instead of which, the dream of the African pontiff was dead and Tedesco was back in the lead – a mere four votes off the forty he needed to deny anyone else a two-thirds majority . . . *The race is not to the swift nor the battle to the strong, but time and chance happen to all* . . . And Tremblay – assuming the Third World vote started to swing his way, might he be poised to become the new front-runner? (Poor Bellini, they whispered, glancing over at his passionless expression – when would his long-drawn-out humiliation be over?) As for Lomeli, presumably his vote reflected the fact that when things started to look uncertain, there was always a yearning for a steady hand. And finally there was Benítez – five votes for a man nobody even knew two days ago: that was little short of miraculous . . .

Lomeli put his head down and continued to study the figures, oblivious to the number of cardinals who had begun staring at him, until Bellini leaned around the back of the Patriarch of Lebanon and gave him a gentle poke in the ribs. He looked up in alarm. There was some laughter from the other side of the aisle. What an old fool he was becoming!

He rose and went up to the altar. 'My brothers, no candidate having secured a two-thirds majority, we shall now proceed immediately to a fifth ballot.'

CHAPTER 12

THE FIFTH BALLOT

In modern times, they usually had a Pope by the fifth ballot. The late Holy Father, for example, had got it on the fifth, and Lomeli could picture him now, resolutely refusing to sit on the papal throne but insisting on standing up to embrace the cardinals as they queued to congratulate him. Ratzinger had won it one ballot earlier, when they voted for the fourth time; Lomeli remembered him, too – his shy smile as his tally reached two-thirds and the Conclave burst into applause. John Paul I had also been a fourth-ballot victor. In fact, apart from Wojtyła, the fifth-ballot rule held true at least as far back as 1963, when Montini had defeated Lercaro and had famously remarked to his more charismatic rival, 'That's how life is, Your Eminence – you should be sitting here.'

An election completed in five ballots was what Lomeli had secretly prayed for – a nice, easy, conventional number, suggestive of an election that had been neither schism nor coronation but a meditative process of discerning God's will. It would not be so this year. He did not like the feel of it.

213

Studying for his doctorate in canon law at the Pontifical Lateran University, he had read Canetti's *Crowds and Power*. From it he had learnt to separate the various categories of crowd – the panicking crowd, the stagnant crowd, the crowd in revolt, and so forth. It was a useful skill for a cleric. Applying this secular analysis, a papal Conclave could be seen as the most sophisticated crowd on earth, moved this way or that by the collective impulse of the Holy Spirit. Some Conclaves were timid and disinclined to change, such as that which elected Ratzinger; others were bold, like the one that eventually chose Wojtyła. What worried Lomeli about this particular Conclave was that it was beginning to show signs of becoming what Canetti might call a disintegrating crowd. It was troubled, unstable, fragile – capable of suddenly heading off in any direction.

That growing sense of purpose and excitement with which they had ended the morning session had evaporated. Now, as the cardinals filed up to vote, and the small area of sky visible through the high windows darkened, the silence in the Sistine became bleak and tomblike. The tolling of the bell of St Peter's for five o'clock might have been the death knell at a funeral. We are lost sheep, Lomeli thought, and a great storm is approaching. But who will be our shepherd? He still thought the best choice was Bellini, and voted for him yet again, but without any expectation that he could win. His tallies in the four ballots

214

so far had been eighteen, nineteen, ten and eighteen respectively: clearly something was preventing him breaking out beyond his core group of supporters. Perhaps it was because he had been Secretary of State, and was too closely associated with the late Holy Father, whose policies had both antagonised the traditionalists and disappointed the liberals.

He found his gaze returning repeatedly to Tremblay. The Canadian, who was nervously fingering his pectoral cross as the voting proceeded, managed somehow to combine a bland personality with passionate ambition – a paradox that was not uncommon in Lomeli's experience. But maybe blandness was what was needed to maintain the unity of the Church. And was ambition necessarily such a sin? Wojtyła had been ambitious. My God, how confident he had been, right from the start! On the night of his election, when he had stepped on to the balcony to address the tens of thousands in St Peter's Square, he had practically shouldered the Master of Papal Liturgical Celebrations out of the way in his eagerness to speak to the world. If it comes to a choice between Tremblay and Tedesco, Lomeli thought, I shall have to vote for Tremblay – secret report or no. He could only pray it would not happen.

The sky was entirely black by the time the last ballot was cast and the scrutineers began to count the votes. The result was another shock:

215

Tremblay 40
Tedesco 38
Bellini 15
Lomeli 12
Adeyemi 9
Benítez 4

As his colleagues turned to look at him, Tremblay bowed his head and placed his hands together in prayer. For once this ostentatious show of piety did not irritate Lomeli. Instead, he briefly closed his eyes and gave thanks. *Thank you, O Lord, for this indication of Your will, and if Cardinal Tremblay is to be our choice, I pray that You may grant him the wisdom and strength to fulfil his mission. Amen.*

It was with some relief that he stood and faced the Conclave. 'My brothers, that concludes the fifth ballot. No candidate having achieved the necessary majority, we shall resume voting tomorrow morning. The masters of ceremonies will collect your papers. Please do not take any written notes out of the Sistine, and be careful not to discuss our deliberations until you are back inside the Casa Santa Marta. Would the Junior Cardinal-Deacon please ask for the doors to be unlocked?'

At 6.22 p.m., black smoke once again began to pour from the Sistine chimney, picked out by the searchlight mounted on the side of St Peter's Basilica. The pundits hired by the television channels professed themselves surprised by the Conclave's failure to agree. Most had predicted that the new Pope would have been elected by now, and the US networks were on standby to interrupt their lunchtime schedules to show the scenes in St Peter's Square as the victor appeared on the balcony. For the first time the experts started to express doubts about the strength of Bellini's support. If he was going to win, he ought to have done so by now. A new collective wisdom began to rise out of the debris of the old: that the Conclave was on the verge of making history. In the United Kingdom – that godless isle of apostasy, where the whole affair was being treated as a horse race – the Ladbrokes betting agency made Cardinal Adeyemi the new favourite. Tomorrow, it was commonly said, might at last see the election of the first black Pope.

As usual, Lomeli was the last cardinal to leave the chapel. He stayed behind to watch Monsignor O'Malley burn the ballots, and then together they made their way across the Sala Regia. A security man trailed them down the staircase towards the courtyard. Lomeli assumed that O'Malley, as the Secretary of the College, must know the results of the afternoon ballots, if only because it was his task to collect the cardinals' notes in order to destroy them – and O'Malley was not the kind of man to avert his eyes from a secret. He must be aware therefore of the collapse of Adeyemi's

217

candidacy and of the unexpected ascendancy of Tremblay's. But he was too discreet to raise the subject directly. Instead he said quietly, 'Is there anything you would like me to do before tomorrow morning, Your Eminence?'

'Such as?'

'I was wondering if perhaps you wanted me to go back to Monsignor Morales and see if I could discover any more about this withdrawn report into Cardinal Tremblay.'

Lomeli glanced over his shoulder at the security man. 'I don't know what would be the point of it, Ray. If he wouldn't say anything before the Conclave started, he's hardly likely to do so now, particularly if he suspects Cardinal Tremblay might be about to be elected Pope. And that, of course, is exactly what he *would* suspect if you raised the matter for a second time.'

They emerged into the evening. The last of the minibuses had gone. Somewhere nearby a helicopter was hovering again. Lomeli beckoned at the security guard and gestured to the deserted courtyard. 'I seem to have been left behind. Would you mind?'

'Of course, Your Eminence.' The man whispered into his sleeve.

Lomeli turned back to O'Malley. He felt weary and alone and was seized by an unaccustomed desire to unburden himself. 'Sometimes one can know too much, my dear Monsignor O'Malley. I mean, who among us doesn't have some secret of which he is ashamed? This ghastly business of shutting our eyes to sexual abuse, for example – I was in the foreign service, so was spared direct involvement myself, thank God, but I doubt I would have acted any more firmly. How many of our colleagues failed to take the complaints of the victims seriously, but simply moved the priests responsible to a different parish? It wasn't that those who turned a blind eye were evil; it was simply that they didn't understand the scale of the wickedness they were dealing with, and preferred a quiet life. Now we know differently.'

He was silent for a moment, thinking of Sister Shanumi and her worn little photograph of her child. 'Or how many have had friendships that became too intimate, and led on to sin and heartbreak? Or poor silly Tutino and his wretched apartment – without a family, one can so easily become obsessed with matters of status and protocol to give one a sense of fulfilment. So tell me: am I supposed to go around like some witch-finder general, searching for my colleagues' lapses of more than thirty years ago?'

O'Malley said, 'I agree, Your Eminence. "Let anyone among you who is without sin be the first to throw a stone." However, I thought in the case of Cardinal Tremblay you were worried about something more recent – a meeting between the Holy Father and the cardinal that took place last month?'

'I was. But I'm beginning to discover that the

Holy Father – may he be joined for evermore to the Fellowship of Holy Pontiffs . . .'

'Amen,' said O'Malley, and the two prelates crossed themselves.

'I am beginning to discover,' continued Lomeli in a quieter voice, 'that the Holy Father may not have been entirely himself in the last few weeks of his life. Indeed, from what Cardinal Bellini has said to me, I gather he had almost become – I speak to you in absolute confidence – slightly paranoid, or at any rate very secretive.'

'As witnessed by his decision to create a cardinal *in pectore*?'

'Indeed. Why in heaven's name did he do that? Let me say at once that I hold Cardinal Benítez in high esteem, as clearly do several of our brothers – he is a true man of God – but was it really necessary for him to be elevated in secret, and in such haste?'

'Especially as he had only just tried to resign as archbishop on the grounds of poor health.'

'And yet he seems perfectly fit in mind and body to me, and last night when I asked after his health, he seemed surprised by the question.' Lomeli realised he was whispering. He laughed. 'Listen to me – I sound like a typical old maid of the Curia, gossiping in darkened corners about appointments!'

A minibus drove into the courtyard and pulled up opposite Lomeli. The driver opened the doors. There were no other passengers inside. A blast of hot air-conditioned air fanned their faces.

Lomeli turned to O'Malley. 'Do you want a lift to the Casa Santa Marta?'

'No, thank you, Your Eminence. I need to go back to the Sistine and put out fresh ballot papers, and make sure everything is ready for tomorrow.'

'Well then, goodnight, Ray.'

'Goodnight, Your Eminence.' O'Malley offered his hand to help Lomeli up on to the coach, and for once Lomeli felt so tired he took it. The Irishman added, 'Of course, I could undertake a little further investigation, if you would like me to.'

Lomeli paused on the top step. 'Into what?'

'Cardinal Benítez.'

Lomeli thought it over. 'Thank you, but no. I don't think so. I've heard enough secrets for one day. Let God's will be done – and preferably quickly.'

When he reached the Casa Santa Marta, Lomeli went straight to the elevator. It was just before seven o'clock. He held the door open long enough to allow the archbishops of Stuttgart and Prague, Löwenstein and Jandaček, to join him. The Czech was leaning on his stick, grey-faced with fatigue. As the door closed and the car began to rise, Löwenstein said, 'Well, Dean, do you think we will finish this by tomorrow night?'

'Perhaps, Your Eminence. It's not in my hands.'

Löwenstein raised his eyebrows and glanced briefly at Jandaček. 'If it drags on much longer, I wonder what the actuarial odds are that one of us will die before we find a new Pope.'

221

'You might mention that to a few of our colleagues.'
Lomeli smiled and gave him a slight bow. 'It may
concentrate minds. Excuse me – this is my floor.'

He stepped out of the elevator, passed the votive
candles outside the Holy Father's apartment and
walked along the dimly lit corridor. From behind
several of the closed doors he could hear showers
running. When he reached his room, he hesitated,
then went on a few paces and stood outside
Adeyemi's. Not a sound came from within. The
contrast between this deep silence and the laughter
and excitement of the previous evening was awful
to him. He felt appalled by the brutal necessity of
his own actions. He tapped lightly. 'Joshua? It's
Lomeli. Are you all right?' There was no reply.

His own room had again been tidied by the nuns.
He took off his mozzetta and rochet, then sat on
the edge of his bed and loosened his shoelaces.
His back ached. His eyes were swimming with
tiredness. Yet he knew that if he lay down, he would
fall asleep. He went to his prie-dieu, knelt, and
opened his breviary to the readings for the day.
His eye fell immediately upon Psalm 46:

Come, behold the works of the Lord;
see what desolations He has brought on
    the earth.
He makes wars cease to the end of the
    earth;
He breaks the bow, and shatters the spear;
He burns the shields with fire.

As he meditated, he began to experience the same premonition of violent chaos that had almost overcome him during the morning session in the Sistine Chapel. He saw for the first time how God willed destruction: that it was inherent in His Creation from the beginning and that they could not escape it – that He would come among them in wrath. *See what desolations He has brought on the earth . . .!* He gripped the sides of the prie-dieu so hard that a few minutes later, when someone rapped loudly on the door behind him, his entire body seemed to jolt, as if he had been given an electric shock.

'Wait!'

He hauled himself back up on to his feet and briefly put his hand on his heart. It kicked against his fingers like a trapped animal. Was this how it had felt for the Holy Father just before he died? Sudden palpitations that turned into an iron band of pain? He took a few more moments to gather his composure before he opened the door.

Standing in the corridor were Bellini and Sabbadin.

Bellini stared at him with concern. 'Forgive us, Jacopo, are we disturbing your prayers?'

'It's of no consequence. I'm sure God will excuse us.'

'Are you unwell?'

'Not at all. Come in.'

He stood aside to let them enter. As usual, the

223

Archbishop of Milan looked as professionally mournful as an undertaker, although he brightened when he saw the size of Lomeli's room. 'Dear me, this is tiny. We both have suites.'

'It's not so much the lack of space as the lack of light and air that I find oppressive. It's giving me nightmares. But let us pray it won't be for too much longer.'

'Amen!'

Bellini said, 'That is what we've come about.'

'Please.' Lomeli removed his discarded mozzetta and rochet from the bed and draped them over the prie-dieu to allow his visitors to sit down. He pulled out the chair from the desk and turned it round so that he was seated facing them. 'I'd offer you a drink, but foolishly, unlike Guttuso, I've failed to bring in my own supplies.'

'It won't take long,' said Bellini. 'I simply wanted to let you know I've come to the conclusion that I don't have sufficient support among our colleagues to be elected Pope.'

Lomeli was taken aback by his directness. 'I wouldn't be so sure, Aldo. It isn't over yet.'

'You are kind, but I'm afraid, as far as I'm concerned, it is. I've had a very loyal cohort of supporters – among whom I've been touched to number you, Jacopo, despite the fact that I replaced you as Secretary of State, for which you would have had every right to harbour a grudge.'

'I have never wavered in my belief that you are the best man for the job.'

Sabbadin said, 'Hear, hear.'

Bellini held up his hand. 'Please, dear friends, don't make this any harder for me than it is. The question now arises: given that I can't win, whom should I advise my supporters to vote for? In the first ballot I voted for Vandroogenbroek – the greatest theologian of the age, in my opinion – even though of course he never stood a chance. In the last four ballots, Jacopo, I have voted for you.'

Lomeli blinked at him in surprise. 'My dear Aldo, I don't know what to say . . .'

'And I should be happy to go on voting for you, and to tell my colleagues to do the same. But . . .' He shrugged.

'But you can't win either,' said Sabbadin with brutal finality. He opened his tiny black notebook. 'Aldo got fifteen votes in the last ballot; you got twelve. So even if we delivered you all of our fifteen in a block – which frankly we can't – you'd still only be in third place, behind Tremblay and Tedesco. The Italians are divided – as usual! – and since we three agree that the Patriarch of Venice would be a disaster, the logic of the situation is clear. The only viable option is Tremblay. Our combined total of twenty-seven, plus his forty, takes him to sixty-seven. That means he only needs another twelve to win a two-thirds majority. If he doesn't get them on the next ballot, my feeling is he'll probably get them on the one after that. Do you agree, Lomeli?'

225

'I do – unfortunately.'

Bellini said, 'I'm no more of an enthusiast for Tremblay than you are. Even so, we have to face the fact that he has demonstrated broad appeal. And if we believe that the Holy Spirit is operating through the Conclave, we have to accept that God – improbable as it may seem – wishes us to give the Keys of St Peter to Joe Tremblay.'

'Perhaps He does – although it's strange that until lunchtime He also seemed to want us to give them to Joshua Adeyemi.' Lomeli glanced at the wall: he wondered if the Nigerian was listening. 'Can I add that I am also slightly troubled by this . . .' he gestured back and forth, 'by the three of us meeting in collusion to try to influence the result? It seems a sacrilege. All we need is the Patriarch of Lisbon with his cigars and we'd be in a smoke-filled room, just like an American political convention.' Bellini gave a thin smile; Sabbadin frowned. 'Seriously, let us not forget that the oath we swear is to cast our ballot for the candidate whom before God we think should be elected. It's not enough for us just to vote for the least-worst option.'

'Oh really, with respect, Dean, that is sophistry!' scoffed Sabbadin. 'On the first ballot, one can take the purist view – good; fine. But by the time we reach the fourth or fifth ballot, our personal favourite is likely to have long since gone, and we are obliged to choose from a narrowed field. That process of concentration is the whole function of the Conclave. Otherwise nobody would change their mind and we would be here for weeks.'

'Which is what Tedesco wants,' added Bellini.

'I know, I know. You are right,' sighed Lomeli. 'I came to the same conclusion myself in the Sistine this afternoon. And yet . . .' He sat forward in his chair, rubbing his palms together, trying to decide if he should tell them what he knew. 'There is one other thing you ought to be aware of. Just before the Conclave began, Archbishop Woźniak came to see me. He said that the Holy Father had fallen out badly with Tremblay – to such an extent that he was intending to dismiss him from all his offices in the Church. Had either of you picked up this story?'

Bellini and Sabbadin looked at one another in bewilderment. Bellini said, 'It's news to us. Do you really believe it's true?'

'I don't know. I put the allegation to Tremblay in person, but naturally he denied it – he blamed the rumour on Woźniak's drinking.'

Sabbadin said, 'Well, that is possible.'

'Yet it can't be entirely a figment of Woźniak's imagination.'

'Why not?'

'Because I discovered afterwards that there *was* a report of some kind into Tremblay, but it was withdrawn.'

There was a moment's silence as they considered this. Sabbadin turned to Bellini. 'If there had been

227

such a report, surely as Secretary of State you would have heard of it?'

'Not necessarily. You know how this place works. And the Holy Father could be very secretive.'

Another silence. It went on for perhaps half a minute, until at last Sabbadin spoke. 'We'll never find a candidate who doesn't have some kind of black mark against his name. We've had a Pope who was a member of the Hitler Youth and fought for the Nazis. We've had Popes who were accused of having colluded with communists and fascists, or who ignored reports of the most appalling abuses . . . Where does it end? If you've been a member of the Curia, you can be sure someone will have leaked something about you. And if you've been an archbishop, you're bound to have made a mistake at one time or another. We are mortal men. We serve an ideal; we cannot always *be* ideal.'

It sounded like a rehearsed speech for the defence – so much so that for a moment Lomeli entertained the unworthy thought that perhaps Sabbadin had already approached Tremblay and offered to try to secure him the papacy in return for some future preferment. He wouldn't put it past the Archbishop of Milan: he had never concealed his ambition to be Secretary of State. But in the end all he said was, 'That was very well put.'

Bellini said, 'So we are agreed, Jacopo? I shall talk to my supporters and you will talk to yours and we'll both urge them to support Tremblay?'

228

'I suppose so. Not that I actually know who my supporters *are*, I might add, apart from you and Benítez.'

'Benítez,' said Sabbadin thoughtfully. 'Ah, now *there's* an interesting fellow. I can't make him out at all.' He consulted his notebook. 'And yet he got four votes on the last ballot. Where on earth are they coming from? You might have a word with him, Dean, and see if you can persuade him to our point of view. Those four votes might make all the difference.'

Lomeli agreed that he would try to see Benítez before dinner. He would go to his room. It was not the sort of conversation he wished to be seen having in front of the other cardinals.

Half an hour later, Lomeli took the elevator to the sixth floor of Block B. He recalled Benítez telling him that his room was at the top of the hotel, in the wing facing the city, but now that he was here, he realised he did not know the number. He wandered the corridor, examining the dozen identical closed doors, until he heard voices behind him and turned to see two cardinals emerging. One was Gambino, the Archbishop of Perugia, who was acting as one of Tedesco's unofficial campaign managers. The other was Adeyemi. They were in the middle of a conversation: 'I am sure he can be persuaded,' Gambino was saying. But the moment they saw Lomeli, they stopped talking.

Gambino said, 'Are you lost, Dean?'

229

'I am, as a matter of fact. I was looking for Cardinal Benítez.'

'Ah, the new boy! Are you *plotting*, Your Eminence?'

'No – or at least no more than anyone else.'

'Then you *are* plotting.' The archbishop pointed along the corridor, greatly amused. 'I think you'll find he's in the end room, on the left.'

As Gambino turned away and pressed the button for the elevator, Adeyemi lingered for a fraction longer, staring at Lomeli. You think I am finished, his face seemed to say, but you can spare me your pity, for I am not without some power, even yet. Then he joined Gambino in the elevator. The doors closed and Lomeli was left staring at the empty space. Adeyemi's influence had been entirely overlooked in their calculations, he realised. The Nigerian had still received nine votes in the last ballot, even though by then his candidacy was plainly doomed. If he could deliver even half of those diehards to Tedesco, then the Patriarch of Venice would be assured of his blocking third.

The thought energised him. He strode along the corridor and knocked firmly on the end door. After a few moments he heard Benítez call out, 'Who is it?'

'It's Lomeli.'

The lock slid back and the door half opened. 'Your Eminence?' Benítez was clutching his unbuttoned cassock together at his throat. His thin brown feet were bare. The room behind him was in darkness.

'I'm sorry to interrupt you while you're dressing. May I have a word?'

'Of course. One moment.' Benítez disappeared back into his room. His wariness struck Lomeli as odd, but then he thought that if he had lived in some of the places this man had, doubtless he too would have got into the habit of not opening his door without first checking who was there.

Along the corridor, two other cardinals had appeared and were preparing to go down to dinner. They glanced in his direction. He raised his hand. They waved back.

Benítez opened the door wide. He had finished dressing. 'Come in, Dean.' He switched on the light. 'Excuse me. At this time of day, I always try to meditate for an hour.'

Lomeli followed him into the room. It was small – identical to his own – and dotted with a dozen flickering candles: on the nightstand, on the desk, beside the prie-dieu, even in the darkened bathroom.

'In Africa I got used to not always having electricity,' explained Benítez. 'Now I find that candles have become essential for me when I pray alone. The sisters kindly found me a few. There is something about the quality of the light.'

'Interesting – I must see if it helps me.'

'You have difficulty praying?'

Lomeli was surprised by the bluntness of the question. 'Sometimes. Especially lately.' His hand

231

motioned a vague circle in the air. 'I have too much on my mind.'

'Perhaps I could be of assistance?'

For a brief instant Lomeli was affronted – was he, a former Secretary of State and Dean of the College of Cardinals, to be given lessons in how to pray? – but the offer was clearly sincere, so that he found himself saying, 'Yes, I would like that, thank you.'

'Sit, please.' Benítez pulled out the chair from the desk. 'Will it disturb you if I finish getting ready while we talk?'

'No, go ahead.'

Lomeli watched the Filipino as he sat on the bed and pulled on his socks. He was struck afresh by how young and trim he looked for a man of sixty-seven – boyish almost, with his lock of jet-black hair spilling like ink across his face as he bent forward. For Lomeli these days, putting on a pair of socks could take ten minutes. Yet the Filipino's limbs and fingers seemed as lithe and nimble as a twenty-year-old's. Perhaps he practised yoga by candlelight, as well as praying.

He remembered why he had come. 'The other night you were kind enough to say that you had voted for me.'

'I did.'

'I don't know whether you've continued to do so – I'm not asking you to tell me – but if you have, I want to repeat my plea to you to stop, only this time I make the plea with even greater urgency.'

'Why?'

'First, because I lack the necessary spiritual depth to be Pope. Secondly, because I can't possibly win. You must understand, Your Eminence, this Conclave is poised on a knife edge. If we don't reach a decision tomorrow, the rules are very clear. Voting will have to be suspended for a day so that we can reflect on the impasse. Then we shall try again for two days. Then we stop for another day. And so on, and so on, until twelve days have passed and a total of thirty ballots have been held. Only after that can the new Pope be elected by a simple majority.'

'So? What is the problem?'

'I would have thought that was obvious: the damage such a long-drawn-out process will do to the Church.'

'Damage? I don't understand.'

Was he naïve, Lomeli wondered, or disingenuous? He said patiently, 'Well, twelve successive days of balloting and discussion, all of it in secret, with half the world's media camped in Rome, would be seen as proof that the Church is in crisis – that it can't agree on a leader to guide it through these difficult times. It would also, frankly, strengthen that faction of our colleagues who want to take the Church back to an earlier era. In my worst nightmares, to speak absolutely freely, I wonder if a prolonged Conclave could herald the start of the great schism that has been threatening us for nearly sixty years.'

'So I take it you have come to ask me to vote for Cardinal Tremblay?'

He was sharper than he seemed, thought Lomeli.

'That would be my advice. And if you know the identities of the cardinals who have voted for you, I would also ask you to consider advising them to do the same. *Do* you know who they are, as a matter of interest?'

'I suspect two of them are my fellow countrymen Cardinal Mendoza and Cardinal Ramos – even though, like you, I have begged everyone not to support me. Cardinal Tremblay has spoken to me about this, in fact.'

Lomeli laughed. 'I'm sure he has!' He regretted his sarcasm at once.

'You want me to vote for a man you regard as ambitious?' Benítez looked at Lomeli – a long, hard, appraising look that made him feel quite uncomfortable – and then, without speaking further, began putting on his shoes.

Lomeli shifted in his seat. He didn't care for this lengthening silence. Eventually he said, 'I am assuming, of course, because of your obviously close relationship with the Holy Father, that you don't want to see Cardinal Tedesco as Pope. But perhaps I'm wrong – perhaps you believe in the same things he does?'

Benítez finished tying his shoelaces and placed his feet on the floor. He looked up again.

'I believe in God, Your Eminence. And in God alone. Which is why I don't share your alarm at the idea of a long Conclave – or even a schism, come to that. Who knows? Perhaps that is what God wants. It would explain why our Conclave is proving to be such a conundrum that even you can't solve it.'

'A schism would go against everything I have believed in and worked for throughout my entire life.'

'Which is what?'

'The divine gift of the single Universal Church.'

'And this unity of an institution is worth preserving even at the price of breaking one's sacred oath?'

'That is an extraordinary allegation. The Church is not merely an institution, as you call it, but the living embodiment of the Holy Spirit.'

'Ah, well here we differ. I feel I am more likely to encounter the embodiment of the Holy Spirit elsewhere – for example in those two million women who have been raped as an act of military policy in the civil wars of central Africa.'

Lomeli was so taken aback it was a moment before he could reply. He said stiffly, 'I can assure you I would never for a moment countenance breaking my oath to God – whatever the consequences for the Church.'

The evening bell rang – a long, jangling note like a fire alarm – to signal that dinner was being served.

Benítez stood and extended his hand. 'I meant no offence, Dean, and I am sorry if I have given it. But I cannot vote for a man unless he is the one I deem most worthy to be Pope. And for me, that man is not Cardinal Tremblay: it is you.'

'How many more times, Your Eminence?' Lomeli struck the side of his chair in his frustration. 'I do not want your vote!'

'Nevertheless, you will have it.' Benítez stretched out his hand further. 'Come. Let us be friends. Shall we go down to dinner together?'

Lomeli sulked for a few more seconds, then sighed and allowed himself to be helped up from his chair. He watched as Benítez went round the room blowing out the candles. The extinguished wicks spurted thin black tendrils of pungent smoke, and the smell of the burnt wax carried Lomeli in an instant back to his days in the seminary, when he would read by candlelight in the dormitory after lights-out and pretend to be asleep when the priest came by to check. He went into the bathroom, licked his thumb and forefinger, and snuffed out the candle beside the washbasin. As he did so, he noticed the little kit of toiletries that O'Malley had provided for Benítez on the night of his arrival – a toothbrush, a small tube of toothpaste, a bottle of deodorant, and a plastic disposable razor, still in its cellophane wrapper.

CHAPTER 13

THE INNER SANCTUM

That night, as they consumed the third dinner of their imprisonment – some unidentifiable fish in caper sauce – a new and febrile mood took hold of the Conclave. The cardinals were a sophisticated electorate. They could 'do the math', as Paul Krasinski, the Archbishop Emeritus of Chicago, was going round urging them. They could see that this had now become a two-horse race between Tedesco and Tremblay: between unyielding principle on the one hand and yearning for compromise on the other; between a Conclave that might drag on for another ten days and one that would probably end the following morning. The factions worked the room accordingly.

Tedesco from the start took up a position alongside Adeyemi on the table of African cardinals. As usual, he held his plate in one hand and hoisted food into his mouth with the other, occasionally pausing to stab the air with his fork as he made a point. Lomeli – who was seated in his customary position with the Italian contingent of Landolfi, Dell'Acqua, Santini and Panzavecchia – didn't need to hear what he was saying to know that he was expounding on his familiar theme of the moral decay of Western liberal societies. And to judge by his listeners' solemnly nodding heads, he was finding a receptive audience.

Tremblay, meanwhile, a Québécois, ate his main course on a table of fellow French-speakers: Courtemarche of Bordeaux, Bonfils of Marseilles, Gosselin of Paris, Kourouma of Abidjan. His campaigning technique was the opposite of Tedesco's, who liked to gather a circle around him and lecture them. Instead, Tremblay spent the evening moving from group to group, seldom staying more than a few minutes with each: shaking hands, squeezing shoulders, indulging in general bonhomie with this cardinal, exchanging whispered confidences with that. He did not seem to have a campaign manager as such, but Lomeli had already overheard several of the coming men – such as Modesto Villanueva, the Archbishop of Toledo – announcing in loud voices that Tremblay was the only possible victor.

From time to time Lomeli allowed his gaze to drift to the others. Bellini was sitting over in the far corner. He seemed to have given up trying to influence the undecided and was indulging himself for once by taking his meal with his fellow theologians, Vandroogenbroek and Löwenstein, no doubt discussing Thomism and phenomenology, or some similar abstractions.

As for Benítez, the moment he had arrived in

the dining room he had been invited to join the Anglophones. Lomeli couldn't see the Filipino's face – he had his back to him – but he could observe the expressions of his companions: Newby of Westminster, Fitzgerald of Boston, Santos of Galveston-Houston, Rudgard of the Congregation for the Causes of Saints. Like the Africans with Tedesco, they seemed to be engrossed in what their guest was saying.

And all the while, between the tables, carrying trays and bottles of wine, moved the blue-habited, downcast-eyed nuns of the Daughters of Charity of St Vincent de Paul. Lomeli was familiar with the ancient order from his years as a nuncio. It was run from a mother house in the rue du Bac in Paris. He had visited it twice. The remains of St Catherine Labouré and St Louise de Marillac were buried in its chapel. Its members had not given up their lives in order to become waitresses for cardinals. Its charism was supposed to be service to the poor.

On Lomeli's table, the mood was sombre. Unless they could bring themselves to vote for Tedesco – which they all agreed they couldn't – they were in the process of gradually reconciling themselves to the fact that they would probably never again see an Italian Pope in their lifetimes. The conversation was desultory all evening, and Lomeli was too preoccupied with his thoughts to pay it much attention.

His dialogue with Benítez had disturbed him

profoundly. He was unable to get it out of his mind. Was it really possible that he had spent the past thirty years worshipping the Church rather than God? Because that, in essence, was the accusation Benítez had levelled against him. In his heart he could not escape the truth of it – the sin; the heresy. Was it any wonder he had found it so difficult to pray?

It was an epiphany similar to that which had struck him in St Peter's while he was waiting to deliver his sermon.

Finally he could stand it no longer and pushed back his chair. 'My brothers,' he announced, 'I fear I have been dull company. I think I shall go to bed.'

There was a muted chorus around the table of 'Goodnight, Dean.'

Lomeli walked towards the lobby. Few noticed him. And of those few, none would have guessed from his dignified tread the clamour resounding in his head.

At the last minute, instead of going upstairs, his footsteps suddenly swerved away from the staircase towards the reception desk. He asked the nun behind the counter if Sister Agnes was still on duty. It was around 9.30 p.m. Behind him in the dining room, dessert was just being served.

When Sister Agnes appeared from her office, something in her manner suggested she had been expecting him. Her handsome face was sharp and pale, her eyes a crystalline blue.

'Your Eminence?'

'Sister Agnes, good evening. I was wondering if it might be possible for me to have another word with Sister Shanumi?'

'That's impossible, I'm afraid.'

'Why?'

'She is on her way home to Nigeria.'

'My goodness, that was quick!'

'There was an Ethiopian Airlines flight to Lagos from Fiumicino this evening. I thought it would be best for all concerned if she was on it.'

Her eyes held his, unblinking.

After a pause he said, 'Perhaps in that case I might have a private talk with you?'

'Surely we are having a private talk at the moment, Your Eminence?'

'Yes, but perhaps we might continue it in your office?'

She was reluctant. She said she was about to go off duty. But in the end she led him around the back of the reception desk and into her little glass cell. The blinds were down. The only light came from a desk lamp. On the table was an old-fashioned radio-cassette machine, playing a Gregorian chant. He recognised Alma Redemptoris Mater: 'Loving Mother of our Saviour'. The evidence of her piety touched him. That ancestor of hers martyred during the French Revolution had been beatified, he remembered. She turned off the music and he closed the door behind them. They both remained standing.

He said quietly, 'How did Sister Shanumi come to be in Rome?'

'I have no idea, Your Eminence.'

'But the poor woman didn't even speak Italian and had never left Nigeria before. She can't simply have turned up here without someone causing it to happen.'

'I received notification from the office of the Superioress General that she would be joining us. The arrangements were made in Paris. You should ask the rue du Bac, Your Eminence.'

'I would, except that, as you know, I am sequestered for the duration of the Conclave.'

'Then you can ask them afterwards.'

'The information is of value to me now.'

She stared him out with those indomitable blue eyes. She could be guillotined or burnt at the stake; she would not yield. If I had ever married, he thought, I would have wanted a wife like this.

He said, gently, 'Did you love the Holy Father, Sister Agnes?'

'Of course.'

'Well, I certainly know he had a special regard for you. In fact I think he was rather in awe of you.'

'I don't know about that!' Her tone was dismissive. She knew what he was doing. And yet a certain part of her could not help but be flattered, and for the first time her gaze flickered slightly.

Lomeli pressed on. 'And I believe he may have had some small regard for me as well. At any rate, let's say that when I tried to resign as dean, he wouldn't let me. I couldn't understand why at the time. To be honest, I was angry with him – may God forgive me. But now I believe I understand. I think he sensed he was dying and for some reason he wanted me to run this Conclave. And, with constant prayer, that is what I'm trying to do – for him. Therefore, when I say I need to know why Sister Shanumi came to be in the Casa Santa Marta, I am asking not for myself but on behalf of our late mutual friend the Pope.'

'You say that, Your Eminence. But how do I know what he would have wanted me to do?'

'Ask him, Sister Agnes. Ask God.'

For at least a minute she did not reply. Eventually she said, 'I promised the superioress I wouldn't say anything. And I shan't say anything. You understand?' And then she put on a pair of spectacles, sat at her computer terminal and began to type with great rapidity. It was a curious sight – Lomeli would never forget it – the elderly aristocratic nun peering closely at the screen, her fingers flying as if by their own volition across the grey plastic keyboard. The percussive blur of clicks built to a crescendo, slowed, became single beats, until with a final aggressive stab, she lifted her hands, stood, and moved away from the desk to the other side of the office.

Lomeli took her seat. On the screen was an email from the superioress herself, dated 3 October – two weeks before the Holy Father died, he noted

– marked 'In Confidence' and reporting the immediate transfer to Rome of Sister Shanumi Iwaro of the Oko community in Ondo province, Nigeria. *My dear Agnes, between us both, and not for public consumption, I would be grateful if you could take particular care of our sister, as her presence has been requested by the Prefect of the Congregation for the Evangelisation of Peoples, His Eminence Cardinal Tremblay.*

After saying goodnight to Sister Agnes, Lomeli retraced his steps and returned to the dining room. He queued for coffee and carried it into the lobby. There he sat in one of the overstuffed crimson armchairs with his back to the reception desk and waited and watched. Ah, he thought, but he was something, this Cardinal Tremblay! A North American who was not an American, a French-speaker who was not a Frenchman, a doctrinal liberal who was also a social conservative (or was it the other way round?), a champion of the Third World and the epitome of the First – how foolishly Lomeli had underestimated him! Already he noticed the Canadian did not have to fetch his own coffee any more – Sabbadin collected it on his behalf – and then the Archbishop of Milan accompanied Tremblay over to a group of Italian cardinals, who deferred to him at once, widening their circle to admit him.

Lomeli sipped his coffee and bided his time. He wanted there to be no witnesses to what he needed to do.

244

Occasionally a cardinal would come over to speak to him, and he would smile up at them and exchange a few pleasantries – nothing in his face betrayed the agitation in his mind – but he found that if he did not stand, they soon took the hint and moved away. One by one they began making their way up to bed.

It was almost 11 p.m. and most of the Conclave had retired for the evening when Tremblay finally ended his conversation with the Italians. He raised his hand in what could almost have been interpreted as a benediction. Several of the cardinals bowed slightly. He turned away, smiling to himself, and walked towards the stairs. Immediately Lomeli tried to intercept him. There was a moment of near-comedy as he discovered his legs had stiffened and he could barely get up from his chair. But after a struggle he managed to rise and limped on stiff legs in pursuit. He caught the Canadian just as he put his foot on the bottom step of the staircase.

'Your Eminence – a word, if I may?'

Tremblay was still smiling. He exuded benignity. 'Hello, Dean. I was just on my way to bed.'

'It really won't take a moment. Come.'

The smile remained, but a wariness appeared in Tremblay's eyes. Nevertheless, when Lomeli gestured to him to follow, he did – the length of the lobby, around the corner and into the chapel. The annexe was deserted and in semi-darkness. Behind the toughened glass, the spotlit Vatican

245

wall glowed greenish-blue, like an opera set for a midnight assignation, or a murder. The only other illumination came from the lamps above the altar. Lomeli crossed himself. Tremblay did the same. 'This is mysterious,' the Canadian said. 'What is it?'

'It's quite simple. I want you to withdraw your name from the next ballot.'

Tremblay peered at him, still apparently amused rather than alarmed. 'Are you feeling all right, Jacopo?'

'I'm sorry, but you are not the right man to be Pope.'

'That may be your opinion. Forty of our colleagues disagree.'

'Only because they don't know you as I do.'

Tremblay shook his head. 'This is very sad. I have always valued your level-headed wisdom. But ever since we entered the Conclave, you seem to have become quite disturbed. I shall pray for you.'

'I think you would do better to save your prayers for your own soul. I know four things about you, Your Eminence, that our colleagues don't. First, I know there was some kind of report into your activities. Second, I know that the Holy Father raised the matter with you only hours before he died. Third, I know that he dismissed you from all your posts. And fourth, I now know why.'

In the bluish half-light, Tremblay's face seemed suddenly stupefied. He looked as if he had been struck a heavy blow on the back of the head. He sat down quickly on the nearest chair. He said nothing for a while, just stared straight ahead, at the crucifix suspended above the altar.

Lomeli took the seat directly behind him. He leaned forward and spoke quietly into Tremblay's ear. 'You are a good man, Joe, I'm sure of it. You wish to serve God to the fullness of your abilities. Unfortunately, you believe those abilities are equal to the papacy, and I have to tell you they are not. I am speaking as a friend.'

Tremblay kept his back to him. 'A friend!' he muttered bitterly and derisively.

'Yes, truly. But I am also the Dean of the College, and as such, I have responsibilities. For me not to act on what I know would be a mortal sin.'

Tremblay's voice was hollow. 'And what exactly is it you know that isn't mere gossip?'

'That somehow – I assume through your contacts with our missions in Africa – you discovered the story of Cardinal Adeyemi's grave surrender to temptation thirty years ago, and arranged for the woman involved to be brought to Rome.'

Tremblay didn't move at first. When at last he did turn round, he was frowning, as if trying to remember something. 'How do *you* know about her?'

'Never mind that. What matters is that you brought her to Rome with the express intention of destroying Adeyemi's chances of becoming Pope.'

'I deny that accusation absolutely.'

247

Lomeli held up a warning finger. 'Think carefully before you speak, Your Eminence. We are in a consecrated place.'

'You can bring me a Bible to swear on if you like. I still deny it.'

'Let me be clear: you deny asking the superioress of the Daughters of Charity to transfer one of her sisters to Rome?'

'No. I asked her. But not on my own behalf.'

'On whose behalf, then?'

'The Holy Father's.'

Lomeli drew back in disbelief. 'To save your candidacy you would libel the Holy Father in his own chapel?'

'It isn't libel, it's the truth. The Holy Father gave me the name of a sister in Africa and asked me, as Prefect for the Evangelisation of Peoples, to make a private request to the Daughters of Charity to bring her to Rome. I asked no questions. I merely obliged him.'

'That is very hard to believe.'

'Well it's true, and quite frankly, I'm shocked that you should think otherwise.' He stood. All his old self-assurance had returned. Now he looked down on Lomeli. 'I shall pretend this conversation never took place.'

Lomeli pushed himself up on to his feet. It took an effort to keep the anger out of his voice. 'Unfortunately, it *has* taken place, and unless you indicate tomorrow that you no longer wish to be considered for the papacy, I shall make it known to the Conclave that the Holy Father's last official act was to dismiss you for attempting to blackmail a colleague.'

'And with what proof will you back up this ridiculous assertion?' Tremblay spread his hands. 'There is none.' He took a step closer to Lomeli. 'May I advise you, Jacopo – and I, too, am speaking here as a friend – not to repeat such malicious allegations to our colleagues? Your own ambition has not gone unnoticed. It might be seen as a tactic to blacken the name of another rival. It could even have entirely the opposite effect to the one you intend. Remember how the traditionalists tried to destroy Cardinal Montini in '63? Two days later he was Pope!'

Tremblay genuflected to the altar, crossed himself, wished Lomeli a cold goodnight, and walked out of the chapel, leaving the Dean of the College of Cardinals to listen to the dwindling echo of his footsteps on the marble floor.

For the next few hours, Lomeli lay on his bed, fully dressed, and stared at the ceiling. The only source of light shone from the bathroom. Through the partition wall came the sound of Adeyemi snoring, but this time Lomeli was so preoccupied with his thoughts, he barely heard him. In his hands he held the pass key Sister Agnes had lent him on the morning he'd returned to the Casa Santa Marta after the Mass in St Peter's, when he'd discovered he had locked himself out of his

249

room. He turned it over and over between his fingers, praying and talking to himself at the same time, so that the two merged into a single monologue.

O Lord, You have charged me with the care of this most sacred Conclave . . . Is it my duty merely to arrange my colleagues' deliberations, or do I have a responsibility to intervene and affect the outcome? I am Your servant and I dedicate myself to Your will . . . The Holy Spirit will surely lead us to a worthy pontiff regardless of any actions I may take . . . Guide me, Lord, I beg You, to fulfil Your wishes . . . Servant, you must guide yourself . . .

Twice he rose from the bed and went to the door, and twice he returned and lay down again. Of course, he knew there would be no flash of insight, no sudden infusion of certainty. He did not expect one. God did not work that way. He had sent him all the signs he needed. It was for him to act upon them. And perhaps he had always suspected what he would have to do in the end, which was why he had never returned the pass key but had kept it in the drawer of the nightstand.

He got up for a third time and opened the door.

According to the Apostolic Constitution, no one was to be left in the Casa Santa Marta after midnight apart from the cardinals. The nuns were taken back to their quarters. The security men were either in their parked cars or patrolling the perimeter. In the Palazzo San Carlo, barely fifty metres away, two doctors were on standby. Should an emergency arise, medical or otherwise, the cardinals were supposed to press the fire alarms.

Satisfied that the corridor was deserted, Lomeli walked quickly towards the landing. Outside the Holy Father's apartment, the votive candles flickered in their red glasses. He contemplated the door. For a final time he hesitated. *Whatever I do, I do for You. You see my heart. You know my intentions are pure. I commend myself to Your protection.* He inserted the key into the lock and turned it. The door opened inwards a fraction. The ribbons, affixed by Tremblay with such speed after the Holy Father's death, tautened, preventing it from opening fully. Lomeli studied the seals. The red wax discs bore the coat of arms of the Apostolic Camera: crossed keys beneath an unfurled parasol. Their function was purely symbolic. They would not survive an instant's pressure. He pushed the door harder. The wax cracked and broke, the ribbons came free, and the way into the papal apartment was open. He crossed himself, stepped over the threshold and closed the door behind him.

The place smelled stale and airless. He felt around for the light switch. The familiar sitting room looked exactly as it had on the night the Holy Father died. The lemon-coloured curtains, tightly drawn. The scallop-backed blue sofa and two armchairs. The coffee table. The prie-dieu. The desk, with the Pope's battered black leather briefcase propped beside it.

251

He sat at the desk and picked up the briefcase, rested it on his knees and opened it. Inside were an electric razor, a tin of peppermints, a breviary and a paperback copy of *The Imitation of Christ* by Thomas à Kempis. It was famously – according to the report issued by the Vatican press office – the last book the Holy Father had been reading before his heart attack. The page he had been studying was marked with a yellowing bus ticket, issued in his home city more than twenty years before:

Of the dangers of intimacy

Do not tell others what is on your mind but seek advice from someone who is wise and fears God. Keep company with young people or strangers sparingly. Do not admire the wealthy, and avoid the company of celebrities. It is better to keep company with the poor and simple, the devout and the virtuous . . .

He closed the book, put everything back in the briefcase and replaced it where he had found it. He tried the central desk drawer. It was unlocked. He pulled it all the way out, placed it on the desk and rummaged through the contents: a spectacles case (empty) and a plastic bottle of lens cleaner, pencils, a box of aspirin, a pocket calculator, rubber bands, a penknife, an old leather wallet containing a ten-euro note, a copy of the latest *Annuario Pontificio*, the thick red-bound directory listing every major office-holder in the Church . . . He slid open the other three drawers. Apart from signed postcards of the Holy Father that he used to give out to visitors, there was no paper of any kind.

He sat back and considered this. Although the Pope had refused to live in the traditional papal apartment, he had made use of his predecessors' office in the Apostolic Palace. He used to walk to it every morning, carrying his briefcase, and invariably he brought work home with him to study in the evening. The burdens of the papacy were never-ending. Lomeli clearly remembered being with him when he was signing letters and documents in this very seat. Either he had given up work entirely in his final days or the desk must have been cleaned out – no doubt by the ever-efficient hand of his private secretary, Monsignor Morales.

He stood and walked around the room, summoning the will to open the bedroom door.

The sheets had been stripped from the massive antique bed, the pillows had no covers. But the Pope's spectacles and alarm clock were still on the nightstand, and when he opened the closet, two white cassocks hung ghost-like from the rail. The sight of these simple garments – the Holy Father had refused to wear the more elaborate papal vestments – seemed to break something inside Lomeli

253

that had been pent up since the funeral. He put his hand to his eyes and bowed his head. His body shook, although no tears came. This dry convulsion lasted barely half a minute, and when it passed, he felt curiously strengthened. He waited until he had recovered his breath, and then turned and contemplated the bed.

It was formidably ugly, centuries old, with big square posts at all four corners and carved panels at the head and foot. Alone of all the fine furniture to which he was entitled in the papal apartment, the Holy Father had chosen to have this ungainly object shipped to the Casa Santa Marta. Popes had slept in it for generations. To get it through the outer door must have required taking it apart and then reassembling it.

Carefully, as he had on the night the Pope died, Lomeli lowered himself to his knees, clasped his hands together, closed his eyes and rested his forehead on the edge of the mattress to pray. Suddenly the terrible solitariness of the old man's life seemed almost too unbearable to contemplate. He reached out his arms in either direction along the wooden frame of the bed, and gripped it.

How long he remained in this position he could not afterwards say with certainty. It might have been two minutes; it might have been twenty. What he was quite sure of was that at some point during this time, the Holy Father entered his mind and spoke to him. Of course, it *could* have been a trick of the imagination: the rationalists had an explanation

254

for everything, even for inspiration. All he knew was that before he knelt he was in despair, and afterwards, when he scrambled to his feet and stared at the bed, the dead man had told him what to do.

His first thought was that there must be a concealed drawer. He got back down on his knees and went round feeling under the frame, but his hands encountered only empty space. He tried lifting the mattress, even though he knew it was a waste of time: the same Holy Father who beat Bellini at chess most evenings would never have done anything so obvious. Finally, when all other options were exhausted, he contemplated the bedposts.

First he tried the one to the right of the head-board. Its top was a dome of thick dark polished oak. At a casual glance it appeared to be all of a piece with its heavy support. But when he ran his fingers around the beading, one of the small carved discs felt slightly loose. He switched on the bedside lamp, climbed up on to the mattress, and examined it. Cautiously he pressed it. Nothing seemed to happen. But when he grasped the bedpost so that he could swing his feet back down to the floor, the top came away in his hand.

Beneath it was an empty cavity with a flat, unvarnished wooden base, in the centre of which, so small as to be barely noticeable, was a tiny wooden knob. He grasped it between thumb and forefinger, pulled, and slowly withdrew a plain wooden case.

There was a wonderful exactness to how it fitted. Fully extracted, it was about the size of a shoebox. He shook it. Something rustled within.

He sat down on the mattress and slid off the cover. Inside, rolled up, were a few dozen documents. He flattened them out. Columns of figures. Bank statements. Money transfers. Apartment addresses. Many of the pages had pencilled notations in the Holy Father's tiny, angular handwriting. Suddenly his own name jumped out at him: *Lomeli. Apartment no.2. Palace of the Holy Office. 445 square metres!!* It appeared to be in a list of official apartments occupied by serving and retired members of the Curia, prepared for the Pope by APSA, the Administration of the Patrimony of the Apostolic See. The names of all the cardinal-electors who had apartments were underlined: *Bellini* (410 square metres), *Adeyemi* (480 square metres), *Tremblay* (510 square metres) . . . At the foot of the document, the Pope had added his own name: *The Holy Father. Casa Santa Marta. 50 square metres!!*

There was an addendum attached:

For the eyes of the Pontiff only

Most Holy Father,

As far as we can ascertain, the overall surface area of the APSA patrimony totals 347,532 square metres, with a potential value in excess of 2,700,000,000, but a stated book value of 389,600,000. The shortfall in revenue would appear to indicate a paid occupancy rate of only 56%. It appears therefore, as Your Holiness suspected, that much of the income is not being properly stated.

I have the honour to be,
Your Holiness's most devoted and obedient child,
D. Labriola (Special Commissioner)

Lomeli turned to the other pages, and here was his name again: to his astonishment, this time when he looked more closely he saw it was a summary of his personal bank records with the Istituto per le Opere di Religione – the Vatican Bank. A list of monthly totals going back more than a decade. The most recent entry, for 30 September, showed he had a closing balance of 38,734.76. He had not even known the figure himself. It was all the money he had in the world.

He ran his eye over the hundreds of names listed. He felt grubby merely to be reading them, yet he couldn't stop himself. Bellini had 42,112 on deposit, Adeyemi had 121,865 and Tremblay 519,732 (a figure that earned another set of papal exclamation marks). Some cardinals had tiny balances – Tedesco's was a mere 2,821, and Benítez seemingly didn't have an account at all – but others were rich men. The Archbishop Emeritus of Palermo, Calogero Scozzazi, who had

257

worked for a time at the IOR in the days of Marcinkus, and who had actually been investigated for money-laundering, was worth 2,643,923. A number of cardinals from Africa and Asia had banked large amounts over the past twelve months. Across one page the Holy Father had scrawled, in shaky pencil, a quotation from St Mark's Gospel: *Is it not written, 'My house shall be called a house of prayer for all the nations'? But you have made it a den of robbers.*

After he had finished reading, Lomeli rolled up the papers tightly, put them back in the box and closed it. He could taste his disgust, like something rotten on his tongue. The Holy Father had secretly used his authority to obtain his colleagues' private financial records from the IOR! Did he think they were *all* corrupt? Some of it came as no surprise to him: the scandal of the Curial apartments, for example, had been leaked to the press years ago. And the personal wealth of his brother cardinals he had long suspected – the other-worldly Luciani, who survived as Pope only for a month, was said to have been elected in 1978 because he was the only Italian cardinal who was clean. No, what shook him most, at first reading, was what the collection revealed about the state of mind of the Holy Father.

He pressed the box back into its compartment and replaced the top of the bedpost. The fearful words of the disciples to Jesus came into his mind: *This is a lonely place, and the hour is now late.* For a few seconds he clung on to the solid wooden upright. He had asked God for guidance, and God had guided him here, and yet he was afraid of what else he might discover.

Nevertheless, once he had calmed himself, he went around the bed to the opposite side of the headboard, and checked the beading beneath the carved dome. Here too he discovered a hidden lever. The top of the bedpost came away in his hand and he drew out a second container. Then he went to the foot of the bed and pulled out a third, and then a fourth.

CHAPTER 14

SIMONY

I t must have been nearly three in the morning when Lomeli left the papal suite. He opened the door sufficiently to enable him to peer beyond the crimson glow of the candles. He checked the landing. He listened. More than a hundred men, mostly in their seventies, were either sleeping or silently praying. The building was completely still.

He pulled the door shut behind him. Attempting to reseal it was pointless. The wax was broken, the ribbons trailed. The cardinals would discover it when they woke; it could not be helped. He crossed the landing to the staircase and started to climb. He remembered Bellini telling him that his room was directly above the Holy Father's, and that the old man's spirit seemed to rise up through the parquet floor: Lomeli did not doubt it.

He found number 301 and knocked softly. He had expected to have difficulty making himself heard without waking half the corridor, but to his surprise, almost immediately he heard movement, the door was opened, and there was Bellini, also dressed in his cassock. He regarded Lomeli with

260

the sympathetic recognition of a fellow sufferer. 'Hello, Jacopo. Can't sleep, either? Come on in.'

Lomeli followed him into his suite. It was identical to the one downstairs. The lights in the sitting room were off, but the door to the bedroom was ajar and it was from there that the illumination came. He saw that Bellini had been in the middle of his devotions. His rosary was draped over the prie-dieu; the Divine Office was open on the stand.

Bellini said, 'Would you like to pray with me a moment?'

'Very much.'

The two men got down on their knees. Bellini bowed his head. 'On this day we remember St Leo the Great. Lord God, You built Your Church on the firm foundation of the Apostle Peter, and You promised that the gates of hell would never overcome it. Supported by the prayers of Pope St Leo, we ask that You will keep the Church faithful to Your truth, and maintain it in enduring peace through our Lord. Amen.'

'Amen.'

After a minute or two, Bellini said, 'Can I get you anything? A glass of water?'

'That would be good, thank you.'

Lomeli took a seat on the sofa. He felt at once exhausted and agitated – no state in which to make a momentous decision. He heard the sound of a tap running. Bellini called out from the bathroom, 'I can't offer you anything to go with

261

it, I'm afraid.' He came back into the sitting room carrying two tumblers of water and offered one to Lomeli. 'So what is keeping you awake at this hour?'

'Aldo, you must continue with your candidacy.'

Bellini groaned and sat down heavily in the armchair. 'Please, no, not that again! I thought the matter was settled. I don't want it and I can't win it.'

'Which of those considerations weighs the more heavily with you – the not wanting it or the not being able to win it?'

'If two-thirds of my colleagues had deemed me worthy of the task, I would have set aside my doubts reluctantly and accepted the will of the Conclave. But they didn't, so the question doesn't arise.' He watched as Lomeli withdrew three sheets of paper from inside his cassock and laid them on the coffee table. 'What are those?'

'The Keys of St Peter, if you are willing to pick them up.'

There was a long pause, and then Bellini said quietly, 'I think I should ask you to leave.'

'But you won't, though, Aldo.' Lomeli took a long drink of water. He hadn't realised how thirsty he was. Bellini folded his arms and said nothing. Lomeli observed him over the rim of his glass as he drained it. He set it down. 'Read them.' He pushed the pages across the table towards Bellini. 'It's a report into the activities of the Congregation for the Evangelisation of

Peoples – more specifically, it's a report into the activities of its prefect, Cardinal Tremblay.'

Bellini frowned at the pages and glanced away. Finally, reluctantly, he unfolded his arms and picked them up.

Lomeli said, 'It's an overwhelming prima facie case that he's guilty of simony – an offence, might I remind you, that's stipulated in Holy Scripture: "Now when Simon saw that the Spirit was given through the laying on of the Apostles' hands, he offered them money, saying, 'Give me also this power, that any one on whom I lay my hands may receive the Holy Spirit.' But Peter said to him, 'May your silver perish with you, because you thought you could obtain the gift of God with money!'"'

Bellini was still reading. 'I am aware of what simony is, thank you.'

'But has there ever been a clearer case of an attempt to purchase office or sacrament? Tremblay only obtained all those votes on the first ballot because he bought them – mostly from cardinals in Africa and South America. The names are all there – Cárdenas, Diène, Figarella, Garang, Papouloute, Baptiste, Sinclair, Alatas. He even paid them in cash, to make it harder to trace. And all of it done in the last twelve months, when he must have guessed the Holy Father's pontificate was coming to an end.'

Bellini finished his reading and stared into the middle distance. Lomeli could see his powerful mind assimilating the information, testing the strength of the evidence. Eventually he said, 'How do you know they didn't use the money for completely legitimate purposes?'

'Because I've seen their bank statements.'

'Good God!'

'The issue at this point isn't the cardinals. I wouldn't even accuse them of being corrupt, necessarily – perhaps they do intend to pass this money on to their churches but haven't got round to it yet. Besides, their ballots have been burnt, so how could we ever prove who they voted for? What *is* absolutely clear, though, is that Tremblay ignored the official procedures and handed out tens of thousands of euros in a manner that was clearly designed to further his candidacy. And the automatic penalty for simony, I need hardly remind you, is excommunication.'

'He'll deny it.'

'He can deny it all he likes: if this report becomes widely known, it will create the scandal to end all scandals. For one thing, surely it establishes that Woźniak was telling the truth when he said that the Holy Father, in his last official act, ordered Tremblay to resign.'

Bellini made no reply. He replaced the pages on the table. With his long fingers he squared them off meticulously, until they were perfectly aligned. 'May I ask where you obtained all this information?'

'From the Holy Father's apartment.'

'When?'

'Tonight.'

Bellini looked up at him, appalled. 'You broke the seals?'

'What choice did I have? You witnessed the scene at lunchtime. I had cause to suspect Tremblay had deliberately destroyed Adeyemi's chances of the papacy by bringing that poor woman from Africa to embarrass him. He denied it, of course, so I needed to see if I could find proof. In all conscience I could not stand back and see such a man elected Pope without at least making some enquiries.'

'And did he? Bring her here to embarrass Adeyemi?'

Lomeli hesitated. 'I don't know. He certainly asked for her transfer to Rome. But he said he did it at the request of the Holy Father. Maybe that part is true – the Holy Father does seem to have mounted some kind of espionage operation against his own colleagues. I found all manner of private emails and telephone transcripts hidden in his room.'

'My God, Jacopo!' Bellini groaned as if he were in physical pain. He threw back his head and gazed at the ceiling. 'What a devil's business this is!'

'It is, I agree. But better we clear it up now, while the Conclave is still in session and we can discuss our affairs in secret, than we only discover the truth after we've elected a new Pope.'

'And how are we to "clear it up" this late in our proceedings?'

'For a start, we must make our brothers aware of the Tremblay report.'

'How?'

'We must show it to them.'

Bellini regarded him with renewed horror. 'Are you serious? A document based on private bank records, stolen from the Holy Father's apartment? It will smack of desperation! It could backfire on us.'

'I'm not suggesting that you should do it, Aldo – absolutely not. You must keep well clear of it. Leave it to me, or perhaps to me and Sabbadin. I'm willing to take the consequences.'

'That's noble of you, and I'm grateful, of course. But the damage wouldn't end with you. Word inevitably would leak out. Think of what it would do to the Church. I couldn't possibly countenance becoming Pope in such circumstances.'

Lomeli could hardly credit what he was hearing. 'What circumstances?'

'The circumstances of a dirty trick – a break-in, a stolen document, the smearing of a brother cardinal. I would be the Richard Nixon of Popes! My pontificate would be tainted from the start, even assuming I could win the election, which I strongly doubt. You do appreciate that the person who stands to gain the most from this is Tedesco? The whole basis of his candidacy is that the Holy Father led the Church to disaster by his ill-thought-out attempts at reform. For him and his supporters, the revelation that the Holy Father

266

was reading their bank accounts and commissioning reports accusing the Curia of institutional corruption would simply prove their point.'

'I thought we were here to serve God, not the Curia.'

'Oh don't be naïve, Jacopo – you of all people! I have been fighting these battles for longer than you have, and the truth of the matter is that we can only serve God through the Church of His Son, Jesus Christ, and the Curia *is* the heart and brain of the Church, however imperfect it may be.'

Lomeli was suddenly conscious of a fearsome headache beginning to form, positioned precisely behind his right eye – it was always brought on by exhaustion and nervous strain. On past form, if he was not careful, he would have to take to his bed for a day or two. Perhaps he should? There was a provision in the Apostolic Constitution for sick cardinals to cast their votes from their rooms in the Casa Santa Marta. Their ballot papers were to be collected by three nominated cardinals known as *infirmarii*, who were required to transfer their votes in a locked box to the Sistine Chapel. He was sorely tempted by the idea of lying in bed with the covers over his head and leaving it to others to sort out the mess. But immediately he asked God to forgive his weakness.

Bellini spoke quietly. 'His pontificate was a war, Jacopo. People have no idea. It started on the first day, when he refused to wear the full regalia of his office and insisted on living here rather than in the Apostolic Palace, and it went on every day thereafter. Do you remember how he marched into that introductory meeting with the prefects of all the congregations in the Sala Bologna and demanded full financial transparency – proper books kept, disclosure of accounts, outside tenders for every tiny bit of building work, receipts? Receipts! In the Administration of the Patrimony they didn't even know what a receipt was! Then he brought in accountants and management consultants to comb through every file, and set them up in their own offices downstairs on the first floor of the Casa Santa Marta. And he wondered why the Curia hated it – and not just the old guard, either!

'So then the leaks started, and every time he looked in a newspaper or at the television, there was some new embarrassment about how much his friends like Tutino were skimming off funds for the poor to have their apartments renovated or fly first class. And all the while in the background there was Tedesco and his gang sniping away at him, practically accusing him of heresy whenever he said anything that sounded too much like common sense about gays or divorced couples or promoting more women. Hence the cruel paradox of his papacy: the more the outside world loved him, the more isolated he became inside the Holy See. By the end, he hardly trusted anybody. I'm not even sure he trusted me.'

'Or me.'

'No, I'd say he trusted you as well as he did anyone, otherwise he would have accepted your resignation when you offered it. But there's no point in us fooling ourselves, Jacopo. He was frail and he was sick, and it was affecting his judgement.' Bellini leaned forward and tapped the report. 'If we use this, we will not be doing his memory a service. My advice is to put it back, or destroy it.' He pushed it across the table to Lomeli.

'And have Tremblay as Pope?'

'We've had worse.'

Lomeli studied him for a moment, then got to his feet. The pain behind his eye was almost blinding. 'You grieve me, Aldo. You do. Five times I cast my ballot for you, in the true belief that you were the right man to lead the Church. But now I see that the Conclave, in its wisdom, was correct, and I was wrong. You lack the courage required to be Pope. I'll leave you alone.'

Three hours later, with the reverberations of the 6.30 bell still echoing around the building, Jacopo Baldassare Lomeli, Cardinal-Bishop of Ostia, wearing full choir dress, let himself out of his room and moved quickly along the corridor, past the apartment of the Holy Father, with its unmistakable signs of forced entry, down the staircase and into the lobby.

None of the other cardinals had yet emerged. Beyond the plate-glass door, a security guard was

269

checking the identity of the nuns who were arriving to prepare breakfast. It was not yet sufficiently light to distinguish their faces. In the pre-dawn gloom they were a line of moving shadows, such as one might see anywhere in the world at that hour – the poor of the earth beginning their day's labour.

Lomeli walked quickly around the reception desk and into the office of Sister Agnes.

It was many years since the Dean of the College of Cardinals had used a photocopier. Indeed, now that he looked at one, he was not sure he ever had. He studied the array of settings, then began pressing buttons at random. A small screen lit up and displayed a message. He bent to read it: *Error.*

He heard a sound behind him. Sister Agnes was standing in the doorway. Her unwavering gaze intimidated him. He wondered how long she had been watching his fumbling efforts. He raised his hands helplessly. 'I am trying to make some copies of a document.'

'If you give it to me, Your Eminence, I'll do it for you.'

He hesitated. The top sheet was headed: *Report prepared for the Holy Father into the alleged offence of simony committed by Cardinal Joseph Tremblay. Executive Summary. Strictly confidential.* It was dated 19 October, the day of the Holy Father's death. Finally, he decided he had no choice and handed it to her. She glanced at it without comment. 'How many copies does Your Eminence require?'

'One hundred and eighteen.'

Her eyes widened slightly.

'And one other thing, Sister – if I may. I would like to preserve the original document untouched, yet at the same time I wish to obscure certain words in the copies. Is there a way of doing that?'

'Yes, Your Eminence. I believe that should be possible.' There was a trace of amusement in her voice. She lifted the lid of the machine. After she had made a copy of each page, she gave them to him. 'You can add your changes to this version, and then this will be the one we copy. The machine is excellent. There will be very little deterioration in quality.' She found him a pen and pulled out a chair so that he could sit at the desk. Tactfully, she turned away and opened a cupboard to take out a new packet of paper.

He went through the document line by line, carefully inking out the names of the eight cardinals to whom Tremblay had given cash. *Cash!* he thought, tightening his mouth. He remembered how the late Holy Father always used to say that cash was the apple in their Garden of Eden, the original temptation that had led to so much sin. Cash sluiced through the Holy See in a constant stream that swelled to a river at Christmas and Easter, when bishops and monsignors and friars could be seen trooping through the Vatican carrying envelopes and attaché cases and

271

tin boxes stuffed with notes and coins from the faithful. A papal audience could raise 100,000 euros in donations, the money pressed discreetly into the hands of the Holy Father's attendants by his visitors as they took their leave while the Pope pretended not to notice. The money was supposed to be taken straight to the cardinals' vault in the Vatican Bank. The Congregation for the Evangelisation of Peoples in particular, obliged to send money to its missions in the Third World, where bribery was rife and banks unreliable, liked to deal in large sums of cash.

When he reached the end of the report, Lomeli went back to the beginning, to make sure he had removed every name. The redactions made it look even more sinister, like some classified file released by the CIA under the Freedom of Information Act. Of course, the thing would reach the press eventually. Sooner or later, everything did. Had not Jesus Christ Himself prophesied, according to Luke's Gospel, that *nothing is hid that shall not be made manifest, nor anything secret that shall not be known and come to light*? It was a fine calculation as to whose reputation would be the more damaged, Tremblay's or the Church's. He gave the amended report to Sister Agnes, and watched as she began to make one hundred and eighteen copies of each page. The blue light of the machine moving back and forth, back and forth, back and forth, seemed to Lomeli to have the rhythm of a scythe.

He muttered, 'God forgive me.'

Sister Agnes glanced at him. She must have known by now what she was printing: she could hardly have avoided seeing it. 'If your heart is pure, Your Eminence,' she said, 'He will forgive you.'

'Bless you, Sister, for your generosity. I believe my heart *is* pure. But how can any of us say for sure why we act as we do? In my experience, the basest sins are often committed for the highest motives.'

It took twenty minutes to print the copies and another twenty to collate the pages and staple them together. They worked alongside one another in silence. At one point a nun came in to use the computer, but Sister Agnes told her sharply to leave. When they were done, Lomeli asked if there were enough envelopes in the Casa Santa Marta to enable each report to be individually sealed and delivered.

'I'll go and find out, Your Eminence. Please sit down. You look exhausted.'

While she was gone, he sat at the desk with his head bowed. He could hear the cardinals making their way across the lobby to the chapel for morning Mass. He grasped his pectoral cross. *Forgive me, Lord, if today I try to serve You in a different way* . . . A few minutes later, Sister Agnes returned carrying two boxes of A4 Manila envelopes.

They started inserting the reports into the envelopes. She said, 'What do you want us to do

273

with them, Eminence? Shall we deliver them to each room?'

'I want to be sure every cardinal has a chance to read it before we leave to vote – I fear we don't have the time. Perhaps we could distribute them in the dining room?'

'As you wish.'

Accordingly, when the envelopes had been filled and sealed, they divided the pile in two and went into the dining room, where the nuns were setting the tables for breakfast. Lomeli worked on one side of the room, placing the envelopes on the chairs, and Sister Agnes on the other. From the chapel, where Tremblay was celebrating the Mass, came the sound of plain-song. Lomeli could feel his heart pounding; the pain behind his eyes throbbed in unison with each beat. Nevertheless, he pressed on until he and Sister Agnes met in the centre of the hall and the last of the reports was gone.

'Thank you,' he said to her. He was touched by the sternness of her kindness and held out his hand, expecting her to grasp it. But to his surprise, she knelt and kissed his ring. Then she rose and smoothed her skirts, and walked away without uttering a word.

After that, there was nothing for Lomeli to do except take a seat at the nearest table and wait.

Garbled accounts of what happened next were to emerge within hours of the end of the Conclave,

274

for although there was a strict injunction of secrecy on every cardinal, many could not resist talking to their closest associates when they returned to the outside world, and these confidantes, mostly priests and monsignors, gossiped in their turn, so that very quickly a version of the story appeared.

Broadly speaking, there were two categories of eyewitness. Those who were among the first to leave the chapel and enter the dining room were struck by the spectacle of Lomeli sitting alone and impassive at one of the central tables, his forearms resting on the tablecloth, his gaze fixed ahead, unseeing. The other thing they recalled was the shocked quiet that fell as the cardinals discovered the envelopes and started reading.

In contrast, those who arrived a few minutes later – the ones who had chosen to pray in their rooms rather than attend the morning Mass, or who had lingered in the chapel after receiving Communion – they remembered most clearly the hubbub in the dining room and the cluster of cardinals who by that time had gathered around Lomeli demanding explanations.

Truth, in other words, was a matter of perspective.

In addition to all these, there was another, smaller group, whose rooms were on the second floor, or who had descended via the two staircases from upper storeys, and who had noticed that the seals on the papal apartment were broken. Accordingly, a new set of rumours started circulating, as a counterpoint to the first, that there had been some kind of burglary during the night.

Throughout it all, Lomeli never moved from his seat. To all the cardinals who came up to him – Sá, Brotzkus, Yatsenko and the rest – he repeated the same mantra. Yes, he was responsible for the circulation of the document. Yes, he had broken the seals. No, he had not taken leave of his senses. It had been brought to his notice that an excommunicable offence might have been committed, and then covered up. He had felt it his duty to investigate, even if that had meant entering the Holy Father's rooms in search of evidence. He had tried to handle the matter responsibly. His brother electors now had the information in front of them. Theirs was the sacred duty. They must decide what weight to attach to it. He had merely obeyed his conscience.

He was surprised both by his own sense of inner strength and by the way this conviction seemed to radiate out from him, so that even those cardinals who approached him to express their dismay often ended up going away nodding in approbation. Others took a harsher view. Sabbadin bent as he was passing on his way to the buffet table and hissed in his ear, 'Why have you thrown away a valuable weapon? We could have used this to control Tremblay after his election. All you have succeeded in doing is strengthening Tedesco!'

And Archbishop Fitzgerald of Boston, Massachusetts, who was one of Tremblay's most prominent supporters, actually strode over to the table and flung the report towards Lomeli. 'This is contrary to all natural justice. You have given our brother cardinal no opportunity to lay out his defence. You have acted as judge, jury and executioner. I am appalled at such an unchristian act.' Several cardinals, listening at the neighbouring tables, murmured agreement. One called out, 'Well said!' and another, 'Amen to that!'

Lomeli remained impassive.

At one point Benítez fetched him some bread and fruit and beckoned to one of the nuns to pour him coffee. He took the seat beside him. 'You must eat, Dean, or you will make yourself ill.'

Lomeli said in a low voice, 'Did I do the right thing, Vincent? What is your opinion?'

'No one who follows their conscience ever does wrong, Your Eminence. The consequences may not turn out as we intend; it may prove in time that we made a mistake. But that is not the same as being wrong. The only guide to a person's actions can ever be their conscience, for it is in our conscience that we most clearly hear the voice of God.'

It wasn't until just after 9 a.m. that Tremblay himself appeared, stepping out of the elevator

277

nearest the dining hall. Someone must have taken him a copy of the report. He was holding it rolled up in his hand. He appeared quite composed as he walked between the tables towards Lomeli. Most of the cardinals stopped talking and ceased eating. Tremblay's grey hair was coiffed; his chin jutted. If it hadn't been for his scarlet choir dress, he might have been a sheriff on his way to a showdown in a Western.

'A word with you, Dean, if I may?'

Lomeli put down his napkin and stood. 'Of course, Your Eminence. Would you like to talk somewhere private?'

'No, I would prefer to speak in public, if you don't mind. I want our brothers to hear what I have to say. You are responsible for this, I believe?' He waved the report in Lomeli's face.

'No, Your Eminence, *you* are responsible for it – because of your actions.'

'The report is entirely mendacious!' Tremblay turned to address the room. 'It should never have seen the light of day – and it wouldn't if Cardinal Lomeli hadn't broken into the Holy Father's apartment to remove it in order to manipulate the outcome of this Conclave!'

One of the cardinals – Lomeli could not see who it was – shouted out, 'Shame!'

Tremblay went on, 'In these circumstances, I believe he should step down from his office as dean, since nobody can any longer have confidence in his impartiality.'

278

Lomeli said, 'If the report is, as you say, mendacious, perhaps you could explain why the Holy Father, in his last official act as Pope, asked you to resign?'

A stir of astonishment went through the room.

'He did no such thing – as the only witness to the meeting, his private secretary Monsignor Morales, will confirm.'

'And yet Archbishop Woźniak insists that the Holy Father told him personally of the conversation, and that he was so agitated over dinner when he was recalling it that his distress may have contributed to his death.'

Tremblay's outrage was magnificent. 'The Holy Father – may his name be numbered among the high priests – was a sick man towards the end of his life, and easily confused, as those of us who saw him regularly will confirm: was it not so, Cardinal Bellini?'

Bellini frowned at his plate. 'I have nothing to say on the matter.'

In the far corner of the dining room, Tedesco held up his hand. 'May someone else be allowed to join in this dialogue?' He rose heavily to his feet. 'I deplore all this gossip about private conversations. The issue is the accuracy or otherwise of the report. The names of eight cardinals have been blacked out. I assume the dean can tell us who they are. Let him give us the names, and let these brothers confirm, here and now, whether or not they received these payments, and if they did, whether Cardinal Tremblay requested their votes in return.'

He sat down again. Lomeli was aware of all eyes upon him. He said quietly, 'No, I will not do that.' There were protests. He held up his hand. 'Let each man examine his conscience, as I have had to do. I omitted those names precisely because I have no desire to create bitterness in this Conclave, which will only make it harder for us to listen to God and perform our sacred duty. I have done what I thought was necessary – many of you will say I have done too much: I understand that. In the circumstances, I would be happy to stand down as dean, and I would propose that Cardinal Bellini, as the next most senior member of the College, should preside over the remainder of the Conclave.'

Immediately voices started shouting out all over the dining room, some in favour, some against. Bellini shook his head vigorously. 'Absolutely not!'

In the cacophony it was hard at first to hear the words, perhaps because they were spoken by a woman. 'Your Eminences, may I be allowed to speak?' She had to repeat them more firmly, and this time they cut through the din. 'Your Eminences, may I speak, if you please?'

A woman's voice! It was scarcely credible! The cardinals turned in shock to stare at the tiny, resolute figure of Sister Agnes advancing between the tables. The silence that fell was probably as much appalled at her presumption as curious at what she might say.

'Eminences,' she began, 'although we Daughters of Charity of St Vincent de Paul are supposed to be invisible, God has nonetheless given us eyes and ears, and I am responsible for the welfare of my sisters. I wish to say that I know what prompted the Dean of the College to enter the Holy Father's rooms last night, because he spoke to me beforehand. He was concerned that the sister from my order who made that regrettable scene yesterday – for which I apologise – might have been brought to Rome with the deliberate intention of embarrassing a member of this Conclave. His suspicions were correct. I was able to tell him that she was indeed here at the specific request of one of your number: Cardinal Tremblay. I believe it was that discovery, rather than any malicious intent, that guided his actions. Thank you.'

She genuflected to the cardinals, then turned, and with her head held very erect, walked out of the dining room and across the lobby. Tremblay gaped after her in horror. He held out his hands in an appeal for understanding. 'My brothers, it is true I made the request, but only because the Holy Father asked me to. I had no knowledge of who she was, I swear to you!'

For several seconds no one spoke. Then Adeyemi rose. Slowly he brought up his arm to point at

281

Tremblay. In his deep, well-modulated voice, which sounded to his listeners, that morning more than ever, like the wrath of God made manifest, he intoned the single word, 'Judas!'

CHAPTER 15

THE SIXTH BALLOT

The Conclave was unstoppable. Like some sacred machine, it ground on into its third day, regardless of all profane distractions. At 9.30 a.m., in accordance with the Apostolic Constitution, the cardinals once again began filing out to the minibuses. They knew the routine by now. As quickly as old age and infirmity permitted, they took their seats. Soon the buses were pulling away, one every couple of minutes, heading west across the Piazza Santa Marta towards the Sistine Chapel.

Lomeli stood outside the hotel, biretta in hand, bare-headed beneath the grey sky. The cardinals' mood was subdued – stunned, even – and he half expected Tremblay to plead ill-health and withdraw from the election altogether, but no: he emerged from the lobby on the arm of Archbishop Fitzgerald and climbed up on to his bus, outwardly quite calm, although his face, which he turned to the window as they pulled away, was a dead white mask of misery.

Bellini, who was standing beside Lomeli, said drily, 'We seem to be running out of favourites.'

'Indeed. One wonders who will be next.'

Bellini glanced at him. 'I should have thought that was obvious: you.'

Lomeli put his hand to his forehead. Beneath his fingertips he could feel a vein throbbing. 'I meant what I said just now in the dining room: I believe it would be best for us all if I stepped aside as dean, and you took over the supervision of the election.'

'No, thank you, Dean. Besides, you must have noticed that the mood of the meeting was with you by the end. You are steering this Conclave – exactly where I do not know, but you are certainly steering it, and that firm hand of yours will have its admirers.'

'I don't think so.'

'Last night I warned you that exposing Tremblay would backfire on whoever did it, but it turns out I was wrong – again! Now I predict it will become a contest between you and Tedesco.'

'Then let us hope you're wrong – again.'

Bellini gave one of his chillier smiles. 'After forty years, we may have an Italian Pope at last. That will please our compatriots.' He gripped Lomeli's arm. 'Seriously, my friend, I shall pray for you.'

'Please do. Just as long as you don't vote for me.'

'Oh, I shall do that as well.'

O'Malley put away his clipboard. 'We're ready to leave, Your Eminences.'

Bellini went first. Lomeli put on his biretta and adjusted it, took one last look at the sky, then climbed up on to the bus behind the billowing red skirts of the Patriarch of Alexandria. He settled himself into one of the pair of vacant seats just behind the driver. O'Malley joined him. The doors closed, the bus vibrated over the cobbles.

As they passed between St Peter's Basilica and the Palace of Justice, O'Malley leaned in and said very quietly, so that no one could overhear him, 'I assume, Your Eminence, given the latest developments, the Conclave is extremely unlikely to reach a decision today?'

'How do you know that?'

'I was in the lobby throughout.'

Lomeli grunted to himself. If O'Malley knew, then sooner or later everyone would. He said, 'Well, naturally, given the arithmetic, you'll appreciate that deadlock is almost inevitable. We shall have to devote tomorrow to meditation and resume voting on . . .' He paused. Shuttling back and forth between the Casa Santa Marta and the Sistine, rarely seeing daylight, he was losing track of time.

'Friday, Your Eminence.'

'Friday, thank you. Four ballots on Friday, another four on Saturday, and then a further meditation on Sunday, assuming we're no further forward. We'll need to make arrangements for laundry, fresh clothes and so forth.'

'That is all in hand.'

They halted to allow the buses ahead of them to offload their passengers. Lomeli stared at the blank wall of the Apostolic Palace, then turned to

285

O'Malley and whispered, 'Tell me, what are they saying in the media?'

'They are predicting a decision either this morning or this afternoon, with Cardinal Adeyemi still considered the favourite.' O'Malley brought his lips even closer to Lomeli's ear. 'Between us, Your Eminence, if there isn't white smoke today, I fear we may start to lose control of things.'

'In what sense?'

'In the sense that we are not sure what the press office can say to the media to stop them speculating that the Church is in crisis. How else will they fill the airtime? And there are security issues as well. There are said to be four million pilgrims in Rome awaiting the new Pope.'

Lomeli glanced up at the driver's mirror. A pair of dark eyes were watching him. Perhaps the fellow could lip-read? Anything was possible. He took off his biretta and used it to shield his mouth as he turned to whisper to O'Malley. 'We have sworn an oath of secrecy, Ray, so I rely on your discretion, but I think you should let the press office know, very subtly, that the Conclave is likely to be longer than any in recent history. Instruct them to prepare the media accordingly.'

'And what reasons shall I give them?'

'Not the real ones, that's for sure! Tell them that we have an abundance of strong candidates and that choosing between them is proving difficult. Say that we are deliberately taking our time, and praying hard to divine God's will, and that it may take us some days yet to settle on our new shepherd. You might also point out that God is not to be rushed simply to suit the convenience of CNN.'

He smoothed down his hair and replaced his biretta. O'Malley was writing in his notebook. When he had finished, he whispered, 'One other thing, Your Eminence. It's very trivial. I needn't bother you with it, if you'd prefer not to know.'

'Go on.'

'I did a little more research into Cardinal Benítez. I hope you don't mind.'

'I see.' Lomeli closed his eyes as if he was hearing confession. 'You'd better tell me.'

'Well, you remember I informed you that he had a private meeting with the Holy Father in January this year, following his request to resign as archbishop on health grounds? His resignation letter is in his file at the Congregation for Bishops, along with a note from the Holy Father's private office to say that his request to retire was withdrawn. There is nothing else. However, when I entered Cardinal Benítez's name into our data search engine, I discovered that shortly afterwards, he was issued with a return airline ticket to Geneva, paid for by the Pope's own account. This is in a separate registry.'

'Is it of any significance?'

'Well, as a Philippine national, he was required to submit a visa application. The purpose of travel was given as "medical treatment", and when I looked up his address in Switzerland for the duration of his stay, I discovered it was a private hospital.'

Lomeli opened his eyes at that. 'Why not one of the Vatican's medical facilities? What was he being treated for?'

'I don't know, Your Eminence – presumably it was in connection with the injuries he sustained in the bombing in Baghdad. Anyway, whatever it was, it can't have been serious. The tickets were cancelled. He never went.'

For the next half-hour, Lomeli gave no further thought to the Archbishop of Baghdad. When he disembarked from the bus, he made a point of letting O'Malley and the others go on ahead, and then walked alone up the long staircase and across the Sala Regia towards the Sistine Chapel. He needed an interval of solitude to clear that space in his mind that was the necessary precondition to the admittance of God. The scandals and stresses of the past forty-eight hours, his awareness of the watching millions beyond the walls who were impatient for their decision – all these he tried to banish by reciting in his head the prayer of St Ambrose:

Gracious God of majesty and awe,
I seek Your protection,
I look for Your healing.
Poor troubled sinner that I am,
I appeal to You, the fountain of all mercy.
I cannot bear Your judgement
But I trust in Your salvation . . .

He greeted Archbishop Mandorff and his assistants in the vestibule, where they were waiting for him beside the stoves, then walked with them into the Sistine. Inside the chapel, not a word was being spoken. The only sounds, magnified by the vast echo, were the occasional cough and the shifting of the cardinals in their seats. It sounded like an art gallery, or a museum. Most were praying.

Lomeli whispered to Mandorff, 'Thank you. I expect we shall see you again at lunchtime.' After the doors had been locked, he sat in his place with his head bowed and let the silence go on. He sensed a collective desire for meditation to restore a mood of the sacred. But he could not rid himself of the thought of all those pilgrims, and the commentators babbling their inanities into the cameras. After five minutes, he rose and walked up to the microphone.

'My most holy brothers, I will now take the roll call in alphabetical order. Please answer "Present" when I read out your name. Cardinal Adeyemi?'

'Present.'

'Cardinal Alatas?'

'Present.'

Alatas, an Indonesian, was sitting halfway down the aisle, on the right-hand side. He was one of those who had taken money from Tremblay. Lomeli wondered who he would cast his vote for now.

'Cardinal Baptiste?' He was two places further along from Alatas. Another of Tremblay's beneficiaries,

289

from St Lucia, in the Caribbean. They were so poor, those missions. His voice was thick, as if he had been weeping.

'Present.'

On Lomeli went. Bellini. . . Benítez. . . Brandão D'Cruz . . . Brotzkus . . . Cárdenas . . . Contreras . . . Courtemarche . . . He knew them all so much better now, their foibles and their weaknesses. A line of Kant's came into his mind: *Out of the crooked timber of humanity, no straight thing was ever made* . . . The Church was built of crooked timber – how could it not be? But by the grace of God it fitted together. It had endured two thousand years; if necessary it would last another two weeks without a Pope. He felt suffused by a deep and mysterious love for his colleagues and their frailties.

'Cardinal Yatsenko?'

'Present.'

'Cardinal Zucula?'

'Present, Dean.'

'Thank you, my brothers. We are all assembled. Let us pray.'

For the sixth time, the Conclave stood.

'O Father, so that we may guide and watch over Your Church, give to us, Your servants, the blessings of intelligence, truth and peace, so that we may strive to know Your will, and serve You with total dedication. For Christ our Lord . . .'

'Amen.'

'Scrutineers, will you take your places, please?'

He looked at his watch. It was three minutes to ten.

While Archbishop Lukša of Vilnius, Archbishop Newby of Westminster, and the Prefect of the Congregation for the Clergy, Cardinal Mercurio, took their places at the altar, Lomeli studied his ballot paper. In the upper half were printed the words *Eligo in Summum Pontificem* – 'I elect as Supreme Pontiff'; in the lower half, nothing. He tapped his pen against it. Now that the moment had arrived, he was not sure what name to write. His confidence in Bellini had been shaken badly, but when he came to consider the other possibilities, none of them seemed much better. He looked up and down the Sistine Chapel and begged God to give him a sign. He closed his eyes and prayed, but nothing happened. Conscious that the others were waiting for him to begin the balloting, he shielded his paper and wrote, reluctantly, BELLINI.

He folded the ballot in half, stood, held it aloft, stepped on to the carpeted aisle and approached the altar. He spoke in a firm voice.

'I call as my witness Christ the Lord, who will be my judge, that my vote is given to the one who before God I think should be elected.'

He placed the paper on the chalice and tipped it into the urn. He heard it strike the silver base. As he returned to his seat, he felt an acute sense of disappointment. For the sixth time God had asked him the same question, and for the sixth time he felt he had returned the same wrong answer.

He had no recollection at all of the remainder of the voting process. Exhausted by the events of the night, he fell asleep almost as soon as he sat down, only waking an hour later when something fluttered on to the desk in front of him. His chin was resting on his chest. He opened his eyes to find a folded note: *And behold there arose a great storm on the sea, so that the boat was being swamped by the waves; but he was asleep. Matthew 8:24.* He looked around to see Bellini leaning forward, looking at him. He was embarrassed to have shown such weakness in public, but no one else seemed to be paying him any attention. The cardinals opposite were either reading or staring into space. In front of the altar, the scrutineers were setting up their table. The balloting must have ended. He picked up his pen and scribbled beneath the quotation: *I lay down and slept; I woke again, for the Lord sustained me. Psalm 3.* Then he tossed the note back. Bellini read it and nodded judiciously, as if Lomeli was one of his old students at the Gregorian who had returned a correct answer.

Newby said into the microphone, 'My brothers, we shall now proceed to count the sixth ballot.'

The familiar laborious routine resumed. Lukša extracted a ballot paper from the urn, opened it and wrote down the name. Mercurio checked it, and then he too wrote it down. Finally, Newby pierced it with the scarlet thread and then announced the vote.

'Cardinal Tedesco.'

Lomeli placed a tick against Tedesco's name and waited for the next ballot to be counted.

'Cardinal Tedesco.'

And then again, fifteen seconds later: 'Cardinal Tedesco.'

When Tedesco's name was read out for the fifth time in a row, Lomeli had a dreadful intuition – that the effect of all his efforts had been to convince the Conclave that it needed strong leadership, and that the Patriarch of Venice was about to be elected outright. The wait for the sixth vote to be announced, which was prolonged by a whispered consultation between Lukša and Mercurio, was torture. And then it came.

'Cardinal Lomeli.'

The next three votes were all for Lomeli, and then came two for Benítez, followed by one for Bellini and another two for Tedesco. Lomeli's hand moved up and down the list of cardinals, and he did not know which alarmed him most: the line of marks accumulating beside Tedesco's name, or the threatening number that had started to cluster next to his own. Tremblay – amazingly – took a couple of votes towards the end, as did Adeyemi, and then it was over and the scrutineers began checking their tallies. Lomeli's hand was shaking as he tried to add up Tedesco's vote, which was all that mattered. Would the Patriarch of Venice

293

reach the forty he needed to deadlock the Conclave? He had to count them twice before he arrived at the result:

Tedesco 45
Lomeli 40
Benítez 19
Bellini 9
Tremblay 3
Adeyemi 2

From the other side of the Sistine Chapel came an unmistakable murmur of triumph, and Lomeli looked over just in time to catch Tedesco quickly putting his hand to his mouth to conceal his smile. His supporters leaned down and across the double row of desks to touch him on the back and whisper their congratulations. Tedesco ignored them as if they were so many flies. Instead he glanced across the aisle at Lomeli and raised his bushy eyebrows in amused complicity. It was between the two of them now.

CHAPTER 16

THE SEVENTH BALLOT

The hiss of a hundred cardinals conferring sotto voce with their neighbours, amplified by the echo from the frescoed walls of the Sistine, evoked in Lomeli a memory that at first he could not place but then realised was of the sea at Genoa – to be exact, of a long withdrawing tide over shingle on a beach he used to swim off as a child with his mother. It persisted for several minutes until at last, after conferring with the three cardinal-revisers, Newby stood to read the official result. At that point the electoral college briefly fell quiet. But the Archbishop of Westminster only confirmed what they already knew, and after he had finished, while the scrutineers' table and chairs were being cleared away and the counted ballots placed in the sacristy, the calculating hiss resumed.

Throughout all this, Lomeli sat, outwardly impassive. He spoke to no one, although both Bellini and the Patriarch of Alexandria tried to catch his eye. When the urn and chalice had been replaced on the altar and the scrutineers were in position, he walked to the microphone.

'My brothers, no candidate having achieved the

necessary two-thirds majority, we shall now proceed immediately to a seventh ballot.'

Beneath the flat surface of his manner, his mind was looping endlessly around and around the same circuit. *Who? Who?* In barely a minute he would have to cast his ballot – *but who?* Even as he returned to his seat, he was still trying to decide what he should do.

He did not wish to be Pope – of that much he was certain. He prayed with all his heart to be spared that Calvary. *My Father, if it be possible, let this cup pass from me.* And should his prayer go unheeded and the cup be offered? In that event he was resolved to refuse it, just as poor Luciani had tried to do at the end of the first Conclave of '78. Refusal to take one's place upon the cross was regarded as a grievous sin of selfishness and cowardice, which was why Luciani had yielded in the end to the pleading of his colleagues. But Lomeli was determined to stand firm. If God had granted one the gift of self-knowledge, then surely one had an obligation to use it? The loneliness, the isolation, the agony of the papacy he was willing to endure. What was unconscionable was to have a Pope who was insufficiently holy. *That* would be the sin.

Equally, though, he had to accept responsibility for the fact that Tedesco had taken command of the Conclave. It was he, as dean, who had connived in the destruction of one front-runner and brought about the ruin of the other. He had removed the

296

impediments to the Patriarch of Venice's advance, even though he was unwavering in his belief that Tedesco had to be stopped. Clearly Bellini couldn't do it: to continue voting for him would be an act of pure self-indulgence.

He sat at his desk, opened his folder and took out his ballot paper.

Benítez, then? The man undoubtedly possessed some quality of spirituality and empathy that marked him out from the rest of the College. His election would have a galvanising effect on the Church's ministry in Asia, and probably in Africa, too. The media would adore him. His appearance on the balcony overlooking St Peter's Square would be a sensation. But who was he? What were his doctrinal beliefs? He looked so slight. Did he even have the physical stamina to be Pope?

Lomeli's bureaucratic mind was nothing if not logical. Once one eliminated Bellini and Benítez as contenders, only one candidate was left who could prevent what otherwise might become a stampede towards Tedesco – and that candidate was himself. He needed to hang on to his forty votes and prolong the Conclave until such time as the Holy Spirit guided them to a worthy heir to the Throne of St Peter. No one else could do it.

It was inescapable.

He took up his pen. Briefly he closed his eyes. And then on his ballot paper he wrote: LOMELI.

Very slowly he got to his feet. He folded the ballot paper and raised it for all to see.

'I call as my witness Christ the Lord, who will be my judge, that my vote is given to the one who before God I think should be elected.'

The full extent of his perjury did not strike him until he stood before the altar to place his ballot paper on the chalice. At that instant he found himself eye to eye with Michelangelo's depiction of the damned being turfed out of their barque and dragged down to hell. *Dear Lord, forgive my sin.* But he could not stop now.

As he tipped his vote into the urn, there was a terrific bang, the floor quivered, and from behind him came the sound of panes of glass shattering and crashing on to stone. For a long moment Lomeli was sure he must be dead, and in those few seconds, when time seemed suspended, he discovered that thought is not always sequential – that ideas and impressions can arrive piled on top of one another, like photographic transparencies. Thus he was at once terrified that he had brought God's judgement down upon his own head and yet simultaneously elated to be given proof of His existence. His life had not been lived in vain! In his fear and joy he imagined that he must have passed on to another plane of existence. But when he looked at his hands, they still seemed solid enough, and suddenly time snapped back to its normal speed, as if a hypnotist had clicked his fingers. Lomeli registered the shocked expressions of the scrutineers, who were staring past him. Turning, he saw that the Sistine Chapel was still intact. Some of the cardinals were rising to find out what had happened.

He stepped down from the altar and strode along the beige carpet towards the back of the chapel. He gestured to the cardinals on either side of him, waving them back into their seats. 'Be calm, my brothers. Let us be calm. Remain where you are.' No one seemed to be hurt. He saw Benítez just in front of him and called out, 'What was it, do you think? A missile?'

'I would say a car bomb, Your Eminence.'

From far in the distance came the sound of a second explosion, fainter than the first. Several cardinals gasped.

'Brothers, please stay where you are.'

He went through the screen into the vestibule. The marble floor was covered in broken glass. He descended the wooden ramp, hoisted the skirts of his cassock and moved forward carefully. Looking up, he saw that on the side where the flue from the stoves protruded into the sky, the two windows had both been blown in. They had been big – three or four metres high, made up of hundreds of panes – and their debris was like a drift of crystallised snow. From beyond the door he heard male voices – panicking, arguing – and then the sound of the key turning in the lock. The door was flung open to reveal two black-suited security men with their guns drawn, O'Malley and Mandorff behind them, protesting.

Appalled, Lomeli stepped over the shattered glass with his arms wide to block their entry.

'No! Out!' He shooed them away with his hands as if they were crows. 'Go away! This is a sacrilege. Nobody is injured.'

One of them said, 'I'm sorry, Your Eminence, we need to move everyone to a safe location.'

'We are as safe in the Sistine Chapel, under the protection of God, as anywhere on earth. Now I must insist you leave at once.' The men hesitated. Lomeli raised his voice. 'This is a sacred Conclave, my children – you are imperilling your immortal souls!'

The security men looked at one another, then reluctantly stepped back over the threshold.

'Lock us in, Monsignor O'Malley. We shall summon you when we are ready.'

O'Malley's normally ruddy complexion was a blotchy grey. He bowed his head. His voice was shaky. 'Yes, Your Eminence.'

He pulled the door shut. The key turned.

As Lomeli returned to the main body of the chapel, the centuries-old glass crunched and snapped beneath his feet. He gave thanks to God: it was a miracle that none of the windows closer to the altar had imploded above their heads. If they had, those beneath could have been sliced to pieces. As it was, several of them were looking up uneasily. Lomeli went directly to the microphone. Tedesco, he noticed, seemed entirely unconcerned.

'My brothers, obviously something serious has

happened – the Archbishop of Baghdad suspects a car bomb, and he has had experience of this evil. Personally, I believe we ought to put our faith in God, who has thus far spared us, and continue with the ballot, but others may think differently. I am your servant. What is the will of the Conclave?'

Tedesco stood at once. 'We shouldn't get ahead of ourselves, Your Eminence. It may not actually be a bomb. It may just be a gas main, or some such thing. We'd look absurd if we fled because of an accident! Or perhaps it *is* terrorism – very well then: we shall best show the world the unshakeable strength of our faith if we refuse to be intimidated and continue with our holy task.'

Lomeli thought it well said. Even so, he could not suppress the unworthy suspicion that Tedesco had only spoken at all in order to remind the Conclave of his authority as front-runner. He said, 'Does anyone else wish to say anything?' Several cardinals were still looking up uneasily at the rows of windows fifteen metres above their heads. None indicated a desire to speak. 'No? Very well. However, before we continue, I suggest we take a moment to pray.' The Conclave stood. Lomeli bowed his head. 'Dear Lord, we offer up our prayers for those who may have suffered, or may be suffering at this moment, as a result of the violent detonation we have just heard. For the conversion of sinners, for the forgiveness of sins, in reparation of sins, and for the salvation of souls . . .'

'Amen.'

He allowed another half-minute for reflection before announcing, 'The voting will now resume.'

Very faintly through the broken windows came the sound of sirens, and then a helicopter.

The voting carried on from where it had been interrupted. First the patriarchs of Lebanon, of Antioch and of Alexandria, then Bellini, followed by the cardinal-priests. It was noticeable how much more quickly they strode up to the altar this time. Some appeared so anxious to get the ballot over with and return to the sealed warmth of the Casa Santa Marta, they almost gabbled their way through their sacred oaths.

Lomeli had placed his hands palm-down on the desk to stop them shaking. When he had been dealing with the security men, he had felt completely calm, but the moment he resumed his seat, the shock had hit him. He was not so solipsistic as to believe that a bomb had gone off merely because he had written his own name on a piece of paper. But he was not so prosaic that he did not believe in the interconnectedness of things. How else to interpret the timing of the blast, which had struck with the precision of a thunderbolt, except as a sign that God was displeased with these machinations?

You set me a task and I have failed You.

The wailing of the sirens was rising to a crescendo like a chorus of the damned: some ululated, some whooped, some emitted a single scream. To the drone of the first helicopter had been added the noise of a second. It made a mockery of the Conclave's supposed seclusion. They might as well have been meeting in the middle of the Piazza Navona.

Still, if one could not find the peace to meditate, one could at least beseech God for help – here the sirens only served to help focus one's mind – and as each of the cardinals passed him, Lomeli prayed for his soul. He prayed for Bellini, who reluctantly had been prepared to accept the chalice, only to have it dashed from his lips so humiliatingly. He prayed for Adeyemi in all his ponderous dignity, who had possessed the capacity to become one of the great figures of history but had been ruined by a squalid impulse of more than thirty years before. He prayed for Tremblay, who slunk past him with a furtive sidelong glance and whose wretchedness would be on Lomeli's conscience for the rest of his life. He prayed for Tedesco, who trudged implacably up to the altar, his stout frame swaying above his short legs, like a battered old tugboat breasting a heavy sea. He prayed for Benítez, whose expression was more serious and purposeful than he had seen it up till now, as if the explosion had reminded him of sights he would prefer to forget. And lastly he prayed for himself, that he might be forgiven for breaking his oath, and that in his hopelessness he might yet be sent a sign telling him what he should do to save the Conclave.

★ ★ ★

It was 12.42, according to Lomeli's watch, when the final ballot was cast and the scrutineers began counting the votes. By then the sirens had become less frequent, and for a few minutes there was a lull. A strained and self-conscious silence settled over the chapel. This time Lomeli left his list of cardinals untouched in its folder. He could not bear again to experience the long-drawn-out torture of following the results one by one. If he hadn't thought it would render him ridiculous, he would have put his fingers in his ears.

O Lord, let this cup pass from me!

Lukša pulled the first vote from the urn and gave it to Mercurio, who gave it to Newby, who stitched it on to his thread. They too seemed to be fumbling in their haste to complete their task. For the seventh time, the Archbishop of Westminster began his recital.

'Cardinal Lomeli . . .'

Lomeli shut his eyes. The seventh ballot ought to be propitious. In the Holy Scriptures, seven was the number of fulfilment and achievement: the day on which God rested after the creation of the world. Did not the seven Churches of Asia represent the completeness of the body of Christ?

'Cardinal Lomeli . . .'

'Cardinal Tedesco . . .'

Seven stars in Christ's right hand, seven seals of God's judgement, seven angels with seven trumpets, seven spirits before God's throne . . .

'Cardinal Lomeli . . .'

'Cardinal Benítez . . .'

. . . seven circuits of the city of Jericho, seven immersions in the River Jordan . . .

He went on for as long as he could, but he was unable to shut out Newby's fruity voice entirely. Eventually he surrendered and listened to it. But by then it was impossible for him to gauge who might be ahead.

'And that completes the voting in the seventh ballot.'

He opened his eyes. The three cardinal-revisers were rising in their places and walking to the altar to check the tallies. He looked across the aisle at Tedesco, who was tapping his list with his pen as he counted his votes. 'Fourteen, fifteen, sixteen . . .' His lips were moving but his expression was impossible to read. This time there was no general murmur of conversation. Lomeli folded his arms and focused on his desk as he waited for Newby to announce his fate.

'My brothers, the result of the seventh ballot is as follows . . .'

Lomeli hesitated, then picked up his pen.

Lomeli 52
Tedesco 42
Benítez 24

He was in front. He could not have been more dumbfounded if the numbers had been written in fire. But there they were, inescapably: they would not change no matter how long he stared at them. The laws of psephology, if not of God, were propelling him remorselessly towards the edge of the precipice.

He was aware of every face being turned towards him. He had to grip the sides of his chair to summon the necessary effort to launch himself to his feet. He didn't bother this time walking to the microphone. 'My brothers,' he said, raising his voice to address the cardinals from where he stood, 'yet again no candidate has achieved the necessary majority. Therefore we shall proceed to an eighth ballot this afternoon. Will you be so good as to remain in your places until the masters of ceremonies have collected your notes. We shall leave as quickly as possible. Cardinal Rudgard, would you please ask for the doors to be unlocked?'

He remained standing while the Junior Cardinal-Deacon performed his duty. Each step of the American's cautious progress across the glass-strewn marble floor of the vestibule was clearly audible. When he hammered on the door and cried, '*Aprite le porte! Aprite le porte!*' he sounded almost desperate. As soon as he came back into the body of the chapel, Lomeli left his place and made his own way down the aisle. He passed Rudgard, who was on his way back to his seat, and tried to give him an encouraging smile, but the American looked away. Nor did any of the seated cardinals meet his eye. At first he thought it was hostility, then he realised it was the first manifestation of a new and terrifying deference: they were beginning to think he might be Pope.

He passed through the screen just as Mandorff and O'Malley were coming into the chapel, followed by the two priests and two friars who served as their assistants. Behind them, loitering in the Sala Regia, Lomeli could see a line of security men and two officers of the Swiss Guard.

Mandorff picked his way gingerly through the glass towards him, his hands outstretched. 'Your Eminence, are you all right?'

'Nobody's hurt, Willi, thank God, but we should clear up this glass before the cardinals come out, in case someone cuts his feet.'

'With your permission, Eminence?'

Mandorff beckoned to the men beyond the door. Four entered, carrying brooms, bowed to Lomeli and immediately started clearing a path, working fast, heedless of the noise they made. At the same time, the masters of ceremonies hurried up the ramp and into the chapel to begin collecting the cardinals' notes. From their haste it was clear that a decision had been taken to evacuate the Conclave as quickly as possible. Lomeli put his arms around the shoulders of Mandorff and O'Malley and drew them in close. He was glad of the physical contact. They did not yet know of the vote; they did not flinch or try to keep a respectful distance.

'How serious is it?'

O'Malley said, 'It is grave, Your Eminence.'

'Do we know yet what happened?'

'It appears to have been a suicide bomber and also a car bomb. In the Piazza del Risorgimento. They seem to have chosen a place packed with pilgrims.'

Lomeli released the two prelates and stood silent for a few seconds, absorbing this horror. The Piazza del Risorgimento was about four hundred metres away, just outside the walls of the Vatican City. It was the closest public place to the Sistine Chapel. 'How many killed?'

'At least thirty. There was also a shooting at the church of San Marco Evangelista during a Mass.'

'Dear God!'

Mandorff said, 'And a gun attack in Munich, Eminence, at the Frauenkirche, as well as an explosion at the university in Louvain.'

O'Malley said, 'We are under attack all across Europe.'

Lomeli remembered his meeting with the Minister of Security. The young man had spoken of 'multiple co-ordinated target opportunities'. So this must be what he meant. To a layman, the euphemisms of terror were as universal and baffling as the Tridentine Mass. He made the sign of the cross. 'May God have mercy on their souls. Has anyone claimed responsibility?'

Mandorff said, 'Not yet.'

'But it will be Islamists, presumably?'

'I'm afraid that several eyewitnesses in the Piazza

del Risorgimento report that the suicide bomber shouted "Allahu Akbar", so there cannot be much doubt.'

'"God is great".' O'Malley shook his head in disgust. 'How these people slander the Almighty!'

'No emotion, Ray,' warned Lomeli. 'We need to think very clearly. An armed attack in Rome is appalling in itself. But a deliberate attack on the Universal Church in three different countries at the very moment when we are choosing a new Pope? If we are not careful, the world will see it as the start of a religious war.'

'It *is* the start of a religious war, Eminence.'

Mandorff said, 'And they have struck us deliberately when we have no commander-in-chief.'

Lomeli wiped his hand across his face. Although he had prepared for most contingencies, this was one he had never envisaged. 'Dear God,' he muttered, 'what a picture of impotence we must be showing to the world! Black smoke rising from the Roman piazza where the bombs exploded, and black smoke issuing from the Sistine chimney, beside a pair of shattered windows! Yet what are we supposed to do? To suspend the Conclave would certainly show our respect for the victims, but it would hardly solve the leadership vacuum – in fact it would prolong it. And yet to accelerate the voting process would break the Apostolic Constitution . . .'

'Break it, Eminence,' urged O'Malley. 'The Church would understand.'

'But then we would be in danger of electing a Pope without proper legitimacy, which would be a disaster. If there was the slightest doubt about the legality of the process, his edicts would be challenged from the first day of his pontificate.'

'There is another problem to consider, Your Eminence,' Mandorff said. 'The Conclave is supposed to be sequestered, and to have no knowledge of events in the outside world. The cardinal-electors really should not know the details of any of this in case it interferes with their decision.'

O'Malley burst out, 'Well surely to God, Archbishop, they must have *heard* what happened!'

'Yes, Monsignor,' replied Mandorff stiffly, 'but they are not aware of the specific nature of the attack on the Church. One could argue that these outrages actually were intended to communicate a message directly to the Conclave. If that is the case, the cardinal-electors must be shielded from news of what has happened in case it influences their judgement.' His pale eyes blinked at Lomeli through his spectacles. 'What are your instructions, Your Eminence?'

The security men had finished sweeping a path through the shattered windows and were now using shovels to transfer the fragments to wheelbarrows. The Sistine echoed like a war zone to the sound of glass on stone – an infernal sacrilegious racket to hear in such a place! Through the screen Lomeli could see the red-robed cardinals rising from their desks and beginning to file towards the vestibule.

'Tell them nothing for now,' he said. 'If anyone presses you, say that you are obeying my instructions, but not a word about what has happened. Is that understood?'

Both men nodded.

'And what about the Conclave, Eminence?' O'Malley said. 'Does it simply continue as before?'

Lomeli did not know what to reply.

He hurried out of the Sistine Chapel, past the phalanx of guards who thronged the Sala Regia, and into the Pauline Chapel. The gloomy cavernous room was deserted. He closed the door behind him. This was the place where O'Malley and Mandorff and the masters of ceremonies waited while the Conclave was in session. The chairs by the entrance had been rearranged to form a circle. He wondered how they passed the time during the long hours of voting. Did they speculate about what was happening? Did they read? It almost looked as if they had been playing cards – but that was absurd; of course they hadn't. Beside one of the chairs was a bottle of water. It made him realise how thirsty he was. He took a long drink, then walked down the aisle towards the altar, trying to order his thoughts.

As ever, the reproachful eyes of St Peter, about to be crucified upside down, stared out at him from Michelangelo's fresco. He pressed on up to

311

the altar, genuflected, then on impulse turned, and walked back halfway down the aisle to contemplate the painting. There were perhaps fifty figures depicted, most of them staring at the well-muscled, near-naked saint on the cross, which was in the process of being hauled upright. Only St Peter himself gazed out of the frame and into the living world, and not quite directly at the observer, either – that was the genius of it – but out of the corner of his eye, as if he had just spotted you passing and was daring you to walk on by. Never had Lomeli felt such an overwhelming connection with a work of art. He took off his biretta and knelt before it.

O blessed St Peter, head and chief of the Apostles, you are the guardian of the keys of the heavenly kingdom, and against you the powers of hell do not prevail. You are the rock of the Church and the shepherd of Christ's flock. Lift me from the ocean of my sins and free me from the hand of all my adversaries. Help me, O good shepherd, show me what I should do . . .

He must have spent at least ten minutes praying to St Peter, sunk so deep in thought that he never heard the cardinals being ushered across the Sala Regia and down the staircase to the minibuses. Nor did he hear the door open and O'Malley come up behind him. A wonderful feeling of peace and certainty had stolen upon him. He knew what he should do.

May I serve Jesus Christ and you, and with your

help, after the close of a good life, may I deserve to attain the reward of eternal happiness in heaven where you are forever the guardian of the gates and the shepherd of the flock. Amen.

Only when O'Malley said politely, and with a hint of concern, 'Eminence?' did Lomeli surface from his reverie.

He said, without looking round, 'Are the ballots burning?'

'Yes, Dean. Black smoke, yet again.'

He returned to his meditation. Half a minute passed. O'Malley said, 'How are you feeling, Eminence?'

Reluctantly Lomeli dragged his eyes away from the painting and glanced up at the Irishman. Now he detected something different in his attitude as well – uncertainty, anxiousness, timidity. That would be because O'Malley had seen the results of the seventh ballot and realised the danger the dean was in. Lomeli held up his hand and O'Malley helped him to his feet. He straightened his cassock and rochet.

'Fortify yourself, Ray. Look at this extra-ordinary work, as I have been doing, and consider how prophetic it is. Do you see, at the top of the painting, the shrouds of darkness? I used to think they were merely clouds, but now I'm sure it is smoke. There is a fire somewhere, beyond our field of vision, that Michelangelo chooses not to show us – a symbol of violence, of battle, strife. And do you see the way Peter is straining to keep his head

313

upright and level, even as he is being hauled up feet-first? Why is he doing that? Surely because he is determined not to surrender to the violence being done to him. He is using his last reserves of strength to demonstrate his faith and his humanity. He wishes to maintain his equilibrium in defiance of a world that, for him, is literally turning upside down.

'Isn't this a sign for us today, from the founder of the Church? Evil is seeking to turn the world on its head, but even as we suffer, the Blessed Apostle Peter instructs us to maintain our reason and our belief in Christ the Risen Saviour. We shall complete the work that God expects of us, Ray. The Conclave will go on.'

CHAPTER 17

UNIVERSI DOMINICI GREGIS

L omeli was returned at speed to the Casa Santa Marta in the back of a police car, accompanied by two security men. One sat next to the driver, the other in the passenger seat beside him. The car accelerated out of the Cortile del Maresciallo and took the corner sharply. Its tyres shrieked against the cobbles and then the vehicle shot forward again through the next three courtyards. The light on its roof flashed lightning against the shadowed walls of the Apostolic Palace. Lomeli glimpsed the startled blue-lit faces of the Swiss Guard turned to stare at him. He clutched his pectoral cross and ran his thumb along the sharp edges. He was remembering the words of an American cardinal, the late Francis George: *I expect to die in my bed, my successor will die in prison, and his successor will die a martyr in the public square.* He had always considered them hysterical. Now, as they pulled into the square in front of the Casa Santa Marta, where he counted another six police cars with their lights flashing, he felt they had the ring of prophecy.

A Swiss Guard stepped forward to open the car

door. Fresh air fanned his face. Hauling himself out, he glanced up at the sky. Grey massy clouds; a couple of helicopters buzzing in the distance with missiles protruding from their underbellies, like angry black insects ready to sting; sirens, of course; and then the massive imperturbable dome of St Peter's. The familiar sight of the cupola strengthened his resolve. He swept past the crowd of policemen and Swiss Guards without acknowledging their salutes and bows, and marched straight into the lobby of the hostel.

It was as it had been on the night the Holy Father died – the same atmosphere of bewilderment and suppressed alarm, small groups of cardinals standing around talking quietly, heads turning as he entered. Mandorff, O'Malley, Zanetti and the masters of ceremonies were in a huddle by the front desk. In the dining room some of the cardinals had taken their seats. The nuns stood around the walls, apparently unsure whether or not to begin serving lunch. All this Lomeli took in at a glance. He crooked his finger to summon Zanetti. 'I asked for the latest information.'

'Yes, Your Eminence.'

He had demanded the plain facts, nothing more. The priest handed over a single sheet of paper. Lomeli glanced at it briefly. His fingers clenched involuntarily, crumpling it slightly. What a horror! 'Gentlemen,' he said calmly to the officials, 'will you be good enough to ask the sisters to withdraw into the kitchen, and please make sure no one else comes into either the lobby or the dining area? I would like complete privacy.'

As he walked towards the dining room, he saw Bellini standing alone. He took him by the arm and whispered, 'I have decided to announce what has happened. Am I doing the right thing?'

'I don't know. You must judge. But I'll support you whatever happens.'

Lomeli squeezed his elbow and turned to address the room. 'My brothers,' he said loudly, 'will you please be seated? I wish to say a few words.'

He waited until the last of them had come in from the lobby and found their places. At recent meals, as they had got to know one another better, there had been some intermingling of the various linguistic groups. Now, in the hour of crisis, he noticed how they had unconsciously reverted to their seating on the first night – the Italians towards the kitchens, the Spanish-speakers in the centre, the Anglophones closest to reception . . .

'Brothers, before I say anything of what has occurred, I would like to have the authority of the Conclave to do so. Under paragraphs five and six of the Apostolic Constitution, it is permitted for certain matters or problems to be discussed in special circumstances, provided that a majority of those cardinals assembled agree.'

'May I say something, Dean?' The man with his hand raised was Krasinski, Archbishop Emeritus of Chicago.

'Of course, Your Eminence.'

317

'Like you, I am a veteran of three Conclaves, and I recall that in paragraph four of the constitution, it also states that nothing can be done by the College of Cardinals that "in any way affects the procedures governing the election of the Supreme Pontiff" – I believe those are the exact words. I submit that the very fact of trying to hold this meeting outside the Sistine Chapel is an interference with procedure.'

'I am not proposing any change to the election itself, which I believe must continue this afternoon as laid down in the rules. What I do wish to ask is whether the Conclave desires to know what has happened this morning beyond the walls of the Holy See.'

'But such knowledge *is* an interference!'

Bellini stood. 'It is quite plain from the dean's manner that something serious has occurred, and I for one would like to know what it is.'

Lomeli gave him a grateful look. Bellini sat to a muted chorus of 'Hear, hear' and 'I agree'.

Tedesco rose and at once the dining room went quiet. He rested his hands above the swell of his stomach – Lomeli thought he looked as if he were leaning on a wall – and took a moment before he spoke. 'Surely if the matter is as serious as all that, it is bound to increase pressure on the Conclave to come to a rapid decision? Such pressure is of course an interference, however subtle. We are here to listen to God, Your Eminences, not to news bulletins.'

'No doubt the Patriarch of Venice believes we shouldn't listen to explosions, either, but we all heard one!'

There was laughter. Tedesco's face flushed and he looked around to see who had spoken. It was Cardinal Sá, the Archbishop of São Salvador de Bahia – a liberation theologian, no friend of Tedesco or his faction.

Lomeli had chaired enough meetings in the Vatican to know when the time had come to strike. 'May I make a suggestion?' He glanced at Tedesco and waited. Reluctantly, the Patriarch of Venice sat down. 'The fairest course is obviously to put the question to a vote, and so with Your Eminences' permission, that is what I shall now do.'

'Wait a moment—'

Tedesco made an attempt to interject, but Lomeli spoke over him. 'Will all those who wish the Conclave to receive this information, please raise their hands?' At once, scores of scarlet-sleeved arms went up. 'And those against?' Tedesco, Krasinski, Tutino and perhaps a dozen others reluctantly raised their hands. 'That is carried. Naturally, anyone who doesn't wish to hear what I have to say is free to leave.' He waited. Nobody moved. 'Very well.'

He smoothed out the sheet of paper. 'Just before I left the Sistine, I asked for a summary of the latest information to be prepared by the press office in conjunction with the security service of the Holy See. The bare facts are these. At eleven

319

twenty this morning, a car bomb exploded in the Piazza del Risorgimento. Shortly afterwards, just as people were fleeing the scene, an individual with explosives strapped to his body detonated himself. Multiple credible eyewitness reports state that he cried, "Allahu Akbar."'

Several cardinals groaned.

'Simultaneous with this attack, two gunmen entered the church of San Marco Evangelista and opened fire on the congregation while Mass was being celebrated – indeed, prayers were being said at that very moment for the welfare of this Conclave. Security forces were nearby, and both attackers are reported to have been shot dead.

'At eleven thirty – that is, ten minutes later – there was an explosion in the library of the Catholic University of Louvain . . .'

Cardinal Vandroogenbroek, who had been professor of theology at Louvain, cried out, 'Oh God, no!'

'. . . and an armed man also opened fire inside the Frauenkirche in Munich. That incident seems to have turned into a siege and the building has been surrounded.

'Information on casualties is still being assessed, but the latest figures appear to be as follows: thirty-eight dead in the Piazza del Risorgimento, twelve dead in San Marco, four at the university in Belgium and at least two in Munich. Those figures I fear are very likely to rise. The wounded must be numbered in the hundreds.'

He lowered the paper.

'That is all the information I have. Let us stand, my brothers, and observe a minute's silence for those who have been killed and injured.'

After it was all over, it was to be obvious, to theologians and canon lawyers alike, that the rules under which the Conclave operated, *Universi Dominici Gregis* – 'The Lord's Whole Flock' – issued by Pope John Paul II in 1996, belonged to a more innocent age. Five years before 9/11, neither the pontiff nor his advisers had envisaged the contingency of a multiple terrorist attack.

But to the cardinals gathered in the Casa Santa Marta at lunchtime on the third day of the Conclave, nothing was obvious. After the minute's silence ended, conversations – hushed, shocked, disbelieving – slowly broke out around the dining hall. How were they to continue with their deliberations after what had occurred? But equally, how were they to stop? Most of the cardinals had sat down immediately after the silence, but some remained standing. Among them were Lomeli and Tedesco. The Patriarch of Venice was peering around him, frowning, evidently unsure of what he should do. If just three of his supporters deserted him, he would lose his blocking third in the electoral college. For the first time, he appeared less than fully confident.

On the far side of the room, Lomeli saw Benítez tentatively raise his hand.

'Your Eminence, I wish to say something.'

The cardinals seated nearest him, Mendoza and Ramos of the Philippines, were calling for quiet so that he could be heard.

Lomeli announced, 'Cardinal Benítez wishes to speak.'

Tedesco flapped his arms in dismay. 'Really, Dean, this cannot be allowed to turn into a general congregation – that phase is over.'

'I think if one of our brothers desires to talk to us, it should be allowed.'

'But under what provision of the constitution is this permitted?'

'Under what provision is it forbidden?'

'Your Eminence, I will be heard!' It was the first time Lomeli had heard Benítez raise his voice. The high-pitched tone cut through the murmur of conversation. Tedesco gave an exaggerated shrug and rolled his eyes at his supporters, as if to say that the whole thing had become ridiculous. Nevertheless, he made no further protest. A hush settled over the room. 'Thank you, my brothers. I shall be brief.' The Filipino's hands were shaking slightly. He transferred them behind his back and clasped them. His voice was soft again. 'I know nothing of the etiquette of the College, so forgive me. But perhaps for the very reason that I am your newest colleague, I feel I must say something on behalf of those millions outside these walls at this moment who will be looking to the Vatican for leadership. We are all good men, I believe – all of us, are we not?' He sought out Adeyemi and Tremblay and nodded to them, and also to Tedesco and Lomeli. 'Our petty ambitions and follies and disagreements vanish to nothing beside the evil that has been visited upon our Mother the Church.'

Several cardinals murmured in agreement.

'If I dare to speak out, it is only because two dozen of you have been good enough, and I would say foolish enough, to cast your ballots in my favour. My brothers, I believe we will not be forgiven if we go on with this election, day after day, until such time as the rules permit us to elect a Pope by a simple majority. After the last ballot we have an obvious leader, and I would urge us to unite behind him this afternoon. Therefore, for my part, I would ask that all those who have voted for me should transfer their support to our dean, Cardinal Lomeli, and that when we return to the Sistine we should elect him Pope. Thank you. Forgive me. That is all I wish to say.'

Before Lomeli could reply, Tedesco interrupted him.

'Oh no!' He shook his head. 'No, no, no!' He started waving his fat, short-fingered hands again, smiling desperately in his alarm. 'Now, you see, this is exactly what I warned you against, gentlemen! God has been forgotten in the heat of the moment and we are reacting to the pressure of events as if we represented nothing more sacred than a political convention. The Holy Spirit is not biddable, to be summoned at will, like a waiter! Brothers, I

323

beg you, remember that we swear an oath to God to elect the one we believe is best fitted to be Pope, not the one we can most easily push out on to the balcony of St Peter's this afternoon to calm the crowd!'

If Tedesco had been able to stop himself there, Lomeli reflected afterwards, he might have swayed the meeting to his view, which was entirely legitimate. But he was not a man who could ever stop himself once launched upon a theme – that was his glory and his tragedy; that was why his supporters loved him and why they had also persuaded him to stay away from Rome in the days before the Conclave. He was like the man in Christ's sermon: *out of the abundance of the heart his mouth speaks* – regardless of whether that heart's abundance be good or bad, wise or foolish.

'And in any case,' Tedesco said, gesturing to Lomeli, 'is the dean the best man for this crisis?' He flashed that awful smile again. 'I revere him as a brother and as a friend, but he is not a pastor – he is not a man to heal the broken-hearted and bind up their wounds, let alone to sound the trumpet. Insofar as he has any doctrinal positions to speak of, they are the very ones that have brought us to our present pass of drift and relativism, where all faiths and passing fancies are accorded equal weight – so that now, when we look around us, we see the homeland of the Holy Roman Catholic Church dotted with the mosques and minarets of Muhammad.'

Someone – it was Bellini, Lomeli realised – shouted out, 'Disgraceful!'

Tedesco wheeled on him – goaded, like a bull. His face blazed red with anger. '"Disgraceful," says the former Secretary of State. It is a disgrace, I agree. Imagine the blood of the innocents in the Piazza del Risorgimento or the church of San Marco this morning! Do you think we are not ourselves in some part responsible? We tolerate Islam in our land, but they revile us in theirs; we nourish them in our homelands, but they exterminate us in theirs, by the tens of thousands and, yea, by the hundreds of thousands – it is the unspoken genocide of our time. And now they are literally at our walls and we do nothing! How long will we persist in our weakness?'

Even Krasinski tried to reach up a restraining hand, but Tedesco brushed him aside.

'No, there are things that have needed saying in this Conclave, and now they must be said. My brothers, each time we file into the Sistine Chapel to vote, we pass, in the Sala Regia, a fresco of the Battle of Lepanto – I looked at it this morning – where the naval forces of Christendom, drawn together by the diplomacy of His Holiness Pope Pius V, and blessed by the intercession of Our Lady of the Rosary, defeated the galleys of the Ottoman Empire and saved the Mediterranean from slavery at the hands of the forces of Islam.

'We need some fraction of that leadership today. We need to hold fast to our values as the

325

Islamists hold fast to theirs. We need to put a stop to the drift that has gone on almost ceaselessly for the past fifty years, ever since the Second Vatican Council, and that has rendered us weak in the face of evil. Cardinal Benítez speaks of the millions beyond the walls looking to us in these terrible hours for guidance. I agree with him. The most sacred task that ever arises within our Mother Church – the bestowing of the Keys of St Peter – has been disrupted by violence in Rome itself. The moment of supreme crisis has come upon us, as foretold by our Lord Jesus Christ, and we must at long last find the strength to rise to meet it: And there will be signs in sun and moon and stars, and upon the earth distress of nations in great perplexity at the roaring of the sea and the waves, men fainting with fear and with foreboding of what is coming on the world; for the powers of the heavens will be shaken. And then they will see the Son of Man coming in a cloud with power and great glory. Now when these things begin to take place, look up and raise your heads, because your redemption is drawing near.'

When he had finished, he crossed himself and bowed his head, then sat down quickly. He was breathing heavily. The ensuing silence seemed to Lomeli to go on for a very long time and was only broken by the gentle voice of Benítez. 'But my dear Patriarch of Venice, you forget I am the Archbishop of Baghdad. There were one and a half million Christians in Iraq before the Americans attacked, and now there are one hundred and fifty thousand. My own diocese is almost empty. So much for the power of the sword! I have seen our holy places bombed and our brothers and sisters laid out dead in lines – in the Middle East and in Africa. I have comforted them in their distress and I have buried them, and I can tell you that not one of them – not one – would have wished to see violence met by violence. They died in the love of, and for the love of, our Lord Jesus Christ.'

A group of cardinals – Ramos, Martinez and Xalxo among them – clapped loudly in agreement. Gradually the applause spread across the room, from Asia through Africa and the Americas to Italy itself. Tedesco glanced around him in surprise and shook his head sorrowfully – whether in regret at their folly, or realisation of his own, or both, it was impossible to tell.

Bellini stood. 'My brothers, the Patriarch of Venice is right in one aspect, at least. We are no longer meeting as a congregation. We were sent here to choose a Pope, and that is what we should do – in strict accordance with the Apostolic Constitution, so there can be no doubt of the legitimacy of the man we elect, but also as a matter of urgency, and in the hope that the Holy Spirit will manifest itself in our hour of need. I propose therefore that we abandon lunch – I'm sure none of us has much appetite in any case – and return at once to the Sistine Chapel and resume voting. I don't believe that is in violation of the sacred statutes, is it, Dean?'

327

'No, not at all.' Lomeli seized the lifeline his old colleague had thrown him. 'The rules merely specify that two ballots must be held this afternoon if necessary, and that if we fail to reach a decision, tomorrow must be set aside for meditation.' He scanned the room. 'Is Cardinal Bellini's proposal, that we should return to the Sistine immediately, acceptable to a majority of the Conclave? Will all those in favour please show?' A scarlet forest of arms sprang up. 'And those against?' Only Tedesco raised his hand, although he looked in the other direction as he did it, as if to dissociate himself from the whole business. 'The will of the Conclave is clear. Monsignor O'Malley, will you make sure the drivers are ready? And Father Zanetti, will you please inform the press office that the Conclave is about to hold its eighth ballot?'

As the meeting dispersed, Bellini whispered in Lomeli's ear, 'Prepare yourself, my friend. By the end of this afternoon, you will be Pope.'

CHAPTER 18

THE EIGHTH BALLOT

In the event, most of the buses were not needed. Some spontaneous, collective impulse seized the Conclave, and those cardinals who were sufficiently able-bodied to walk elected to travel on foot from the Casa Santa Marta to the Sistine Chapel. They marched in a phalanx, some linking arms, as if they were staging a demonstration, which in a sense they were.

And by a stroke of providence – or divine intervention – a helicopter hired on a pooled basis by several television news companies was at that moment hovering above the Piazza del Risorgimento, filming the blast damage. The airspace of the Vatican City was closed, but the cameraman, using a long lens, was able to film the cardinals as they processed across the Piazza Santa Marta, past the Palazzo San Carlo and the Palazzo del Tribunale, past the church of Santo Stefano and along the edge of the Vatican Gardens before they disappeared into the courtyards within the complex of the Apostolic Palace.

The shaky images of the scarlet-clad figures, broadcast live around the world and repeated endlessly throughout the day, put a little heart back into the Catholic faithful. The pictures conveyed a sense of purpose, of unity and defiance. Subliminally they also suggested that very soon there would be a new Pope. From all over Rome, pilgrims began to make their way to St Peter's Square in anticipation of an announcement. Within an hour, a hundred thousand had gathered.

All this, of course, Lomeli only discovered afterwards. For now, he walked in the centre of the group, one hand clasping that of the Archbishop of Genoa, De Luca, the other holding on to Löwenstein. His face was raised to the pale light of the sky. Behind him, faintly at first, Adeyemi began singing the Veni Creator in his magnificent voice, and soon it was taken up by them all:

Far from us drive our deadly foe;
True peace unto us bring;
And through all perils lead us safe
Beneath Your sacred wing . . .

As Lomeli sang, he gave thanks to God. In this hour of deadly trial, in the unlikely setting of this cobbled courtyard, with nothing more elevating for the Conclave to contemplate than bare brick, he could at last sense the Holy Spirit moving among them. For the first time, he felt at peace with the outcome. Should the lot fall to him, so be it. *Father, if thou art willing, remove this cup from me; nevertheless, not my will, but Thine, be done.*

Still singing, they climbed the steps to the Sala Regia. As they crossed the marble floor, Lomeli glanced up at Vasari's vast fresco of the Battle of Lepanto. As ever, his attention was drawn to the lower right-hand corner, where a crudely grotesque representation of Death as a skeleton wielded a scythe. Behind Death, the rival fleets of Christendom and Islam were drawn up for battle. He wondered if Tedesco would ever again be able to bear to look at it. The waters of Lepanto had surely swallowed his hopes of the papacy as completely as they had the galleys of the Ottoman Empire.

In the vestibule of the Sistine, the broken glass had been removed. Sheets of timber were stacked ready to board up the windows. The cardinals filed in pairs up the ramp, through the screen, along the carpeted aisle, and then dispersed to find their places behind the desks. Lomeli walked to where the microphone was set up beside the altar and waited until the Conclave was assembled. His mind was entirely clear and receptive to God's presence. *The seed of eternity is within me. With its aid I can step out of the endless chase; I can dismiss everything that does not belong here in God's house; I can grow still and whole so that I can honestly reply to His summons: 'Here I am, Lord.'*

When the cardinals were all in position, he nodded to Mandorff, who was standing at the back of the chapel. The archbishop's bald dome dipped in return, and he and O'Malley, followed by the masters of ceremonies, left the chapel. The key turned in the lock.

Lomeli began the roll call. 'Cardinal Adeyemi?'

'Present.'

'Cardinal Alatas?'

'Present . . .'

He did not hurry. The recital of the names was an incantation, each one a step closer to God. As he finished, he bowed his head. The Conclave stood.

'O Father, so that we may guide and watch over Your Church, give to us, Your servants, the blessings of intelligence, truth and peace, so that we may strive to know Your will, and serve You with total dedication. For Christ our Lord . . .'

'Amen.'

The rituals of the Conclave, which three days earlier had felt so strange, were now as familiar to the cardinals as a morning Mass. The scrutineers came forward unbidden and set up the urn and chalice on the altar, while Lomeli stepped down to his desk. He opened his folder, took out his ballot paper, uncapped his pen and stared into the middle distance. For whom should he vote? Not himself – not again; not after what had happened last time. That left only one viable candidate. For a second he held his pen poised above the paper. If he had been told four days ago that on the eighth ballot he would vote for a man whom he had never met, whom he was not then even aware was a cardinal, and who even now was largely a mystery to him, he would have dismissed the notion as a fantasy. But he did it even so. In a firm hand, in capital letters, he wrote: BENÍTEZ, and when he looked at it again, it felt strangely right, so that when he stood and flourished his folded ballot paper for all to see, he was able to make his oath with a clean heart.

'I call as my witness Christ the Lord, who will be my judge, that my vote is given to the one who before God I think should be elected.'

He placed it on the chalice and tipped it into the urn.

While the rest of the Conclave voted, Lomeli occupied himself by reading the Apostolic Constitution. It was among the printed material issued to each cardinal. He wanted to make sure he had the procedure for what was to happen next straight in his head.

Chapter 7, paragraph 87: once a candidate had achieved a two-thirds majority, the Junior Cardinal-Deacon was required to ask for the doors to be unlocked, and Mandorff and O'Malley would come in with the necessary documents. Lomeli, as dean, would ask the victorious candidate, 'Do you accept your canonical election as Supreme Pontiff?' As soon as the winner had consented, he was required to ask him, 'By what name do you wish to be called?' Then Mandorff, acting as notary, would fill out the certificate of acceptance with the chosen name, and two of the masters of ceremonies would be brought in to act as witnesses.

After his acceptance, the person elected was immediately Bishop of the Church of Rome, true Pope and head of the College of Bishops. He thus acquired and could exercise full and supreme power over the Universal Church.

One word of assent, one name provided, one signature appended, and it was done: in its simplicity was its glory.

The new Pope would then retire to the sacristy known as the Room of Tears to be robed. Meanwhile, the papal throne would be set up in the Sistine. Upon his re-emergence, the cardinal-electors would queue up 'in the prescribed manner, in order to make an act of homage and obedience'. White smoke would be sent up the chimney. From the balcony overlooking St Peter's Square, Santini, Prefect of the Congregation for Catholic Education and also the Senior Cardinal-Deacon, would make the announcement, *'Habemus papam'* – 'We have a Pope' – and shortly afterwards the new pontiff would appear before the world.

And if, thought Lomeli – it was almost too momentous a possibility for him to allow his mind to encompass it, but it would be irresponsible for him not to do so – if Bellini's prediction proved to be correct, and the chalice passed to him, what would happen then?

In that event, it would fall to Bellini, as the next

most senior member of the Conclave, to ask him by what name he wished to be known as Pope.

The idea was dizzying.

At the start of the Conclave, when Bellini had accused him of ambition and insisted that every cardinal secretly knew the name they would choose if they were elected, Lomeli had denied it. But now – God forgive him for his dissimulation – he acknowledged to himself that he had always had a name in mind, although he had consciously avoided giving voice to it, even in his head.

He had known what he would be for years.

He would be John.

John in honour of the blessed disciple, and of Pope John XXIII under whose revolutionary pontificate he had grown to manhood; John because it would signal his intention to be a reformer; and John because it was traditionally a name associated with Popes whose reigns were short, as he was certain his was bound to be.

He would be Pope John XXIV.

It had a weight to it. It sounded real.

When he stepped out on to the balcony, his first act would be to give the Apostolic Blessing, *Urbi et Orbi* – 'to the City and the World' – but then he would have to say something more personal, to calm and inspire the watching billions who would be yearning for his lead. He would have to be their shepherd. To his amazement, he realised the prospect did not terrify him. There had come into his head, unbidden, the words of

335

our Saviour Jesus Christ: *Do not be anxious how you are to speak or what you are to say; for what you are to say will be given you in that hour.* Even so, he thought (the bureaucrat in him being never far away), it would be best to make at least some sort of preparation, and so for the final twenty minutes of the balloting, casting his eyes occasionally to the Sistine's ceiling for inspiration, Lomeli sketched out what he might say as Pope to reassure his Church.

The bell of St Peter's tolled three times.

The voting was over.

Cardinal Lukša lifted the urn full of ballots from the altar and showed it to both sides of the chapel, then shook it firmly enough for Lomeli to hear the papers inside it stir.

The air had become chilly. Through the broken windows came a strange, soft, immense sound – a murmur, a sigh. The cardinals looked at one another. They couldn't comprehend it at first. But Lomeli recognised it immediately. It was the noise of tens of thousands assembling in St Peter's Square.

Lukša held out the urn to Cardinal Newby. The Archbishop of Westminster thrust his hand into it, pulled out a ballot paper, and said loudly, 'One . . .' He turned to the altar and dropped it into the second urn, then swung back to Lukša and repeated the process. 'Two . . .'

Cardinal Mercurio, his hands clasped to his chest

336

in prayer, moved his head slightly as he watched each movement.

'Three . . .'

Until that moment, Lomeli had felt detached – serene, even. Now each counted ballot seemed to tighten an invisible band strapped around his chest, making it hard for him to breathe. Even when he tried to fill his head with prayer, all he could hear was the steady, inescapable intonation of the numbers. It went on like a water torture until at last Newby plucked out the last ballot paper.

'One hundred and eighteen.'

In the silence, rising and falling like a giant wave in the distance, came again the low, faint cry of the faithful.

Newby and Mercurio left the altar and went into the Room of Tears. Lukša waited, holding the white cloth. They returned carrying the table. He covered it carefully, caressing the fabric, smoothing it flat, and then from the altar he lifted the urn full of votes and placed it reverentially in the centre. Newby and Mercurio set out the three chairs. Newby collected the microphone from its stand. The trio of scrutineers sat.

Across the Sistine Chapel, the cardinals shifted in their seats and reached for their lists of candidates. Lomeli opened his folder. Without noticing it, he held the tip of his pen poised above his own name.

'The first ballot is cast for Cardinal Benítez.'

His pen travelled up the column and made a

337

mark against Benítez's name, then returned to his own. He waited, not looking up.

'Cardinal Benítez.'

Again his pen traversed the list, made a mark, and returned to its default position.

'Cardinal Benítez.'

This time, after he had awarded the tick, he looked up. Lukša was feeling for the next ballot paper from deep inside the urn. He pulled it out, unfolded it, noted the name, and passed the paper to Mercurio. The Italian also wrote the name down carefully, then gave the ballot to Newby. Newby read it and leaned across the table to speak into the microphone.

'Cardinal Benítez.'

The first seven votes were all for Benítez. The eighth was for Lomeli, and when the ninth was as well, he thought that perhaps the early run for Benítez had been one of those flukes of distribution they had seen throughout the Conclave. But then came another spell of Benítez, Benítez, Benítez, and he felt God's grace draining from him. After a few minutes he started counting up the Filipino's votes, putting a line through each group of five. Ten lots of five. He had fifty-one . . . fifty-two . . . fifty-three . . .

After that, he no longer bothered with his own tally.

Seventy-five . . . seventy-six . . . seventy-seven . . .

As Benítez approached the threshold that would make him Pope, the air in the Sistine seemed to tauten, as if its molecules were being stretched by some magnetic force. Dozens of other cardinals had their heads bent over their desks and were making the same calculation.

Seventy-eight . . . seventy-nine . . . *eighty*!

There was a great collective exhalation of breath, a half-ovation of hands being tapped on desktops. The scrutineers paused in their counting and looked up to see what was happening. Lomeli leaned out of his seat to peer along the aisle at Benítez. His chin was on his chest. He appeared to be praying.

The counting of the ballot resumed.

'Cardinal Benítez . . .'

Lomeli took up the sheet of paper on which he had roughed out the notes for his speech and tore it into tiny fragments.

After the last ballot paper had been read out – as it happened, it had been cast for him – Lomeli sat back in his chair and waited while the scrutineers and revisers went over the official figures. Afterwards, when he tried to describe his emotions to Bellini, he said that he felt as though a great wind had briefly lifted him off his feet and whirled him into the air, only to set him down abruptly and go whirling off after someone else. 'That was the Holy Spirit, I suppose. The sensation was terrifying and exhilarating and certainly unforgettable – I am glad to have experienced it – but when it was over, I felt nothing except relief.' It was the truth, more or less.

Newby said into the microphone, 'Your Eminences, here is the result of the eighth ballot . . .'

Out of habit, Lomeli lifted his pen for the final time and wrote down the figures:

Benítez 92
Lomeli 21
Tedesco 5

The end of Newby's announcement was lost in the outbreak of applause. None clapped more loudly than Lomeli. He looked around him, nodding and smiling. There were a few cheers. Opposite him, Tedesco was bringing his palms together very slowly, as if beating time for a dirge. Lomeli, redoubling his clapping, stood, and it was taken as a signal for the entire Conclave to get to its feet in an ovation. Benítez alone remained seated. With the cardinals at his back and on either side looking down at him, applauding him, he appeared, at his moment of triumph, even smaller and more out of place than before – a tiny figure, head still bowed in prayer, his face obscured by a tumbling lock of black hair just as it had been the first time Lomeli saw him with his rosary in Sister Agnes's office.

Lomeli went up to the altar, holding his copy of the Apostolic Constitution. Newby handed him the microphone. The clapping died away. The cardinals sat. He noticed that Benítez had not moved. 'The necessary majority has been achieved.

Will the Junior Cardinal-Deacon please summon the Master of Papal Liturgical Celebrations and the Secretary of the College?'

He waited as Rudgard went into the vestibule and called out for the doors to be opened. A minute later, Mandorff and O'Malley appeared at the back of the chapel. Lomeli stepped down into the aisle and walked towards Benítez. He was conscious of the expressions on the faces of the archbishop and the monsignor. They were standing discreetly just inside the screen and staring at him in astonishment. They must have presumed he would be Pope and were wondering what he was doing. He reached the Filipino and stood before him. He read from the constitution.

'In the name of the whole College of Cardinals, I ask you, Cardinal Benítez, do you accept your canonical election as Supreme Pontiff?'

Benítez seemed not to have heard. He did not look up.

'Do you accept?'

A long silence followed, as more than a hundred men held their breath, and it crossed Lomeli's mind that he was about to refuse. Dear God, what a disaster that would be! He said quietly, 'May I quote to you, Your Eminence, the Apostolic Constitution, written by St John Paul II himself? "I ask the one who is elected not to refuse, for fear of its weight, the office to which he has been called, but to submit humbly to the design of the Divine Will. God who imposes the burden will sustain him with his hand, so that he will be able to bear it."'

At last Benítez raised his head. His dark eyes contained a glint of resolution. He stood. 'I accept.'

Spontaneous exclamations of pleasure erupted along both sides of the chapel, followed by more applause. Lomeli smiled, and patted his heart, to indicate his relief. 'And by what name do you wish to be called?'

Benítez paused, and suddenly Lomeli guessed the reason for his apparent detachment: he had spent the last few minutes trying to decide his papal title. He must have been the only cardinal who had come into the Conclave without having a name in mind.

In a firm voice he said, 'Innocent.'

CHAPTER 19

HABEMUS PAPAM

T he choice of name took Lomeli by surprise. To derive one's papal title from a virtue – innocence, piety, clemency – rather than from a saint was a tradition that had died out generations ago. There had been thirteen Popes named Innocent, none of them in the last three centuries. But the more he considered it, even in those first few seconds, the more he was struck by its aptness – by its symbolism at such a time of bloodshed, by the boldness of its declaration of intent. It seemed to promise both a return to tradition and yet a departure from it – exactly the sort of ambiguity the Curia relished. And it fitted the dignified, childlike, graceful, softly spoken Benítez to perfection.

Pope Innocent XIV – the long-awaited Third World Pope! Lomeli privately gave thanks. Once again, miraculously, God had guided them to the right choice.

He was aware that the cardinals had started clapping again, in approval of the name. He knelt before the new Holy Father. Smiling in alarm, Benítez raised himself out of his seat, leaned across

343

the desk and tugged at Lomeli's mozzetta, indicating that he should get back on his feet. 'It should be you in this place,' he whispered. 'I voted for you in every ballot and I shall need your advice. I would like you to continue as Dean of the College.'

Lomeli grasped Benítez's hand as he hauled himself up. He whispered in return, 'And my first piece of advice, Your Holiness, would be to make no promises of office just yet.' He called to Mandorff: 'Archbishop, would you be so good as to bring in your witnesses and draw up the deed of acceptance?'

He stepped back to allow the formalities to be conducted. It would take five minutes at most. The document had already been written out; it was necessary merely for Mandorff to insert Benítez's birth name, his pontifical name and the date, and then for the new Holy Father to sign it and for it to be witnessed.

It was only as Mandorff placed the paper on the desk and began filling in the blank spaces that Lomeli noticed O'Malley. He was staring fixedly at the deed of acceptance, as if in a trance. Lomeli said, 'Monsignor, I'm sorry to interrupt you . . .' When the Irishman failed to react, he tried again: 'Ray?' Only then did O'Malley turn and look at him. His expression was confused, almost frightened. Lomeli said, 'I think you should start gathering the cardinals' notes. The sooner we can light the stoves, the sooner the world will know we have a new Pope. Ray?' He reached out his hand in concern. 'Are you all right?'

'I'm sorry, Your Eminence. I'm fine.' But Lomeli could see he was having to make a great effort to act as if nothing was wrong.

'What is it?'

'It's simply not the outcome I was expecting . . .'

'No, but it's wonderful all the same.' He dropped his voice. 'Listen, if it's my position you're worried about, my dear fellow, let me assure you I feel nothing but relief. God has blessed us with His mercy. Our new Holy Father will make a much greater Pope than ever I would have done.'

'Yes.' O'Malley managed a kind of stricken half-smile, and gestured to the two masters of ceremonies who were not involved in witnessing the deed of acceptance to begin gathering the cardinals' papers. He walked a few paces further into the Sistine, then halted and quickly returned. 'Eminence, I have a great burden on my conscience.'

It was at that moment that Lomeli once again felt tendrils of alarm begin to curl around his chest. 'What on earth are you talking about?'

'May I speak with you in private?' O'Malley grasped Lomeli's elbow and tried to guide him urgently towards the vestibule.

Lomeli glanced around to see if anyone was watching. The cardinals were all looking at Benítez. The new Pope had signed the deed of acceptance and was leaving his seat in order to be taken to the sacristy to be robed. Lomeli surrendered

345

reluctantly to the monsignor's pressure and allowed himself to be conducted through the screen and into the cold, deserted lobby of the chapel. He glanced up. A wind was blowing through glassless windows. Already it was starting to get dark. The poor man's nerves had obviously been affected by the explosion. 'My dear Ray,' he said, 'for heaven's sake calm yourself.'

'I'm sorry, Your Eminence.'

'Just tell me simply what it is that's troubling you. We have much to do.'

'Yes, I realise now I should have spoken to you earlier, but it seemed so trivial.'

'Go on.'

'On that first night, when I took Cardinal Benítez the toiletries he was lacking, he told me I needn't have bothered with a razor, as he never shaved.'

'What?'

'He was smiling when he said it, and to be frank, given everything else that was going on, I thought nothing of it. I mean, Your Eminence, it's not uncommon, is it?'

Lomeli squinted at him, uncomprehending. 'Ray, I'm sorry, but you are making no sense to me.' Dimly he recalled blowing out the candle in Benítez's bathroom and seeing the razor in its cellophane wrapper.

'But now that I've discovered about the clinic in Switzerland . . .' His voice trailed away helplessly.

'The clinic?' repeated Lomeli. Suddenly the

346

marble floor began to feel like liquid. 'You mean the hospital in Geneva?'

O'Malley shook his head. 'No, that's the point, Eminence. Something kept on niggling away in my mind, and this afternoon, once I saw that there was a chance the Conclave might move towards Cardinal Benítez, I decided I should look it up. It turns out it isn't a normal hospital. It's a clinic.'

'A clinic for what?'

'It specialises in what they call "gender reassignment".'

Lomeli hurried back into the main part of the chapel. The masters of ceremonies were moving along the rows of desks, collecting every scrap of paper. The cardinals were still in their places, talking quietly among themselves. Only Benítez's seat was empty, along with his own. The papal throne had been set up in front of the altar.

He walked the length of the Sistine to the door of the sacristy and knocked. Father Zanetti opened the door a crack. 'His Holiness is being robed, Your Eminence,' he whispered.

'I need to speak with him.'

'But Your Eminence—'

'Father Zanetti, if you please!'

Startled by his tone, the young priest stared at him for a moment before withdrawing his head. Lomeli heard voices within, then the door was opened briefly and he slipped inside. The low vaulted chamber looked like the props room

347

backstage at a theatre. It was cluttered with discarded clothes and the table and chairs that had been used by the scrutineers. Benítez, already clothed in the white watered-silk cassock of the Pope, was standing with his arms held wide, as if nailed to an invisible cross. Kneeling at his feet was the papal tailor from Gammarelli, pins in his teeth, stitching the hem, so intent on his work he did not look up.

Benítez gave Lomeli a resigned smile. 'Apparently even the smallest vestments are too large.'

'May I speak to Your Holiness alone?'

'Of course.' Benítez peered down at the tailor, 'Have you finished, my child?'

Through clenched teeth and pins the reply was unintelligible.

'Leave that,' ordered Lomeli curtly. 'You can finish it later.' The tailor looked round at him and spat his pins into a metal tin, then unthreaded his needle and bit through the gossamer line of spun white silk. Lomeli added, 'You too, Father.'

The two men bowed and left.

When the door was closed, Lomeli said, 'You must tell me about this treatment at the clinic in Geneva. What is your situation?'

He had anticipated various responses – angry denials, tearful confessions. Instead, Benítez looked more amused than alarmed. 'Must I, Dean?'

'Yes, Your Holiness, you must. Within the hour you will be the most famous man in the world. We can be certain the media will try to find out

348

everything there is to know about you. Your colleagues have a right to know it first. So if I may repeat: what is your situation?'

'My situation, as you call it, is the same as it was when I was ordained a priest, the same as when I was made an archbishop and the same as when I was created a cardinal. The truth is, there was no treatment in Geneva. I considered it. I prayed for guidance. And then I decided against it.'

'And what would it have been, this treatment?'

Benítez sighed. 'I believe the clinical terms are surgery to correct a fusion of the labia majora and minora, and a clitoropexy.'

Lomeli sat down on the nearest chair and put his head in his hands. After a few moments, he was aware of Benítez pulling up a chair next to him.

'Let me tell you how it was, Dean,' Benítez said softly. 'This is the truth of it. I was born to very poor parents in the Philippines, in a place where boys are more prized than girls – a preference I fear is still the case all over the world. My deformity, if that is what we must call it, was such that it was perfectly easy and natural for me to pass as a boy. My parents believed that I was a boy. *I* believed that I was a boy. And because the life of the seminary is a modest one, as you know well, with an aversion to the uncovering of the body, I had no reason to suspect otherwise, and nor did anyone else. I need hardly add that all my life I have observed my vows of chastity.'

349

'And you really never guessed? In sixty years?'

'No, never. Now, of course, when I look back, I can see that my ministry as a priest, which was mainly among women who were suffering in some way, was probably an unconscious reflection of my natural state. But I had no idea of it at the time. When I was injured in the explosion in Baghdad, I went to a hospital, and only then was I fully examined by a doctor for the first time. The instant the medical facts were explained to me, naturally I was appalled. Such darkness came upon me! It seemed to me that my entire life had been lived in a state of mortal sin. I offered my resignation to the Holy Father, without giving him the reasons. He invited me to Rome to discuss it and sought to dissuade me.'

'And did you tell him the reasons for your resignation?'

'In the end, yes, I had to.'

Lomeli stared at him, incredulous. 'And he thought it was acceptable for you to continue as an ordained minister?'

'He left it up to me. We prayed together in his room for guidance. Eventually I decided to have the surgery and to leave the ministry. But the night before I was due to fly to Switzerland, I changed my mind. I am what God made me, Your Eminence. It seemed to me more of a sin to correct His handiwork than to leave my body as it was. So I cancelled my appointment and returned to Baghdad.'

'And the Holy Father was content to allow that?'
'One must assume so. After all, he made me a cardinal *in pectore* in full knowledge of who I am.'

Lomeli cried out, 'Then he must have gone mad!'

There was a knock at the door.

Lomeli shouted, 'Not now!' but Benítez called, 'Come!'

It was Santini, the Senior Cardinal-Deacon. Lomeli often wondered afterwards what he must have made of the scene: the newly elected Holy Father and the Dean of the College of Cardinals sitting on a pair of chairs, knees practically touching, in the middle of what was obviously a profound conversation. 'Forgive me, Your Holiness,' Santini said, 'but when would you like me to go out on to the balcony to announce your election? There are said to be a quarter of a million in the square and the surrounding streets.' He gave Lomeli an imploring look. 'We are waiting to burn the ballot papers, Dean.'

Lomeli said, 'Give us one more minute, Your Eminence.'

'Of course.' Santini bowed and withdrew.

Lomeli massaged his forehead. The pain behind his eyes had returned, more blinding even than before. 'Your Holiness, how many people know of your medical condition? Monsignor O'Malley has guessed it, but he swears he has mentioned it to no one apart from me.'

'Then it is only we three. The doctor who treated

me in Baghdad was killed in a bombing shortly after he examined me, and the Holy Father is dead.'

'What about the clinic in Geneva?'

'I was only booked in for a preliminary consultation under an assumed name. I never went. Nobody there would have any idea the prospective patient was me.'

Lomeli sat back in his chair and contemplated the unthinkable. But then, was it not written in Matthew, Chapter 10, Verse 16: *Be wise as serpents and innocent as doves . . .?* 'I'd say there's a reasonable chance that we can keep it secret in the short term. O'Malley can be promoted to archbishop and sent away somewhere – he won't talk; I can deal with him. But in the long term, Your Holiness, the truth will emerge, we may be sure of it. I recall there was a visa application for your stay in Switzerland, giving the address of the clinic – that might be discovered one day. You will get old, and require medical treatment – you may have to be examined then. Perhaps you will have a heart attack. And eventually you will die, and your body will be embalmed . . .'

They sat in silence. Benítez said, 'Of course, we are forgetting: there is one other who knows this secret.'

Lomeli looked at him in alarm. 'Who?'

'God.'

★   ★   ★

It was nearly five when the two emerged. Afterwards, the Vatican press office let it be known that Pope Innocent XIV had refused to receive the traditional pledges of obedience while seated in the papal throne but instead had greeted the cardinal-electors individually, standing before the altar. He embraced them all warmly, but especially those who had at one time dreamed of being in his place: Bellini, Tedesco, Adeyemi, Tremblay. For each he had a word of comfort and admiration; to each he pledged his support. By this demonstration of love and forgiveness he made it plain to every man in the Sistine Chapel that there were to be no recriminations – that no one would be dismissed and that the Church would face the perilous days and years ahead in a spirit of unity. There was a communal sense of relief. Even Tedesco grudgingly acknowledged it. The Holy Spirit had done its work. They had picked the right man.

In the vestibule, Lomeli watched O'Malley cram the paper sacks of ballot papers and all the notes and records of the Conclave into the round stove and set fire to them. The secrets burnt easily. Then into the square stove he released a canister of potassium chlorate, lactose and pine resin. Lomeli let his eyes travel slowly up the length of the flue to the point where it exited through the glassless window and into the darkened heavens. He could not make out the chimney or the white smoke, only the pale

353

reflection of the searchlight in the shadows of the ceiling, followed a moment later by the distant roar of hundreds of thousands of voices raised in hope and acclamation.